WORLDS APART

Max Salt

This book is a work of fiction. It should be understood that, except for the occasional passing reference to a public figure, the names in this book are made up and the characters are fictional and not intended to represent anyone real, living or dead. There are factual inaccuracies in this novel, some of them deliberate, and undoubtedly some unintentional ones as well. The author is responsible for all of them.

ISBN 978-0-6152-0760-5

Published by the Zelkova Press in 2008

For Andrew Vachss,
a true defender of children.

He who fights with monsters might take care lest he thereby become a monster. And if you gaze for long into an abyss, the abyss gazes also into you.
Friedrich Nietzsche

WORLDS
APART

Prologue

Carpinteria, California
26 September 1996

*P*ain.
The sharp cramping hurt registers in my unconscious brain, abruptly pulling me out of a deep stage of sleep. My eyes pop open to the darkness of my tent interior at night, and the next second I'm grabbing for the handgun hidden under my rolled-up jacket. Despite my fear, I keep my finger outside the trigger guard—the only real safety on the Glock— and sit up in my sleeping bag, the gun leveled at the zipped up door flap just beyond my feet. The pain in the scar just below my breastbone is already fading again, and I become aware of the sounds of a large passing vehicle: the rumble of a diesel engine and the more subtle bumping and creaking of the chassis. It's most likely a recreational vehicle or a truck pulling a trailer, driving slowly down the campground's packed dirt road to the area with the RV hookups.

"Fuck," I breathe out quietly as the nausea builds in my stomach and the pain in my scar fades from a cramp to a scratch. "Fuck." I slide out of the sleeping bag and crab-walk a few feet toward the tent's entrance. I was sleeping in my clothing, so all I'm lacking are shoes. I put the Glock in my lap and feel around for my canvas high-top sneakers in the dark, not using the flashlight so as to preserve my night vision. My sneakers are right where I left them of course, and I pull them on and knot the laces blindly, automatically.

Outside the air is cool and the sky is mostly clear and starry. I tuck the gun into the top of my jeans over my abdomen, then zip up the tent. The last of the grogginess is slipping away as I walk over to the dirt road and turn in the direction I heard the diesel go, deeper into the campground. My scar was only itchy when I stepped out of the tent, but further down the road it starts to hurt again, following the familiar pattern. A year and a half ago I still didn't completely understand or believe in the significance of this pain. Five dead bodies and a bullet wound since have changed that. Now I know someone very bad drove past my tent a couple minutes ago, and is still close by.

The campground is at a little more than half capacity, so there are a fair number of RV's and trailers around, but the one I'm interested in is obvious because it's the only one with interior lights on. The motor home is parked nose-in to the space, and its engine is off now, so the night is quiet again except for the crickets. My eyes are naturally drawn to the light coming from the side windows, but all the curtains are pulled shut. The rear window is completely dark, and at my angle of approach I can't see in the front windows, which are much more dimly-lit anyway. The vehicle is long—maybe forty feet—and looks like an older model; the name Airstream occurs to me, but I really don't know. It has rounded edges, and the color, as best I can tell in the dimness, is sort of green or maybe blue with some chrome thrown in.

When I've come even with it on the road, I stop walking. Standing about thirty feet from the vehicle, the pain in my upper abdomen is sharp again. I want to double-over, but I don't; it wouldn't help anyway. I remind myself the sensation isn't real; at least, it doesn't represent any damage to my body. I listen and watch, directing my gaze away from the lighted windows now, checking to see if the owner of the RV is out walking around. There are no wires running to the electrical hookup, so I expect someone to come out and change that, and I'm ready to resume walking. But there's no sign of anyone besides me outside the vehicle, and a couple times I notice a shadow passing across the curtains in the side windows.

The RV goes dim, then dark. I look up and down the road I'm standing on, check behind me, then draw closer. The sandy, pebbly soil crunches softly beneath my feet. I scan the windows, but all the ones I can see appear closed. I glance down and notice how much the white toes on my Converse All-Stars stand out, even in the dim light, and I make a mental note to blacken them with a laundry marker or something. As I get near the back I notice there's no license plate. This would seem odd if I didn't know what must be inside. It does surprise me, though, that he—the person triggering my sense is most likely a guy—can get away with driving around without plates. I continue my approach until I'm pressed against the vehicle's skin. Now the pain has escalated to a stabbing intensity; I start to sweat. I concentrate on staying upright and keeping my breathing soft and regular. Besides the doors to the driving area, RV's usually have another door somewhere around the middle or toward the rear, but on this model that door is apparently on the other side—the driver's side. Hopefully, if anyone does leave the vehicle, he'll use that door, and I'll have time to get away.

I spread my hands over the sheet metal, my palms listening for vibrations but feeling nothing. I lean in close and turn my head, pressing my right ear to the vehicle. I hear nothing but the blood moving through my head and the crickets around me in the night. Everything seems normal and innocuous: a person or people, tired from a long day of driving, pull the RV into the next campground and more or less go right to bed. I didn't really expect a re-run of what happened with the van in northern Florida a year and a half ago, not here in this relatively crowded place, but I thought I might hear some telltale sound from within, of someone being held prisoner, or someone being hurt. Instead, it's absolutely quiet.

Shit. I know someone bad, possibly more than one, is inside, but without some corroborating evidence beyond the pain in me, I can't do anything about it. I've crossed a lot of lines since Florida, but killing people purely on the basis of gut feeling is not one of them. That's too much like killing because a voice inside my head told me to, and then it'd be harder to find differences between me and the predators I sense. So there's nothing to do about it now. I listen a while longer, then step away and walk to the dirt road again, easing the pain in my scar. I turn around and pause, gazing at the RV in the starlight, thinking about phoning it in anonymously to the police. But without an emergency to report, calling 911 is out. Calling a regular police number would make sense if there were some ongoing investigation I could link this sighting to, but I haven't been reading newspapers, and only just arrived in the Los Angeles area yesterday, so I have no idea what's going on around here in terms of unsolved murders. Probably there's a lot of them, and a lot of wacko anonymous tips to go with them.

I yawn; now that the initial scariness is sliding away, I'm feeling tired again. I press the light button on my watch and see it's about midnight. I yawn again. The best I can do is track the motor home when it leaves here. If I can keep in contact with it, that'll buy me time to get a newspaper and listen to the radio, see what I can learn about killings around here that fit the psychopath profile. Then again, maybe he hasn't done anything yet, but if I follow him, I'll be able to—

My stomach squeezes involuntarily at the thought. If I follow and catch him going after his prey, there might not be time for calling 911. Then it'll be up to me.

After the Bad, the incident memorialized by the scar on my upper abdomen, I structured my life around two rules, the first being Avoid Violence. That was before I realized the Bad's legacy to me. What happened in Florida a year and a half ago made clear the meaning of the scar's occasional pain—that sensory flashback to the Bad. What I know about this weird sense means avoiding violence isn't always an option. So when I can't obey Rule One, there's Rule Two: Be Ready. Hence the chunk of metal and plastic stuck between my jeans and my belly. I didn't have the Glock in Florida, or on my first trip to New Orleans a year ago when two more innocent people were killed on my watch and I took a bullet myself because I wasn't ready. So I armed myself. That's one of the lines I've crossed. Another was carrying the weapon back to New Orleans on my second visit, but I still haven't shot anyone. That line's still out in front of me somewhere, and I hate it.

I don't see any other way. I'll have to follow this guy, see what he does, and be ready to stop him myself if I can't get the cops to do it.

I turn and start back toward my tent, then realize I should pee first. I remember where the bathrooms are from earlier in the day, and take the turn down a dirt path cutting through the middle of the campground. When I get there, the pain in my scar has faded to an itch again—annoying, but a lot better than the extreme pain when I'm close. As I sit letting the fluid drain out of my bladder, I absently scratch lightly at the old memory of injury. The scar is just part of me now; I try not to think about how I got it almost eleven years ago, when I was fifteen and—

I try not to think about it. The scar is just part of me, and I rub my fingertips over it, but the itching persists.

Back in my tent, I set the alarm on my digital watch for four, planning to get up early, pack everything, and maybe make some instant oatmeal so I'm ready to go if the RV leaves early. Then I slide into my sleeping bag, the Glock once again under the jacket I'm using as a pillow. I lie awake for a few minutes, wondering and worrying what will happen tomorrow.

* * *

The pain and the sounds of the motor home passing by wake me again. It's still dark. I extract myself from the sleeping bag, jump into my sneakers, and bolt out of the tent, the Glock in one hand, my keys in the other. Looking down the street, I see the RV's brake lights go on as it reaches the paved road running by the campground entrance. By the time I jump in my car, start the engine, and look up again, the motor home is gone. I take off after it, but US-101 is close, and when I reach the on-ramps there's no sign of the old vehicle. *North or south?* There's no telling where he's going now, but not far to the south are suburbs of L.A.—Ventura, Oxnard, Simi Valley. Guessing a predator will be pulled by the nearest and biggest center of human gravity, I head south, driving as fast as I think I can get away with. Getting pulled over will definitely kill my chances of staying with the bad guy, so I only do about 75 in the 55 zone. Even so, my little Geo Metro hatchback is the fastest vehicle I see on the highway, which is quiet because it's—I check my watch quickly—three-thirty-seven in the morning.   I do not, however, see or sense the motor home.

After a couple miles or so I see an exit for State Route 150—another choice. It's too dark to look at a map without turning the dome light on, and there isn't time for that anyway. 101 is a big, fast road aimed directly at the heart of Los Angeles and, for the predator in the RV, millions of potential targets, so I stay with it.

After another ten miles, though, I realize I probably should have gone north, away from L.A. Or taken Route 150. Unless he's really hauling ass in that big old bus of a motor home, I would have caught up with him by now. I take the next exit, the junction with Route 33 just outside Ventura, get turned around, and drive like a mad woman north on 101.

I tap the brakes when I get to Santa Barbara, figuring speed enforcement is more likely in city limits, then pick up the pace again when I come out the other side. When I get to a town called Las Cruces there's an exit for Highway 1, which I remember from looking at the map yesterday. I was thinking of taking the curvy, scenic coastal route for the next leg of my trip. Highway 1 is a much smaller, slower road, and I'm now acting on the assumption he's headed for some population center to the north, possibly San Francisco, but at least somewhere beyond this relatively quiet stretch of coast, so I figure he'll stay on the much faster 101.

It feels hopeless, though. Thanks to my wrong guess earlier, he has at least forty minutes on me. Probably he hasn't been driving as fast, but my pursuit is depending on vague guesses about his travel plans. I go for another half hour, until I reach a small city called Santa Maria. The sky is beginning to lighten now, but there's still no sign of the predator's RV. *Shit.* I take the next exit and pull into the first parking lot I come to, which happens to belong to a Denny's. I pull into a space facing the road, put my car in neutral, and engage the parking brake.

Somewhere between L.A. and San Francisco there's a killer on the loose, and I lost him. Now I don't know where he is, where he's headed, or, and maybe this is a good thing for my sanity, what he's doing. "Shit!" I shout as I slam my fists on the steering wheel, and instantly regret it. There are few things more pathetic than throwing a temper tantrum at your own incompetence. "Sorry Stacey," I mumble quietly to my car.

Yeah, my car's name is Stacey and I talk to her sometimes, more since I started on this long, lonely road trip. I'm not crazy; I know this because she doesn't talk back to me.

"Well, now what?" I say quietly, more to myself than to Stacey.

I was planning to head north today anyway; in fact, my plan is to work my way up the coast to Oregon, and eventually to Washington, so I figure I'll keep my eyes open as I go, in case I cross paths with the old RV again. "Shit."

The laces on my sneakers are still loose from when I ran out of the tent. I tie them, then pull out of the parking lot and head back down the road the way I came in. I look at the 101 North on-ramp, slowing slightly, then shake my head.   I continue down the road and get back on the highway, heading south.

Later in the day, after I get another hour of sleep, I go into town and get breakfast and a copy of the *Los Angeles Times* at a diner. The paper reports a couple murders, but nothing like what I'd expect from a sociopath; in fact, the police characterize the shootings as "probably gang-related"—quick shootings, not the sadistic or sexual brutality culminating in death typical of recreational killers.

I re-fold the paper and lay it on the vacant side of the small, yellow Formica table for two, then eat some more granola cereal and soy milk. It's not easy to eat vegan on the road, but it's been a lot easier here in California. I consider the possibility of settling here. Having just gotten out of the Army and finally finished my masters degree in computer science after two years of night school, I'm now free to start a new life anywhere. This road trip I'm on is part vacation—my first real go-somewhere-and-see-something-new vacation in…well, since before the Bad I guess. But it's also an opportunity to re-evaluate my life, figure out where to go and what to do next.

Besides whatever my weird sense demands of me, that is.

Realistically though, while I'm open to the possibility of finding someplace else I like so much I decide to stay, I'll probably keep going until I end up back in Boston or thereabouts. You'd think, given the bad memories there, I'd want to start someplace new, but there's something drawing me back to New England. I guess there's enough good memories from my childhood there to counter-balance the memory of the Bad. New England still feels like home to me.

One

The smooth surface of Spy Pond is the same light gray color as the sky. The morning is quiet, mostly colorless, and cold, though I'm sweating after working the hills in Arlington Heights for the past thirty minutes, pumping my legs up some intensely steep side streets before leaning back and letting gravity draw me down again. Now I'm almost home, jogging easily along the flat dirt road through the small park on the northern shore of Spy Pond, which is more the size of a lake since it must be about a mile long and contains an island with a small grove of trees on it.

When I hit the start of Linwood Street I turn and follow it up away from the pond, past the Little League field and across the bike path. There are old houses lining the street here, mostly triple-deckers that were built in the first half of the century when the population really began to overflow from Boston and Cambridge into the surrounding towns. I see a brightly-lit Christmas tree in a front window. The interiors of these homes must be a sharp contrast to the morning out here. I imagine little kids screaming and laughing, wrapping paper tearing, music playing. Out here I glimpse colored lights in the windows, but the houses are all sealed against the winter, so all I can hear is my breathing and my feet lightly tapping the pavement as I trot by through the gray chill. This quiet is the best part of Christmas morning for me. Even though it's later than I usually go out running—it's probably about seven-thirty now—it's too early for people to begin visiting, and almost no one commutes to work Christmas morning, so I have the outside world to myself.

I turn down my street—Belknap Street. I can see the white triple-decker that's been home for a couple months.

There's a lighted Christmas tree here too, in the front window of the first floor unit, and as I turn down the driveway and slow to a walk, I can just barely hear "Jingle Bell Rock" when I go by the living room's side window. Around back is where we tenants park our cars—there's one space for each of the four units. Stacey is sitting there with the bright new red white and blue Massachusetts license plate on her butt. The space next to her, for the other third floor unit, is empty, and so is the slot for the people on the second floor. They're all away for the holiday, and that's good because it means my apartment, surrounded by unoccupied space, is quiet. My neighbors are mostly pretty considerate, but it's cool being the only person on the top two floors of the house.

It's kind of tricky getting to my apartment, and I like that. I climb three steps to the back porch and go in one of the two doors there. Inside there's a door to the basement, but I take a flight of stairs up to the second floor. There's a door to the second floor unit, and across the landing from it a door to that unit's back porch. I go out on the porch and walk the length of it to yet another door. I unlock the deadbolt I had installed, then the knob lock, enter, and pull the door shut behind me. I key the deadbolt home, lock the knob, hook the chain into the heavy-duty eyebolt I installed low on the door, and climb a flight of stairs up into my apartment. Each stair tread near the top has a pair of shoes or sneakers on it. I sit on the stairs, take my running shoes off, and put them on the vacant step second from the top, right below my Chuck Taylors, then leave the stairs and step onto the brownish-orange shag carpeting that came with the place.

It's just one room and a bathroom. Every apartment I've lived in as an adult has consisted of one room. They're cheaper to rent and, more importantly, it's easy to tell at a glance that no one else is in here with me. Of course, given my ability to sense the really bad ones, I guess I'd know before I even entered the building if one of them was waiting to harm me. Still, I prefer small apartments lacking in hiding places for intruders. I sweep my eyes over the contents of the room: a table and desk chair, a low bookcase, a basket chair, and a futon mattress on the floor. Except for the mattress, it's all from a used furniture store in Porter Square, or picked up from the side of the road on trash collection day. It's amazing the good stuff people throw out: I didn't even have to repair any of it; I just cleaned it up.

No Christmas decorations here; holidays are pointless when you're alone, but that's not so terrible. For a long time after my parents died, after the Bad, holidays really sucked. I still miss my parents, and I'll carry the guilt and remorse for my part in what happened until I'm dead, but after years of practice I've learned to think of holidays simply as time off from work.

Being alone isn't a problem. What was hard was living with my grandparents while I finished high school. At first they were really supportive; I guess they figured the attack on my family was purely random. But once they found out the bastard who killed their son and daughter-in-law was the photographer hired by my high school to take pictures of sports teams, including my field hockey team, they seemed to decide I did something to attract his attention, to *invite* the attack. Obviously I didn't want the Bad—that's crazy. But it's also clear the monster picked me out of the hundreds of girls he photographed that fall, so I must have done *something* to stand out. I don't debate that point; I even have a good idea what I did wrong. I had no idea of the consequences, but that doesn't change what I did or the shame I feel for it. So I don't blame my grandparents for hating me, but I also don't need their resentment to remind me of my guilt—I do just fine on my own.

Like the first and second floor units, this apartment has its own porch, and I look out the window set into the porch door. The porch is empty, but I think I might try growing a container garden out there in the spring. It faces more or less south, so it gets lots of light. I look further out, and to the right of the big Spy Pond Condominiums building I can see, through bare tree branches, the pond itself, slate gray and smooth.

I can also see the deadbolt on this door is still engaged. I try the knob and find it locked.

Two

*M*onday... Feeling groggy, Mike Maniotes surveys his coffee mug collection: There's the one from Worcester Polytech, his alma mater, next to the heavy white one from Chubby's Paradise Diner back home in Lowell. Next is the *X-Files* mug with Mulder's face on one side and Scully's on the other—when he uses that one he holds it in his left hand so Gillian Anderson's face is toward him. Yeah, she's a babe. Then there's the one from *The Annals of Improbable Research*—issuer of the Darwin Awards and the Ig-Nobel Prizes. Seeing that reminds him of the awards ceremony last October, in Harvard's surprisingly vertical Sanders Theatre where he was part of the almost medievally-raucous crowd. That was a good time. He considers the Kanter Mabry Architects mug, but he's not feeling much like a company man today, not on a Monday. Next is *Star Trek: the Next Generation* with the whole crew from season four; then another Worcester Polytech, this one from his five-year reunion; another *Star Trek* mug, this one with Worf's face on one side and Data's on the other; and finally one from the Boston Society of Architects. It's been a while since he used the Worf-Data mug, so he takes it now and heads for the kitchen.

Fortunately, someone's already made a pot of coffee; he smells it even before he enters the kitchen. He fills his mug with black goodness, stirs in a couple sugar packets, and starts to put the spoon in the sink before remembering Kate The Office Manager's email about leaving dirty dishes in the sink. He rinses the spoon and puts it in the drainer, then takes a sip before heading back to his desk.

Even the mere taste of coffee starts to dispel the cobwebs from his brain—obviously psychosomatic since it can't be the caffeine yet, can it? Maybe it gets absorbed through the gums. He's heard of people rubbing cocaine on their gums, and isn't caffeine chemically similar or something? He sits down and watches the steam rise off the smooth ebony surface of the liquid, deciding he's still just not ready for work. The phrase "seasonal affective disorder" occurs to him.   He read somewhere that the short days, cold temperatures, weak sunlight, and general lack of color typical of winter, especially in northerly places like New England, can actually affect people's emotions, and he wonders if that's his problem today. After all, it's February, so he's been dealing with cold and darkness for something like four months now. Maybe what he needs is a little sunshine.

Mike leans sideways and peers around the side of his big monitor. Looking down the length of Kanter Mabry's large open office, he can see at the far end of the space a spot of color: Shailene's dark yellow hair. He pretty much tripped all over himself when he first met Shailene a couple months ago; he still cringes at the memory. It took him until January before he convinced himself she probably didn't even remember him from her first day since she met two dozen other people that same morning. Over the past few weeks, he's made a hobby of looking for excuses to cross paths with her. Not that he'd date her; it's a bad idea to date co-workers. But he definitely doesn't mind seeing her up close, and there's nothing wrong with that. *I need a little Shailene today*, he thinks. She isn't exactly full of color and light—she's quiet and he has yet to see her really smile, but her green eyes would be welcome now.

It's been at least a week since he did anything to get her to come by and look at his computer. Deep down he knows this thing he does is pretty childish, but he doesn't let himself think about it. He just does it. *Let's see, already did the loose power cord on the computer...and on the monitor...* He at least tries to vary the issue when he calls on her for help. Bad enough he must be making himself look like a complete technological moron, without also looking like he has no capacity for learning from experience.

He opens his email program, gets a couple pieces of spam and a message from Kate The Office Manager about submitting time sheets for the previous week. Email is working fine, so nothing to complain about there. *Changed the screen resolution...what can I break this time?* It's important he doesn't do any real damage, or create a problem that eats up a lot of her time. He doesn't want to make her life difficult; he just wants her to stop by for a few minutes.

He wouldn't have to bother with this game if she were more approachable. While she's always polite and seems to be a good listener, she's not much for small talk. Plus, the office is like a freakin' fish bowl, with someone always nearby to hear what he says to her, so he's not comfortable asking her out.

Not that he would, since he doesn't date co-workers.

She'd say no anyway—she definitely gives off a "not available" vibe. *Maybe she's already seeing someone.* Another thought occurs to him: *Maybe she's a dyke.* He pauses on that idea. The image of her making out with another hot babe is not unpleasant.

He actually shakes his head to clear it, looks around to see if anyone is paying attention to him, but the other desks in his end of the room are unoccupied—most of the people who sit near him are on a site visit this morning, and Fran is on vacation. He clicks the Start button on his screen and looks at the options. *Let's see, let's see...* He drags the mouse up and clicks on the Printers icon. This opens a window showing the four printers he has to choose from. One of them he recognizes as the printer he normally sends stuff to. *A printer probably isn't that hard to reinstall.* He right-clicks on it and chooses delete from the pop-up menu. A message appears in the middle of the screen, asking him if he's sure he wants to do this. "Yep." Another message comes up telling him the large format plotter is now his default. Not wanting to accidentally print something to that and waste the big roller paper and the plotter's ink, he decides to delete that one too, making the color laser printer his default, but he doesn't want to piss off Kate The Office Manager by printing to that one unnecessarily. *Ah, what the hell.* He deletes that one and the fourth and final printer too. He looks at the empty printers window, then closes it.

Now I need something to print. He brings up the email window again and looks at the list of messages. There's one from yesterday listing the division of labor for the Stuart Mills project—this would actually be handy to print and stick on his little cork board. Knowing it won't work, he tries to print the text, gets the message about not having any printers installed, and leaves the message up on his screen.

Mike picks up his mug and walks the length of the large room. *It's too bad she sits way on the other end*, he thinks. If she sat closer he could just turn and talk to her casually from time to time, instead of going through this elaborate scheme. His view of her is temporarily eclipsed by a long three-quarter-height wall in the middle of the room, on which are hung the dozens of awards Kanter Mabry has won over the years. Once he gets past that Shailene comes back into view. She's leaning forward slightly and staring intently at her computer's screen, earnestly moving her mouse around.

Normally Mike prefers women with long hair, but Shailene's hair is really short on the sides and back, and a little bit of a mop on top. On her it's wicked cute, though that doesn't stop him from wondering how'd she'd look with long hair. And glasses. He thinks glasses on women can be very sexy, but he's never seen her wear them. The serious expression she usually has is kind of appealing too, but he's set it as a goal to see her smile. He's still working on that one, but it probably won't happen this morning since he's being a pain in her ass.

She looks over at him when he enters her peripheral vision. Her eyes lock with his. This almost stops him in his tracks, but he recovers and smiles a little as he continues to walk toward her desk. She's attractive to begin with, but her eyes are what really kill Mike. Green eyes are already rare, but then to see such a bright, intense tint—it's striking. At first he figured she was wearing colored contacts, but now he doesn't think so. She doesn't seem the type. She never wears makeup, as far as he can tell, and her clothes are mostly brown, gray, dark blue, or black. She doesn't wear any jewelry either; in fact, her ears aren't even pierced. So he can't imagine she'd make an exception to all this and wear colored contacts. Her eyes are naturally accented by her eyebrows, which are a slightly darker tint of amber than her hair. Almost perfectly straight, they angle down as they approach the center of her face, making her look a little angry, especially since she doesn't really smile. Now, though, the eyebrow on the right arches up a tick.

"Hey Mike, what'd you break now?"

He wonders if she means this literally, if she's caught on to what he's been doing. It is kind of a lot to be purely coincidental, but he sticks to his story. "What'd I *break*? It's not my fault I have bad computer karma."

The right eyebrow climbs another notch. "'Bad computer karma'?" she asks skeptically.

There's a twinge of trepidation in Mike's chest. Could he get in trouble for this? Is she on to him, and getting pissed off about it? Does this count as sexual harassment? "Uh...," he says, hesitating.

"I'm just kidding," she says, almost completely deadpan. Well, there might be slight tightening of her lips which could count as a sort of proto-smile. "What's up?"

"Um," he says, still a little off balance, "I, uh, my printers are gone."

"Gone?"

"That's what it says—I went to print an email, and it tells me I don't have any printers."

Her brow furrows a little. "Weird. I wonder where they went?"

Mike shrugs. "The Cape?" he offers, trying for the smile after all.

Instead she frowns slightly and shakes her head. "I doubt it—not in February."

He laughs, more out of surprise than amusement.

But she still doesn't smile. Instead, her eyes go wide for a moment as she stands up and says "Guess I'd better take a look."

They walk back across the office, Shailene leading the way, Mike surreptitiously checking her out as he follows behind. She's wearing loose-fitting jeans, somewhat faded, but not worn out, and a black, kind of baggy sweater that looks really soft and comfortable. He realizes he's checking out the curve the top of her ass makes under the bottom of the sweater, and drops his eyes to her feet. She's wearing her usual old-style black canvas high top sneakers, the kind with the big circle and star on the inside of each ankle. Hers are a little different though in that the rubber parts on the sole and toe are black instead of white. On the toes he's noticed streaks that make it look like she colored them with a black marker. He looks at the back of her head. "So how was your weekend, Shailene?"

She shrugs and turns her head a little toward him, saying over her shoulder "Fine, I guess. How 'bout yours? Do anything interesting?"

"Um..." The question catches him off guard. His intent was to get her talking and be a spectator, not to be put on the spot himself. His mind flashes to what his weekend actually was like, then briefly considers making up something like rock climbing or white water rafting, but he's always sucked at lying, and he's just not that quick at inventing stuff. "Uh, well, my 'scrip came in at the comic store, so I had to pick that up."

They've arrived at Mike's desk now, and Shailene walks around it and sits down in Mike's chair, looking up at him as she does. "Your 'scrip'? Like 'prescription'?"

"Huh? No—no, my *sub*scription." *This is so lame; I should have made something up.* "I, uh, subscribe to a few comics," he says, his voice trailing off.

"Really? I didn't know you could do that. You mean 'subscribe' like to a magazine, right?"

"Yeah," he nods, "yeah, exactly."

"Hmmm—neat." She looks at his computer screen and starts moving his mouse around. "Weird." She looks back up at him. "You have no printers installed."

Mike looks back, his face, he hopes, completely blank and innocent. "Really? I had them yesterday."

"Yeah, I figured you probably did." She looks back at the screen. "But now you have none—none printers installed."

Mike smiles. "*Spinal Tap*, right?"

She doesn't say anything; she just starts installing printers. "Fortunately, these are wicked easy to put back, but it's weird they'd just disappear like that."

She finishes installing the first printer, starts on the next. He watches her pale, slender hand riding around on top of his mouse, her long delicate fingers with the short-trimmed nails clicking the buttons. He shifts his eyes up to the side of her face. At this angle he can't see her eyes well, but he looks at the small ear with the unpunctured ear lobe, the way her honey-colored hair falls across her forehead, the smooth softness of her cheek, and he suddenly wants to kiss that cheek. "Yeah, I guess it's just my bad computer karma again."

Something suddenly changes in her—he can't say exactly what, but her whole body seems to tense, and her hand stops moving the mouse. She sits quietly for a couple long seconds, then asks, "Would that be the same bad computer karma that loosened the power cord on your computer one time, your monitor the next, the network cable after that, and changed your screen resolution last week?"

He looks away from her face, at the computer screen, suddenly feeling guilty and exposed. "Um..."

She turns to look at him. He meets her eyes for a second, sees something bright and scary in them, and looks down. "Sorry," he says, then glances sideways to see if anyone is nearby, paying attention to them, but no one is. She isn't saying anything, but she's still looking at him. He meets her gaze again. "I'm sorry. I—I just, I dunno, I guess I like you," he says, his voice trailing off to mumbling again.

Her face darkens; Mike takes a step back, but doesn't dare look away.

"Why—" she cuts the word short before she even finishes speaking it, and shakes her head. "Never mind." She turns back to the computer and resumes her work, installing another printer, moving and clicking the mouse rapidly.

Mike watches her, feeling shitty about the way this is going, trying to think of a way to recover. "Look, I'm sorry— let me buy you a cup of coffee or something after work. I owe you."

She finishes the third printer, starts on the fourth. "I don't think so...I—that's OK, let's just forget it, all right?"

He watches helplessly as she clicks through the procedure to install the last printer. "Look, this won't happen again—I mean...you know what I mean. I *am* sorry; the last thing I wanted to do was offend you somehow. That wasn't my intention. And I really would like to make it up to you."

She shakes her head as she closes the printer window, then stands up. "No, it's me. Let's just forget it." She's looking down at the computer screen, then glances up at him briefly, then away again, and says in a brighter, more friendly voice, "Should be all set now." She turns and walks away.

Shit. I'm so stupid, stupid, stupid.

Three

I stand on the bus platform beneath Harvard Square, waiting for the 77 bus that'll take me home. Since coming back to Massachusetts, the first couple times I stood here I remembered standing in this same spot, waiting for the same bus, over ten years ago. That was the first time I experienced the sense—that revisited pain on and behind the scar just below my sternum. I didn't know what it meant then; if I had, it would've scared me even more than it did. At the time I was told it was another symptom of post-traumatic stress disorder. They offered me meds to deal with the psycho-logical wounds, but I didn't take them. I don't let anything diminish my alertness; if I didn't have to sleep, I wouldn't do that either.

Anyway, now that I'm working at Kanter Mabry here in the square, this platform and the 77 bus are part of my everyday routine again, and I don't normally think about that time back in 1986. Today I'm thinking about Mike and the weirdness at work this morning. *What is* up *with these guys? What else can I do?* All that's really left is the hair on top of my head; maybe I should just cut it all off. *Shave* it off. Or maybe get really fat—that'd work. But I wouldn't be ready to fight if I were out of shape, and that'd break Rule Two—Be Ready. That's all the more important now that, because of the sense, I occasionally have to break Rule One—Avoid Violence.

The bus arrives and I get on, swipe my pass through the slot, and find a seat halfway back by a window on the right side. I prefer this side because it's better for looking out at the buildings and sidewalk going by on the trip home. I hear someone dump a handful of change into the fare box; more people get on. A woman sits down next to me, which is good since this time of day there's almost always going to be someone sitting next to me, and I don't like sitting close to guys. The bus doors close and we drive up the ramp and onto Massachusetts Avenue, headed home through the cold winter night, the light from the stores, other vehicles, and street lamps passing across my face.

I'm mainly a rational person; I know most men are not threats, and I've had a fair number of guy friends—well, not friends really, but guys I was friendly with and comfortable around—in the Army. And there was Remi, that cop down in New Orleans who asked me out. I didn't go, but his asking me out didn't bother me either. What made that different? The thing is, if I'm ever going to be close—really close—to someone, it's going to have to be with a guy. I cringe at the thought, but it's true.

When I was living in Alabama I was in the only romantic, and sexual, relationship I've ever experienced. I met Miranda at night school while we were both working on our computer science degrees. We had a good five months together, but unfortunately I'm not much of a lesbian. Anyone who says sexual orientation is a choice is full of shit because I really, *really* wanted to be with her, but I wasn't into the sex part of our relationship. She broke up with me two years ago this month.

So women really aren't an intimacy option with me, but I don't know that guys can be either. I think about Mike again. He seems pretty harmless; maybe I over-reacted. Probably I over-reacted. It wouldn't be the first time, although the episode that occurs to me now was a lot more embarrassing. I was with Miranda when it happened. We were both into weight lifting, and a few times we worked out at the gym where she had a job as a trainer, rather than at the considerably less swank Army gym where I normally trained.

The details are still vivid in my memory, I guess because of what happened. That morning—a Saturday—it was getting crowded, but fortunately we were almost done since we'd started a couple hours earlier. We were working biceps, spotting each other through multiple sets of barbell curls. I still remember Miranda adjusting her grip, her short, almost black hair hanging in front of her face while she was looking down at the bar, then looking up with those dark blue, almost violet eyes and smiling before taking up the weight.

Miranda did most of the lifting set on her own before I helped her get one last repetition in, then we switched and I did my set with the bar. Sometimes, when I'm in the middle of a set, with the lactic acid burning my muscles and my strength ebbing, something clicks over in my head and it's like I'm fighting for my life again. Suddenly, all that matters is moving the weight, and the pain in my body becomes irrelevant, or in a bizarre way actually desirable. A sort of rage fills me, and I'll be fucked if I'm going to give in to the pain and the weakness. The set I did then was one of those sets, and probably contributed to what happened next. I had just finished having Miranda force me through several reps until there was absolutely nothing left.

"You're insane," Miranda said as she helped me rack the barbell.

My arms felt like they were vibrating, but I managed a shrug. "It felt good, so I went with it."

Miranda shook her head. "Well, you may be crazy, but at least you maintain good form, even when you're tired. I really admire your discipline—you almost never cheat or throw the weight."

"Thanks, but it'd be kind of crazy to resort to bad form, wouldn't it?" I replied. "Unless you didn't have a training partner and wanted to force through some extra negative reps like we did just now. I mean, the idea is to make the movement hard and stress the muscle: that's how it gets stronger, right? I think it's mostly guys that throw weights around, trying to show off and make themselves seem stronger than they actually are."

"Like that guy that's been following us around in here, trying to impress you?"

"What guy?"

"You haven't noticed him? He was doing straight bar curls two racks down from us. Look—he's coming back from the water fountain now."

I looked over my shoulder and saw a beefy guy winding his way through the equipment. He wasn't very tall for a man—maybe five-eight, and while he was bulky with muscle, he wasn't sculpted like a body builder, but more thick and smooth like a football player or bouncer. He held his arms out from his body as he walked. The biggest bodybuilders are so muscular their mass prevents their arms from hanging naturally, but this guy looked more like he was actually holding his arms out away from his sides, pretending to be that big. I turned my head back toward Miranda, but continued to watch the man's reflection in the mirror on the wall. "You mean that guy, in the black tank with the brown flat top?"

"That's him."

"I guess I saw him a few times, but I didn't realize he was following us." I shouldn't have, but for some reason I continued to watch him in the mirror and saw him glance over at us as he approached the rack he was using.

"See—he's been doing that for the last half hour— following us around and constantly checking to see if we're checking him," she said quietly enough so he wouldn't be able to hear her over the gym's sound system. "What a dork—he has no idea he is so barking up the wrong tree."

I didn't say anything; I just watched the man's image. I was peripherally aware of Miranda turning to watch the mirror too, but I stayed focused on him. His eyes flicked toward me and I realized he was checking out my reflection too. Brief check, then a longer look punctuated with a sudden smile and wink as he looked at me via the reflective surface.   He mouthed something, slowing and exaggerating the articulation to make it easy for me to read his lips: *You're hot*. My head swam and a hand grabbed my heart and squeezed it hard.

I was vaguely aware of Miranda starting to laugh a little and saying something dismissive, but by then I'd already halved the distance between me and the guy. "Back off, you fuck!" I shouted.

The grin vanished from the guy's face as he turned his whole body toward me, obviously having a hard time mentally catching up.

"You think I'm hot?   You think I'm fuckin' *hot*?!"   At some deep level I realized the situation was out of control and I was, amazingly, inches from the man's face, leaning in and shouting at him, fists balled, my face burning and contorted. A demon had me and I didn't know what would happen next. "*I'm not hot!*"

"Shailene!"

The still lucid part of me heard Miranda yelling, but was unable to respond. I continued shouting, spraying the stunned man's face with spittle—I actually remember seeing the little white specks land on his face below his eyes. Arms clamped around me from behind and I exploded against them, almost breaking free before I heard Miranda's voice close in my left ear.

"Shailene, it's me—Miranda! It's OK—let's go!"

"You *fuck!*" I screamed, straining against Miranda's embrace, but the sane part of me, hearing Miranda's voice, was beginning to reassert itself.

"*Shailene!* C'mon, girlfriend, let's go, let it go, c'mon, *please*!"

I stopped fighting Miranda and let myself be dragged backward. Back a few steps and then Miranda was turning me around, putting her face close to mine and speaking quietly. I began to feel shaky, exhausted, and embarrassed. I allowed Miranda to lead me back to where our gym gear was piled by the rack we'd been using. I noticed I was breathing hard and tried to get it under control while something cold and wet ran down the hot skillet of my cheek. I heard Bruce Springsteen singing *Santa Claus is Coming to Town* on the sound system and sensed that otherwise the gym was now very quiet, with everyone looking at me. Behind me I heard a male voice say "crazy bitch", not directed at me exactly but, somewhere between a stage whisper and a shout, a simple declaration. I ignored it; I just wanted to go home.

"It's OK, honey. Let's just get our stuff and go, OK? Everything is all right now."

I nodded, looking down at the black-speckled, dull red hard rubber floor tiles. I sensed someone else come near and felt anger boil up again.

"It's all right, Dave—we're leaving."

He said nothing in response, but remained near as I put on my sweatshirt, and we picked up our towels, spring collars, and notebooks. I kept my eyes down and avoided looking at him, pretended he wasn't there and focused instead on the arm Miranda kept around my shoulders as we were escorted out the front door.

Miranda unlocked the passenger door of her Jeep and we threw our gear on the floor in front of the seat. I started to get in but Miranda touched my shoulders, gently stopping and turning me so we were facing each other. "Are you OK, sweetie?"

I briefly met the blue-violet eyes and then, feeling horribly embarrassed, looked back down at the pavement and nodded, mostly so Miranda would stop looking at me. "He should have just left me alone. I just want to be left alone," I said quietly.

Miranda hugged me again, then guided me into the Jeep.

We traveled in silence back to Miranda's apartment. I kept my head turned away, looking safely out the window at the streets of Dothan going by. Miranda pulled the Jeep into the parking lot behind her building, in a space next to my car. There were a couple seconds of silence. I was still too embarrassed to look at Miranda, and instead gazed longingly at my car, wanting only to go home and be alone, but feeling I needed to say something.

"I'm sor—" and "Are you—" we said, accidentally stepping on each other's words.

I looked over and saw Miranda smiling gently.

"Let's go inside."

"Miranda, I'm really sorry."

"You don't need to apologize."

"Yes I do—"

"Let's go in and talk."

"I think I should just go home."

"Don't make me guilt you into staying. C'mon, one glass of water and then you can go back to your place; you need to rest before you go." Before I could respond, Miranda was out and around to the passenger side by the time I was sliding off my seat. Miranda grabbed my free hand and we walked into the building and down the stairs to her basement apartment.

I immediately started gathering my things into my overnight bag, but Miranda took me by the hand again and sat me down at the little round table we ate at. "Just sit." Miranda got us each a tall glass of ice water and sat down across from me. "Drink up," she said, holding up her own glass as if making a toast, then taking a big gulp. I picked up my glass, sipped some water, put it back down.

"I'm sorry, Miranda."

"Look, it's my fault too—you hadn't even noticed him before I said anything. I just, I dunno, I thought it was *funny*—I didn't realize it would upset you."

"He should have left me alone—he had no business checking us out, or...I wasn't doing anything—why was he bothering me?"

"Shailene, what was it? I mean, he was an ass, but what set you off? I've never seen you so upset—I don't think I've ever seen *anyone* so upset."

I glanced up quickly before resettling my eyes on the ice floating in my glass of water. "He just...reminded me of someone...I met once. Someone bad. I dunno...I really think I should go home."

"Shailene, *talk* to me. We're s'posed to be able to help each other out and trust each other, right?" she exclaimed, suddenly sounding exasperated.

I looked up at her, startled.

She took a deep breath and added more quietly, "I'm sorry—I don't mean to shout, but it would be easier to deal with this if I understood what it was about. I always feel walled off from some big part of you. Why do you keep shutting me out?"

I looked back at my glass of water. I felt I *did* owe her an explanation, and I *wanted* her to understand. But years of habit...except for Sarah, the counselor who'd helped me right after the Bad, I'd never spoken to anyone about...that. But this was Miranda. "I—" I stopped, wondering if Miranda would be disgusted by the truth, wondering what her reaction would be. But it was clear not telling her was becoming a wedge between us. *If only I hadn't noticed that guy—why did she point him out?* I thought, looking for someone else to blame and immediately regretting it. *Why was he looking at me?* I had no answer I wanted for this one. *Fuck it.* I spoke very quietly, trying to minimize the words as I said them. "I was—" That word—I never use that word in reference to myself. "I was atta—" I closed my eyes and swallowed. "I was raped," I felt the tears start to roll, but I persisted, "when I was fifteen."

"Oh honey, I'm so sorry."

I heard Miranda get up and come around the table, felt her arms embrace me, her chin touch the top of my head. I felt at once grateful and unworthy, wanted to keep the arms there and to throw them off.

"A…" I paused. I wanted to get it all out now, but I wasn't sure what to call the monster. "He broke into our house in the middle of the night. To get to me, he…" I felt my face contort involuntarily and was glad Miranda couldn't see. I swallowed again, got my voice under control. "He killed my parents. Then he raped me."

"My god! Honey, I'm so sorry."

No! No sympathy! I suddenly felt Miranda shouldn't be holding me. I didn't deserve it and didn't want it, but also didn't want to hurt her feelings.

"So, your, uh, that scar—did he do that?"

I nodded. There are actually two visible scars on my skin from the Bad, but I knew the one Miranda meant, the bigger one at the top of my abdomen, the one that hurts sometimes. Miranda had seen it a few weeks earlier when we were trying on some of Miranda's retro jazz age clothes. "You, uh, you don't have to hold me."

"I'm sorry," she said, letting go.

I felt bad; I didn't want or merit an apology. "I just need to wipe my nose," I said matter-of-factly, suddenly under control again, as if I were talking about someone else's nose.

Miranda walked to the bathroom, returned with a box of tissues which she placed on the table. She hesitated a moment, then sat down across from me.

I took a tissue, blew my nose, took another and wiped my cheeks and eyes, wishing none of this had happened, wishing I were alone.

"Did they get him?"

I continued to look at the wadded up tissues in my hands, resting on the table top. "I got him," I said flatly.

"What? You mean—what do you mean?"

"I mean I…killed him." This was something else I hadn't said since giving my statement to the police back when it happened.

"Whoa, really? I—that's great!" She paused a beat; I stayed focused on my fists. "Isn't it?"

I shook my head. "It's not like that. I'd be lying if I said there wasn't some consolation in him being dead, but I don't like to think about it—about any of it, really. Sometimes I dream about what happened—nightmares—but not as much as I used to, which is a relief." I paused, noticing that talking about this hadn't made me feel any better; there was no catharsis. Then again, talking about it hadn't changed anything, so why should I have felt different? "The damage is done, you know? There's no undoing it." I shuddered involuntarily, sniffed, and looked up at Miranda. "That's it. I haven't told anyone since then." Maybe saying that last part sounded manipulative, but I did want Miranda to know.

Miranda reached across the table and her fingertips touched my hands, still clutching their wet ball of tissues. "Thank you. That means a lot to me. Does it make you feel better to talk about it?"

I dropped my eyes again. "I guess it's kind of a relief that now you know. But talking about it doesn't make me feel better. I think I'm past that stage and what I feel now is what I feel—I don't think that's going to change." But I did sense a barrier between us had been removed. I took the used tissues away with my left hand, and gripped Miranda's hand with my right. "I hope telling you is good for us, though. You mean a lot to me."

The bus is approaching my stop; I press the rubber strip between the windows and the "Stop Requested" sign at the front of the bus lights up.

Even two years later, I still miss Miranda. Not the sex part, but the companionship. I wonder what she's doing now, how she's doing.

I get up and start walking down the aisle, touching the seats for balance as the bus rolls to a stop. "Thanks, have a good one," I say to the driver as I disembark.

"See ya," I hear him say behind me, and then the doors close and the bus roars off down Mass Ave. I wait for a break in traffic, then cross the street diagonally and head down Marion Road, which leads to my street. It feels cold after being on the warm bus, but I walk quickly, and I'll be in my apartment in two or three minutes.

Anyway, I realize I can be quick to anger. But to be fair, that guy in the gym's word choice—the phrase he mouthed to me in the mirror—carries extra baggage with me. "Because you're hot" is the answer the fifteen-year-old me got when she asked her attacker "why?" *Because you're hot* has echoed in my head ever since, and I've tried hard to show how wrong he was, but that dickhead in the gym was telling me I'd failed.

Is Mike telling me the same thing? Not in so many words…but why all the weirdness with breaking stuff on his PC if he just wants to be friends?

Well, it's true I don't make friends easily. Over the past several years, especially since I graduated from the Military Academy and left behind the enforced companionship of cadet life, I've gotten in the habit of keeping to myself. The thing about solitude is the longer you're alone, the harder it is to be with other people. I guess social interaction is like any ability: when neglected, it atrophies. I know I should force myself to make nice with people, and at some level I think I want to, but mostly I find the idea really unappealing. What would I talk about? Why would anyone want to talk to me?

Mike apparently wants to talk to me; he *did* invite me out for coffee. That seems pretty safe: A cup of coffee in a busy place after work, and then we part company. No harm in that;

coffee isn't sex. And I could ask him about his comic book subscription. *How strange that sounds.* So, yeah, maybe he wants something else—maybe he does want to...date or...whatever—but it doesn't have to be that way, does it? Maybe we can just be friends. *That does happen, right? People do sometimes become friends without having to have sex eventually. Right?*

Four

"I am so ready for spring," Mike says to Shailene as they step out the door to the office building they work in. They pause to button their coats in the building's broad covered entryway at the edge of the sidewalk. "By the end of February every year, I am done—*done* with winter."

"Yeah, but unfortunately winter couldn't care less what we think."

Mike looks over at her as he finishes buttoning his coat and smiles. Shailene isn't smiling; he still hasn't seen the smile for real yet, though he's tried to imagine it a few times. If anything, she looks a little nervous: a couple small lines have appeared between her eyebrows, and she's looking around a lot, but doesn't look back at him. He wonders if she could be as nervous as he is, and if she is, what it might mean. "So, where to?"

She looks at him, and there's a sharpness in her eyes. "I don't know—this is *your* idea; I don't go out for coffee."

Mike mentally takes a step back. He's wanted to go out with her for weeks, but not if she's going to be like this. "Listen, we don't—"

"I'm sorry," she says, looking down and shaking her head. She looks back up at him, meeting his eyes. "I'm just a little..." she looks away, "...edgy. I, uh, I don't socialize a lot, so this is a little awkward for me." She meets his eyes again. "Look, let's start this over, OK? I'll be right back— wait here." She turns and goes back in the building.

Mike, surprised, turns and looks through the glass door into the lobby, watches her as she walks across the foyer to the elevator doors and stands facing them. *Is she going back upstairs?* After two or three seconds she turns and walks back toward him, pushes through the glass door, and walks up to him.

"Hi," she says, making a short, declarative sentence out of it. "Let's go somewhere for coffee, OK?"

"Uh, sure," Mike says, half smiling, thinking how weird this is.

"The Au Bon Pain in Harvard Square sound good to you?" she asks.

"Au Bon Pain—perfect."

"OK, let's go." She steps into the bustle of the sidewalk and starts walking toward the square.

Mike hurries after her.

"I realize I should have asked where you live," she says when he pulls even with her. "Is this taking you way out of your way?"

"Um, well, not *way* out—I live in Inman Square."

"Oh, great—so this is like the opposite direction from home for you."

"Really, it's OK. Where do you live?"

She smiles her lopsided, tight, ironic smile—not a real smile, but it's something. "I live in East Arlington, so this is perfect for me. I take the bus from the square home, so I go this way every day. Sorry. If you want we can go somewhere more centrally-located—I just don't know any coffee shops here in Cambridge that aren't in the square. I don't really pay attention to them."

"No, this is fine. Afterwards, you'll still have to take the bus home, and I'll walk home—Probably about twenty minutes for each of us, so it's even."

"OK, thanks. You're a good guy, Mike."

He looks down at her—she's about a half foot shorter than him, and she glances up at him, makes eye contact briefly, then looks back in front of her in time to avoid colliding with a group of Asian students walking toward them. Mike falls behind to make more space for her to move over to the right, and as he does this he replays the words she just said, and the look that followed them. He reminds himself not to read too much into it, which is his usual problem with women he finds attractive.

The crowded sidewalk and noise from the rush hour traffic beside them on Massachusetts Avenue makes talking difficult, so they don't say any more until Mike holds the door for her at Au Bon Pain and says "After you."

"Thanks," she says—small, closed smile, but with both corners of her mouth this time: no irony.

Inside Shailene tries to buy her own cup of tea, but Mike insists on paying. "The whole point of this is for me to pay you back for, you know...that thing with my computer."

"Oh yeah—I forgot about that. Pay the man," she says, nodding at the counter and stepping back with a mug in her hands, which are red from the cold outside.

"See if you can snag us a table." Mike gets himself a simple cup of black coffee, pays, then looks around to see Shailene raise her hand from a two-top a third of the way across the big, crowded seating area. He walks toward her wondering what to talk about, and reminding himself to ask questions—get her to talk about her.

As he sits down, she raises her mug to him. "So, thanks Mike. You really didn't have to do this."

"It's just a cup of tea—no big deal. And I *wanted* to do this, so," he raises his mug to her, "thank *you* too." He takes a small sip because it's still very hot. When the liquid hits the back of his tongue, the bitterness causes him to grimace. "Ugh—I forgot to add sugar." He reaches for the little plastic caddy with the paper packets of sweeteners.

"Used to be I couldn't drink coffee straight either, but back in school, during exams, we'd get what we called 'survival rations' in the barracks, and the sugar would always run out before the coffee. After a while, I got to like it better without the sweet."

"The 'barracks'? Where did you go to school?"

Ironic smile. "Sorry, I forgot to translate; I'm still getting used to this civilian thing. We called our dorms 'barracks'; I went to the Military Academy."

He looks at her blankly, feeling like he should know what she means, but not making the connection.

"You know, uh, West Point," she says, gesturing dismissively.

Mike feels his eyebrows go up. "Really? You went to West Point?"

Her right eyebrow cocks, and a trace of the ironic smile appears again. "Is that surprising?"

"Well, yeah, it kind of is...I mean, aren't you kind of, well, small?"

"There is a height requirement, but the standard for women encompasses normal female heights, including my five-feet four inches. I'm not that short, am I?"

"It's not just your height. I'd have expected an Army woman to be more...*burly* I guess." He wants to add "and less pretty," but he senses that would be a mistake—too much, too forward.

"I'm not as dainty as you might think. So how 'bout you? Where'd you learn to be an architect?"

"Worcester Polytech."

She nods. "Good school, I've heard."

"I liked it, though it's not as interesting as West Point. Why'd you decide to go there?"

She looks down at her tea and shrugs. "It seemed like the best place for me to go." She looks back up at him quickly. "So are you from around here?"

"Lowell, actually. My parents immigrated from Greece, and my uncle, who immigrated before my parents, was in Lowell, so they settled there too."

"Were you born in Greece?" she asks, leaning forward and looking at him.

Mike wishes he could say yes, since she seems so interested in this. "No, I was born here—well, in Lowell. But growing up in my neighborhood was a little like being from Greece. Most of the store signs in my old neighborhood are in Greek, and you hear more Greek than English being spoken there. But I've never been to Greece myself. Hopefully someday."

"Are you bilingual?

"Yeah, I am that. At home my parents mostly spoke Greek, but they taught me a lot of English before I started school."

"Well, you should definitely go to Greece—you wouldn't be confined to the touristy places because you'd be able to speak to the normal people there. I bet you could have a really interesting trip."

"Yeah, I'd like to take my parents there someday. They haven't been back since they came here, and they still have relatives over there. I know they'd like to visit, but they don't take vacations because they have to run their pastry shop. They wanted me to work in the business too, and hand it off to me eventually, but I like to have down time once in a while, you know?"

She nods. "Sure. I think it'd be really hard to be self-employed, and especially to own a store or have people working for you. I think it'd be stressful."

"Well it's definitely a lot of work—they're open Monday through Saturday, and even on Sunday they often go in there early or in the afternoon to take care of stuff. Pretty much the only time they consistently aren't in the shop is late each Sunday morning, when they're at church. They never miss that."

"Pretty religious?"

Mike takes a sip of the coffee and nods. "They are. They wish I were too, but...I don't know. In a way, *I* wish I were more religious, but it's hard for me to..." he pauses, searching for the right phrase, "…accept things on faith. You know what I mean?"

She's nodding and meets his eyes when he looks at her. "Absolutely. I think it's essential to question, especially with big issues like morality and religion. I was raised attending church and Sunday school, but some stuff happened when I was a teenager and I saw how…wrong—you know: just plain incorrect—a lot of what I'd been taught was, so I became an atheist."

"You're an atheist?" Mike asks, surprised.

Crooked smile, but with some real amusement in her eyes. "Does that bother you?"

Mike looks away as he tries to sort out what he feels. "It's just that I've never met an atheist before. Well, probably I've met plenty of atheists, but no one has actually come out and said it before. In my family, atheism is probably the ultimate taboo—right up there with laziness." He smiles, and wonders if he's on thin ice with her here.

She nods, the half smile still on her face. "Yeah, well now I'm a lapsed atheist. Some stuff happened about a year and a half ago, and I lost my faith in my lack of faith, started to question the randomness of the universe. Now I'm more of an agnostic, I guess. I've been intending to try to figure this out, to figure out what I really think, but it's hard to know where to begin. Plus, I've been kind of busy, what with becoming a civilian again, finishing my masters, and moving back up here. How 'bout you? You said you're not all that religious, but I guess you're not an atheist either."

"I'd say I'm still a Christian—I like the message of Christianity. Real Christianity anyway, not the 'we're better than you and you're going to hell' kind. I'm not really into all the pomp and circumstance either, and there's a lot of that in the Greek church. I don't know—maybe I'm in the same situation as you, sort of. I feel like I should figure this out, but it's hard—there's always other stuff to do."

"Like what? What else do you like to do? Besides design buildings, I mean."

He smiles. "Well, you already know about my comic subscription; I can't believe I told you that."

"Why?"

"I generally try to avoid the extreme geek image for myself."

And then it happens—just for a second—but she flashes a real smile, teeth and all. "Mike, I think you already blew that with your mug collection. I mean, *Star Trek* and *The Annals of Improbable Research*? C'mon!" There's almost a laugh in her voice as she says this, and the real smile comes out again.

Mike smiles back. "You mean, not everybody's into the *Annals*?"

"The only reason I know about it is because I listen to Public Radio, and they broadcast the—what is it? The Ig-Nobel Prize ceremony every year on the day after Thanksgiving. 'Will the undergraduates bar the doors!'" she says, imitating the over-the top commanding tone of the Ig-Nobels' MC.

"'Recognizing scientific achievements which can not, or should not, be reproduced,'" Mike replies, matching her tone. "But doesn't the fact that you know about this, and listen to Public Radio, make *you* a geek?"

She looks up and to the side and puts a finger to her lips in an exaggerated look of thoughtfulness. "Hmmm, gee, who'd have thought that the person who takes care of your computers is…a *geek*?!"

Mike laughs a little, partly because he thinks what she said is funny, and partly because he's pleased and surprised by her making a joke.

"So what were you saying—before I interrupted, I mean. Oh yeah—the comics; tell me about the comics."

"Damn, I thought you'd dropped that. Well, the comics; what can I say? I try to remember to refer to them as 'graphic novels'—then it sounds intellectual and trendy. 'Comics' sounds like I never grew up."

"Not to me—I thought it sounded cool and interesting. Made me want to know more."

"If you want, I can loan you some. I don't know what you're interested in, but I tend to prefer the crime story stuff more than super hero. Have you heard of Frank Miller?"

"No, who's he?"

"He does this series called *Sin City*—it's pretty intense crime fiction. You can borrow some if you like—they really are graphic novels, so each one is a lot longer than a standard comic book, and contains a complete story arc."

"Yeah, I don't know; the crime stuff might not be my thing."

"There's also Garth Ennis' Preacher series. That's hard to categorize, but it's sort of an adventure story with supernatural elements, about a guy with the 'voice of God' power he can use to compel anyone to do anything, just by commanding them. There's a lot more to it than that, but it'd probably be easiest to just read the first one."

"Sure, I'd give that a shot—thanks!"

Mike remembers he'd meant to show her he's actually *not* a total geek. "So anyway, besides the comics, I'm into karate."

Her eyebrows go up. "Really?"

Yes! She seems suitably impressed, but he manages to keep nonchalant about it and simply nods. "Yeah, you've heard of it?"

"Of 'karate'?" she asks giving him a weird look.

Of course she's heard of karate—*who hasn't?!* "Er, I mean, of *shotokan* karate—I meant to say that. That's the style I'm learning."

She nods and then shakes her head. "Oh, no—I'm not really familiar with the different styles. Except tae kwon do— that's like Korean karate. I knew some guys, Korean guys mostly, when I was stationed in Korea." She rolls her eyes. "Of course, 'Korean, Korean, Korea'—sorry. Anyway, I always meant to get them to teach me some moves, but it never worked out. Maybe you could show me some stuff?"

This surprises him. "Uh—you want me to teach you?"

"Yeah, I'm interested in martial arts. I've never committed to learning one, but I try to pick up a move or two here and there and learn them. You never know—might come in handy sometime."

Is this happening? "Sure, I'd like that," he says, working hard to sound casual. Maybe we could meet tomorrow at the Y in Central Square? That's where my classes are, but there's also usually a quiet area someplace where we could practice for a little while."

"All right." She nods sharply once. "Tomorrow it is. What time?"

"Ten a.m. OK with you?"

"Ten a.m." She nods again, then pushes away from the table. "I really should get going—get home and get some dinner. Thanks again for the tea, Mike." She gives the small, closed-lip, non-ironic smile, what Mike is starting to think of as the "sweet" smile.

"Totally my pleasure—really," he says, standing up, surprised at her sudden departure. He feels like he should shake hands or something, but just the thought of that seems painfully awkward. "I'm really glad we could talk like this."

She flashes the sweet smile again. "Me too. So where do I take this?" she asks, picking up her mug and looking around.

"Just leave it—I'll take it up."

"No, I like to clean up after myself—I see it." She turns back to him. "So thanks, and see ya tomorrow, Mike."

"OK, see ya."

She turns and passes by the counter on her way out, leaving her mug there. Mike watches her go, then realizes he's been standing in the middle of the place, turning to follow

her departure.   He looks around and sees no one is paying
attention to him.   As he carries his mostly empty mug up to
the counter, he wonders why she suddenly had to leave, and
worries he said something wrong just now.   But she did ask if
they could get together again on Saturday—actually set a time
with him, so that's something.

He replays their conversation in his head, trying to recall
each expression that crossed her face, each word she said.   He
thinks about the sound of her voice—deep for a small, slender
woman like her, but still feminine.

He's halfway home before he even realizes where he is.

Five

Paul Tomasi relishes the quiet. The loudest sound is his boots crunching through the icy, granular patches of snow in the shady parts of the sand road, and the cawing of several crows somewhere in the middle distance up ahead. He loves this time of year because so few people visit the Pine Barrens now. Except for an elderly couple he passed on the sand road leading from the Atsion parking area, he hasn't seen anyone else since he got here today. For Paul the lack of other humans is one of the main attractions of the forest. He doesn't hate people, but he believes the key to good time off is to get away from whatever it is you do during the week to earn a living. In Paul's case, this means getting away from the streets and traffic and people in Trenton, where he works maintaining the electric grid. On the weekend, he likes to see trees and hear quiet. He's not able to do this every weekend, especially now with his wife Gina so far along in her pregnancy, but the time he does get out here is like gold.

Today it's sunlight he has on him, and it feels warm. The cold spell they had after the snow storm that blew through last week broke yesterday, and in the sunny areas the snow has already melted away. Even in the shady places the four inches of fluff has become an inch or two of packed ice crystals. Paul looks up and admires the brilliant, deep blue of the sky, contrasting with the dark green of the pines which line the road and frame his view. Some crows fly across the strip of blue, their shiny blackness catching the light as they go. Paul wonders where they're headed, what they're doing.

He's intrigued by animals that stay through the winter. He wonders how they survive and what their lives are like. Maybe he should have been a naturalist, though he really doesn't know how a person gets paid to do that. Maybe you have to teach, and then the university pays you to take time off and study nature? He also wonders, had he become a naturalist, if it would have ruined his appreciation of nature. If you do something you love to earn a living, does that thing become "work"? Do you end up disliking it and wanting, on your weekends, to get away from it? Maybe not. He shrugs his shoulders slightly. It doesn't matter now; at thirty-five, with a mortgage to pay and a kid on the way, he's not going to suddenly fork over their savings to go back to school, and he's not going to change careers. Now he's saving to put little Marie, his soon-to-be-born daughter through school. He smiles at the thought of telling Gina he's going back to college to be a naturalist—that'd get a reaction. Maybe he'll tell her anyway, just to mess with her.

He hears wings overhead and looks up to see a couple more crows, flying the same way as the others. *Where are they all going?* He's seen crows—big masses of them— gather in trees and caw at each other. He wonders what they're talking about, if it's like some kind of town meeting for them.

He remembers hearing some crows around this point on his way out a couple hours ago. At the time he hadn't paid much attention; then he was just glad to be in the woods, stretching his legs and breathing the clean, chilly air. And he'd felt much colder then, before the sun came up and before he'd really gotten going. Getting warm had been a motivation to step out. Now, with the sunlight angling through the trees on his back and his heart rate slightly up, he's plenty warm, and can afford to be curious.

There's more raucous cawing in the woods on his left. He stops and peers through the pines, but there are too many trees and shrubs, and a slight incline, blocking his view. He can't see the crows, just lots of thin-trunked gangly pines, a few thicker hardwoods, and a scattering of green in the understory—mountain laurel. He wonders again about what the crows do when they gather together. *Maybe they're plotting the overthrow of humans and the corvid conquest of the planet,* he thinks, smiling at the idea, and pleased that he remembers the scientific name for the family of birds which includes ravens and crows. He read in *National Geographic* that corvids are especially smart, and have even been observed using rudimentary tools. He glances at his watch and says "what the hell?" under his breath before stepping between the nearest two trees.

About twenty feet in he thinks he remembers there's a side trail a little closer to the parking area that leads up this way, but he continues on through the woods. There are a lot of pines, and some very low, twiggy undergrowth he thinks might be low-bush blueberry, but he really doesn't know. Despite this, the going isn't very difficult. He weaves his way through, occasionally looking back over his shoulder, though he's not really concerned about getting lost. He can still make out the pale sand of the road behind him, and he's pretty certain he'll eventually hit that side trail, which is itself wide enough for a car, if he remembers correctly.

He smells the fresh odor of the pines all around him. It's like smelling the life force of the forest, hiding just below the surface. In a couple months when he comes here that energy will be bursting forth everywhere: plants pushing up out of the ground, leaves popping out on these bare twigs at his feet, insects buzzing through the air. The songbirds will start showing up again, filling the air with their music. Spring is the most exciting time of year here, and Paul loves it.

Gina has her own springtime going on, with the life of their daughter just below her surface. *Marie.* He forms the name in his mind, still getting used to the sound of it, to the idea of being a father.

After going a hundred feet or so into the trees, he sees a brown break in the vegetation up ahead, a place the size of a large room, maybe thirty feet across. In this area there are no pines or undergrowth, just the mat of fallen needles that's everywhere. He stops, thinking about his earlier idea of the crow conference, and of that Hitchcock movie *The Birds*. Through the branches and trunks he sees a whole gang of crows—maybe two dozen of them—clustered on the ground around something near the middle of the small clearing.

Then he notices the smell. It's faint, but distinctive: that ripe sweetness garbage gets when bones and meat scraps have been sitting in the barrel almost the full week since the last pickup. His first thought is that some asshole dumped his trash here. People can be such dolts. Then it occurs to him it could be a dead animal. *Maybe it's a deer*, he thinks, looking at the large number of birds on it, but the cluster of black bodies prevents him from seeing what they're standing on. The would-be naturalist in him is curious, but he also doesn't want to disturb the birds' meal or them fulfilling their role in the forest. He quietly steps closer.

The clearing is not large enough to be actually sunny, but everything is brightly lit by the brilliant sunlight all around, which the bare-branched hardwoods and thin pines cannot completely block. He peers at the cluster of birds. As they peck and flap at each other, jockeying for position, he catches a glimpse of red: such a bright shade of red it surprises him. *Could that be blood?* he thinks, simultaneously repulsed and fascinated. He slowly, quietly steps closer; the crows pay no attention to him.

The crows move again, and now he sees the red more clearly. It's too bright to be meat or blood. The edge of the red, silhouetted against the brown background of dirt and dead grass, is a smooth curve, not ragged, and Paul thinks clothing, like an insulated coat—something sufficiently thick and stiff to keep its shape. He continues moving closer, and some of the crows spook and take flight. Paul notices one of the bolder crows pulling at the red, and tossing something white and fluffy aside. *Insulation—it's a winter coat. What...* He thinks there could be a discarded or lost coat here, that it could just happen to be lying near or on a dead animal, but he quickens his pace. More crows hop away, cawing angrily, and fly up into the trees all around the clearing.

The red shape is partially obscured by some scattered sand, dead branches, pine needles, and a few pine boughs, but the clear shape of a hood and what could be a sleeve, both child-sized, stops him. The pine branches are out of place, concentrated as they are in the middle of the clearing, away from the surrounding trees. Paul thinks the piled debris could have been a makeshift blanket or shelter. He rushes the last few steps and, waving his arms and yelling, shoos the remaining crows away. Standing over the exposed red coat, he can see inside the hood. It takes Paul a moment to process the image of empty eye sockets, exposed bone, and remnants of flesh; then he stumbles backward, the garbage smell sticking in his nostrils and getting in his mouth. "Oh shit," he says quietly. He moves his gaze away from the head. Right next to the partially buried child, in a smaller depression amidst more scattered dirt, is the tattered carcass of what might have been a very small dog.

He turns away, pulls out his cell phone, and dials 911. Paul doesn't know who this kid was, but even as he begins speaking to the emergency services operator he silently vows Marie will never be found lying dead in the woods like this.

Six

Mario runs up a ramp, leaps across a chasm, and crosses a platform, managing to grab some coins on his way. Then he's down a flight of stairs, jumps on a Koopa Trooper, and begins ascending another staircase.

Wayne Lambert works the Nintendo's joystick and buttons. He's only rescued the princess—he likes to think of her as Dana—once, but it looks like he might be about to do it again. He leans his body, trying to get over an obstacle. After all this time playing, Wayne really doesn't think of the little character on the screen as Mario anymore. The guy in the overalls and hat is *himself*. Wayne is the hero, and he's going to rescue—no, *not* Dana. This time it's not Dana he's rescuing, but a little boy. Wayne is going to do it, too. He's going to rescue this boy from the people who are messing him up.

Most of these people don't care about the boy, pay no attention to him. That eats away at him, at who he thinks he is, until he feels like he's no one. All that's bad enough, but then a man, *Todd*, takes an interest in the boy and makes him feel special. Because of this the boy loves Todd and does anything for him. Todd knows this, and he and the boy do loving, secret things together. At first, doing these things makes the boy feel good—important and loved. But eventually the vine that grows from this seed will choke and crush the boy.

But not this time. This time Wayne is going to save him. Wayne is going to get him out of here and take him someplace better where he'll be happy and loved, and where no one will ever do secret things to him again.

Wayne faces Bowser—*Todd*—for the last time, and hits him with a series of fireballs, killing him and saving the boy. Some stories have happy endings; sometimes it comes out all right in the end. He turns off the Nintendo and the TV, then carefully wraps the wires around the control unit and puts it away neatly on the shelf below the television, next to the Nintendo box, then closes the cabinet's doors.

All the heroic effort has made him hungry, and he wonders what's for breakfast. He stands up and pads across the room, thinking of Apple Jacks cereal.

The way to the kitchen leads past the bookcase where he keeps almost all his *Star Wars* toys—six shelves worth. He stops and looks at the cantina set up he has, with all the band members that were in the original movie scene, plus Han Solo and Greedo. He picks up Greedo and examines him closely. A lot of collectors would say Wayne is wrong to take the figures out of their packaging—"off card"—but Wayne likes to play with them. Toys are for playing; keeping them in their packages and storing them away so they never fade or get damaged is weird.

He puts Greedo back and looks at the next shelf up, where he has all the toys from the battle scene on the planet Hoth in *Empire Strikes Back*, including three AT-AT Walkers firing at Rebel Snowspeeders in front of a Hoth Ice Planet playset. Wayne repositions the tall, armored AT-ATs so they look, if possible, more threatening to the rebel vehicles, then backs them off again—too scary.

Satisfied, he steps back so he can take in the entire bookcase more or less all at once. All the little figures, dozens of them, carefully arranged, re-creating scenes from the movies. *What am I doing?* He sees a man in his late twenties staring at shelves full of little plastic figures. He spent countless hours finding and purchasing them, setting them up, rearranging them, imagining the scenes and re-enacting them.

But suddenly here he is, twenty-nine years old, standing in his apartment staring at a bookcase full of toys. *What am I doing?*

Then he remembers, and it's like everything snaps back into place. He would have been so psyched to have even a few of these toys when he was a kid. All he had then was a beat-up Chewbacca and a Darth Vader with only one arm he found on the edge of the playground at school. He found the Darth Vader first; after that he checked in the weeds and trash two, three, or more times a week for what must have been months, but only found the Chewbacca in all that time. What was he supposed to do with them? They weren't even really together in any scenes. He'd had to invent an alternate story in which Chewie fights Vader and tears his arm off. *I'm making up for what I missed—that's what I'm doing.*

Feeling good again, Wayne turns and goes into the kitchen to make breakfast.

Seven

"The skills you learn today might save your ass."

One of my mentors at the Military Academy, Sergeant Pike, said this to me and the Ranger School aspirants one cold Saturday afternoon in March as we were embarking on another training mission in the rocky, forested high ground surrounding West Point. There was half a foot of old, icy snow on the ground and it was cold enough to freeze the snot in my nose, but I paid attention because I knew he was right. That's why I was there. The training was preparation for Ranger School, one of the Army's most difficult challenges, but being a woman, I wasn't allowed to attend. I was sort of auditing the course, standing in the snow that day for the same reason I came to West Point in the first place: to learn skills that might save my ass.

Anyway, I repeat these words silently to myself as I walk into an empty dance room at the big YMCA near Central Square in Cambridge. I repeat them not because I'm some crazy, gung-ho yahoo, but because I'm wondering what the hell I've gotten myself into by asking Mike to teach me karate moves. I'd asked it impulsively, almost instinctively, when he told me about his hobby. Now that I'm here, I wish I'd just nodded, said something polite, and moved on. *Will he interpret this as some kind of step on the way to dating or (shudder) becoming physical with each other? Is that why I asked him to do this? Do I subconsciously want something to happen with him?!*

Just calm down and try to learn something, I tell myself, wishing my brain would shut up for once.

"So, OK, here we are—this is the room my class usually meets in. You know, there are some women in the class—it's

definitely cool that way, and Mr. Asihara, the instructor, is
great. We meet every Tuesday evening, and the last Saturday
of every month."

"Thanks, I'll think about it," I say, meaning it. I tend to
keep to myself, and I'm not interested in martial arts as sport
or hobby, but if it would make me stronger…

The room is maybe thirty feet by thirty feet—about like
the aerobics room at the gym where I do my weight training.
The walls are white, with a few large mirrors spaced along
them, and the floor is covered with black hard rubber tiles.
We walk along the wall to a corner, drop our winter coats,
then sit on the floor to remove our shoes. The room isn't very
warm, but fortunately I have a sweatshirt on, so only my face
and my legs, which are clad in the thin cotton baggies I wear
when I lift weights, really feel the chill. I look at Mike's
clothes: gray sweatpants and a dark blue Worcester Polytech
sweatshirt. "You're not dressed the way I thought you'd be.
Don't you have that white karate suit?"

He smiles a little sheepishly. "I wear that for class, but I
thought it'd look kind of dorky to wear it today."

I shrug. "Karate clothes look comfortable, but they're
probably not all that warm. Is it always this chilly in here?"

"It's better when there's a bunch of us. Once you start
doing stuff, it's perfect. Let's run a few laps around the room
to get warmed up, then stretch. Being limber is really
critical."

We start jogging around the edge of the room. "How
long have you been doing karate?" I ask.

"About a year. It's a pretty good fit for me. I realized I
needed to do something physical—something to get in shape.
All those hours on my ass drawing buildings was taking a toll
on my body. But I wanted to do something interesting and
new to me. I knew if I tried to just go running a few times a
week I wouldn't stay with it. As it turns out, Mr. Asihara
wants us to run twice a week, but there's a few of us in the

class who get together to do that. Knowing someone is expecting me to show up keeps me disciplined." We continue jogging, then he asks "How 'bout you? Have you done any martial arts?"

I tip my head to the side, considering the question. "Not really—not martial arts exactly. In school we had to take a PE class—you know, phys. ed.?"

He glances at me and nods.

"We had to take a PE class every quarter. For women in their freshman year, two of those classes were close-quarter combat—we called it CQC. The guys had to take boxing and wrestling. After freshman year we got to choose our PE classes, and I took all the advanced CQC they offered—I figured that was better than taking something lame like squash or golf. But I never signed up for any of the martial arts clubs we had there."

"Why not?"

"Well, I guess I didn't so much *like* learning how to fight as I felt it was an important skill for me to have, you know, in case I'm ever in trouble..." I almost say "again," but stop short. Given the turn my life took a year and a half ago, the again is more likely than ever, but obviously I don't talk about that. "I need to be able to take care of myself. The CQC classes were good because they were pretty practical in their approach: if someone does this, you can do *this* to get on top of the situation, get away or whatever. I talked to some folks in the tae kwon do club, and they were really cool and all, but the emphasis was on perfecting technique and competing in their matches, and it was a big time commitment. It just wasn't my thing. So I took the classes and tried to practice a little on my own or with other people in the classes, and once in a while I'd get someone to teach me some useful stuff. Like there was this guy in my unit at the academy who was on our intramural boxing team. He was really good, so I got him to teach me some boxing techniques. I didn't want to *be* a boxer, or do it a lot, but by getting him to teach me a few things, I felt like I could maybe pick up something useful."

"Like with me today," he says.

"Exactly.   I'm not looking for anything fancy or complicated, just how to kick or punch effectively, or anything else you think might come in handy."

"Yeah, but you're missing out on so much. The coolest thing about karate is the attitude—the whole philosophy of focus and concentration that goes along with it. Plus, it's fun—it's a really good group in my class, and a lot of the time we go out together afterwards for dinner at an Indian place down the street."

I hate it when people try to convert me. There was this group of evangelical Christians at West Point, and a couple of those guys tried to scare me into throwing in with them by telling me stories about eternal damnation and other such nonsense. They were really annoying. Mike isn't coming across to me like that, but I'm still pretty stubborn about people telling me how to be. I decide to make nice, though. "That sounds great, but let's just do this today and see how it goes. I'm a pretty private person; it'd take me a while to warm up to the whole group fun thing.

"So I'm also interested in your stretching routine," I add, trying to shift our focus.

"OK, yeah, we've probably jogged enough. I won't take you through the whole stretching thing, because that can take a while—some days we spend over half an hour on flexibility."

"I'm not in a hurry if you aren't."

He looks at me and I try to read his expression: a little surprised, but not unhappy—maybe even pleased. "Cool," he says. "Well, we start with the neck, then work down from there." Mike leads us through a whole series of stretches, some familiar to me from when I was running track and cross country in high school, and some totally new to me. "Something Mr. Asihara taught us, which I never realized before, is that for stretches to be effective, you have to hold them for at least twenty seconds. He has us do half a minute. Sometimes it—well, it doesn't hurt, but sometimes it's hard to hold the stretch, but it feels a lot better afterwards, like my body is so much more relaxed and loose."

I already knew about holding stretches, but it's always good to have something you know confirmed by an additional source. The back stretches feel great, and I make a point of remembering them. "So Mike," I say as I lay on my back, my bent knees pointed left and my head pointed right, "how did you hit on karate as something to do? I know you said you wanted to get in shape while also doing something interesting, but why karate?"

"Well..." His voice sounds a little disembodied because his face is turned away from me and pressed against the towel he spread on the floor. "I guess, if I have to be honest..."

"Oh you do, you do."

"If I have to be completely honest, it was the movies."

"The movies?"

"Yeah...I really like those karate movies—you know, Bruce Lee, Jackie Chan, Jet Li, even Jean Claude van Damme. They always look so cool—"

"You like—sorry to interrupt, but you like van Damme movies?" I ask, sitting up and looking over at him.

He sits up too. "Well, not for the acting, just for the fight scenes," he says defensively. "Have you seen even one of his flicks? You shouldn't criticize them until you've seen them."

"Yeah—well, I've seen parts of them. They were very popular with my soldiers; I saw a lot of action and horror flicks that way. It was the same at West Point—we had one TV and VCR for my entire company—that's over a hundred of us, and ninety-percent male, so you can imagine what was usually showing in our day room—karate, horror, action. I don't know how many times I've seen *The Highlander*."

"I love that flick!" he says, smiling.

"Yeah, I liked it too, the first three or four times. I just don't know why we had to *keep* seeing it. I actually like so-called guy movies, but van Damme's stuff—I don't know…"

We go back to stretching, but continue to talk about movies for maybe another fifteen minutes before standing up and facing each other.

"OK, I guess the best thing to start with is stance—that'll give you a base to work from. Normally we'd start with the most basic, like the attention stances and the natural stance, but since I'm picking and choosing, we'll start with the basic front stance, which is better for throwing punches and kicks because it orients your power forward. You're right-handed, right?"

I nod.

He has me stand up straight, then step forward with my left foot while keeping my right planted. "OK, a little further—your feet should be shoulder-width wide, but two shoulder widths apart. Yeah. Move your left knee so it's over your left toes—good."

It feels a little awkward, mainly because it feels strange to stand like a statue in a configuration I don't normally assume. It's a stable, balanced position, though—I don't feel shaky or like I might fall over. He takes a step back, studying me, which makes me feel self-conscious. Then he steps around behind me, and I shift my eyes and turn my head to keep him in sight.

"Keep your head forward," he says.

I turn back to the front, but my eyes stay pegged to the left, even though he's now out of range behind me. "Uh—" I start to say, when suddenly I feel his fingertips on my shoulders. I press off with my right foot, stepping forward and spinning around to face him at the same time.

"Whoa, what happened?" he asks, startled, his hands now held up on either side of his head.

"I didn't know you were going to touch me," I say. I can hear the sharpness in my tone, even though I'm trying to keep the emotion out.

"Just your shoulders—just to square them to the front—honest."

There's a look in his eyes like you see when someone has just spilt a full glass of grape juice on a white carpet—that "shit—is there any way I can fix this before it's too late?!" look. I can see he probably *is* innocent, meant no harm or offense, that this is just my craziness, and I feel bad.

"I was just—"

I put my hand up and shake my head, cutting him off. Even as I do this, I realize this might look like I'm angry with him, so I say "No, it's OK; I just—touching makes me nervous. Ask me before you touch me, OK?" I meet his eyes briefly, see he's still feeling anxious.

"I'm sorry, I didn't—"

I look down and nod. "I know," I begin, cutting him off and realizing I actually don't know what he was going to say. "You didn't mean anything, and you didn't realize how I'd react. I understand, and it's OK. Just—well now you *do* know, so just warn me—ask me—before you touch me, OK?" My face feels warm, and this awareness makes it feel warmer.

He nods. "Sorry. I'll—I won't touch you without asking first."

"I know. OK, so I'm sorry too. Let's just—how were my feet supposed to be?"

Mike gets by with only verbal instructions for a while, but I'm not getting something he's telling me about punching, and he asks if he can guide my arm.

"All right," I agree.

Gently, using only his fingers, he takes hold of my right fist and elbow. The touch makes me a little nervous, but not only in a bad way: a little, tiny, rebel part of me wishes I weren't still wearing my sweatshirt so his fingers would be touching the skin on my elbow instead of the sleeve. I'm not wearing gloves, so he is touching my hand directly, and I notice the heat where his fingertips contact me.

"...your elbow in, pointed toward the center of your back. Does this bother you?"

"Huh? No—no it's fine. So then, when I punch—"

"Keep your arm close to your body—you want your arm to travel through the shortest distance possible on its way to the target in front of you."

He lets go, and I practice punching the air until I earn his praise. Then he shows me how to do a basic snap kick, which I remember from my CQC classes, so I get it pretty quickly.

"Let's spar a little," I say.

"You sure?"

I nod eagerly. "I just want to practice this stuff before I forget what you showed me—it'll help me remember it." *That's all, right?* It's got nothing to do with wanting more physical interaction with him.

"OK, but no contact, right?" he asks.

"Right—well, we're not going to actually hit each other, but blocking—that's OK. Let's go at half speed first."

We take turns slowly attacking each other and parrying the punches and kicks. He shows me the importance of attacking with combinations of moves, anticipating my defenses. I already knew this, but it's good to be reminded. Now I'm glad I did this. "I really should train like this more often," I say.

"Anytime you want, Shailene," he says, smiling.

"All right, let's try a full-speed sequence, but still pulling our strikes."

"OK, you want to attack first?"

I shrug. "Let's just see what happens—attack if you want." I get into the stance he showed me earlier, and he does the same maybe five feet in front of me. He's taller than me, by about half a foot. Given my shorter reach, I know I have to get in really close to him to negate his size advantage. *Train like it's real.* Sergeant Pike was always telling us this when we were patrolling, and I applied it to learning fighting skills too. With this in mind, I'm playing for keeps: I don't wait, but instead launch a fast kick attack with my right leg. As I expected, he blocks my kick, but the kick was really just to distract him and get me in close. I block with my left arm like a boxer and throw a straight right punch the way Mike just showed me, except I'm leading with the heal of my hand instead of the knuckles, aiming for a point a few inches short of the tip of his nose. His arms graze mine, but now that I'm right up in his face, it's hard for him to respond. My attack stays on course, and I stop the heel of my hand just below his nose. If I had followed through, the bridge of his nose would be in his brain. This is a potentially, though not reliably, fatal blow, so I bring my left knee up, stopping a few inches shy of his groin while grabbing his shoulders. I retreat, pulling his shoulders with me while pushing them down, bringing his face almost onto my right knee, then I pivot to his side and try to throw him to the ground, but instead he half stumbles, half jogs a few feet past me.

"Whoa!" he exclaims, straightening up and turning to face me, an incredulous smile on his face. "Wow."

At first it occurs to me maybe I shouldn't have been so aggressive, maybe I hurt his feelings or pissed him off. But his smile remains and it's a good smile—genuinely surprised, and a little amused. I feel one side of my mouth tighten into a grin, pleased my training didn't fail me.

"I think you should be teaching me something," he says.

Now I feel a little embarrassed. I wave him off and look away. "No, let's go again," I say.

"No, really—I'm curious about what you learned in the Army. Did they teach you quick kill techniques?"

"Mostly they taught us to fight dirty—use whatever we can to win: eye gouging, crotch kicking, nose ripping…"

"'Nose ripping'?"

"Nothing fancy—you have to do it from behind, but you stick your fingers in the guy's nostrils and pull back and up, try to tear his nose off, which probably won't happen, but once you have a guy by the nose, it's easier to move him where you need to do something else."

"Like quick kills?"

"Yeah…like that," I say, realizing I don't really want to talk about that stuff.

"So, show me something—show me how you could kill me."

He looks excited, like a child, in his curiosity. "I…why don't we just spar again? Show me how I just got lucky."

"OK, but first show me one quick kill technique." He walks over so we're standing a few feet apart again.

"Well, I kinda already did—that first punch I threw would have put your nose in your brain—mighta killed you, or at least lobotomized you."

"Cool! But show me something else."

Automatically, I start thinking of what we were taught as "sentry removal techniques"—quick, quiet ways, some with knives, some with just our hands, to eliminate human obstacles. But for me those thoughts start to associate with memories I don't want.

"Just one thing—show me just one technique, and then we'll spar again."

"OK, just one—I'll show you a way to knock someone out. It's not a quick kill, but it can put someone down quickly and quietly, and could kill them if you held it long enough. Turn around."

He hesitates, then turns his body away, but looks back over his shoulder at me.

"Look away—pretend you're guarding something."

"What are you going to do? Will it hurt?" He sounds a little nervous now.

"No, no—it's not going to hurt at all. In fact, we're not going to follow through with it. If I do it right, you'll start to feel woozy, and when you do, tap out—tap my leg with one of your hands—and I'll let go, OK?"

"OK." He turns his head away from me.

"So it's the middle of the night, and you're bored, standing around in front of a shed full of ammunition and explosives, guarding it, like you have for the last three hours."

"Yep." He relaxes, starts humming some little tune.

I focus on a spot between his shoulder blades; we were taught to not stare at the back of a target's head, so as to not set off the target's "somebody's staring at me" feeling. I see the step I'll take to get close, see my arms going where they need to go, and then, staying loose and relaxed and empty, I do it: step, snake my left arm up and around his neck while my right arm comes up, elbow just behind his shoulder, hand behind his head. My left hand grabs my right forearm, and I lock on, pressing his head forward into the crook of my left arm, my tightened biceps and forearm pressing onto the carotid arteries on either side of his neck, closing them off. My whole body is pressed against his, holding him in place, keeping us locked together, and suddenly I feel a little thrill, even as I'm waiting for his tap on my leg.

He doesn't tap me. "Sorry, I must be doing it wro—" Suddenly I feel his weight pulling us down to the floor. "Oh shit!" I stop pressing with my right hand and try to take the pressure off his throat even as I'm holding on so he doesn't just hit the floor, but now he's really heavy and unconscious. I shoot my right leg out, trying to brace us, but I can't hold him, and we go down in a semi-controlled way, me protecting his head as it gets near the floor. We end up in a heap, and I immediately pull free, roll him on his back, and lift his knees, propping them up with his feet. "Mike! Mike, wake up!" I feel pressure from my stomach climbing up into the back of my throat. "Mike!" His face is pale as I put my hands on it, lightly—or maybe not so lightly—slapping his cheek. "Mike!" *Shit what do I do?*

I'm about to start CPR when his eyes pop open. They're blank at first, then shift over to look at me, and transition to confused. "What happened?"

"Mike, I'm so sorry! Are you all right?"

"I think so." He blinks. "Yeah, I feel fine." He starts to sit up. "What—"

"Just lay here for a minute." I push gently on his chest and he lies back and relaxes again. I study his face, which has regained its normal color.

"What happened?"

"You passed out. Remember me telling you that when you felt woozy, you were supposed to hit my leg with your hand?"

"Uh...yeah?"

"You didn't."

"Oh."

"Why didn't you tap out?"

He shrugs. "I dunno—I, I guess I kinda liked it." He smiles a little mischievously.

"You idiot!" I slap his chest. "You scared the shit out of me."

"Really? Cool. I've never seen you this emotional."

"I'll show you fucking emotional." I raise my hand to slap his chest again, but then just make like I'm dusting him off before turning a little from him and sitting my butt on the floor.

"So you really do know commando stuff. What happened—how did that work?"

"I cut off most of the blood flow to your brain, which means almost no fresh oxygen for your brain cells. Unlike most cells in our bodies, brain cells only have an aerobic energy process, so they can't go very long without oxygen—

no oxygen, no functioning, and before long brain cells start to die."

"How long was I out for?"

"I dunno—several seconds I guess. Not long enough to kill anything, just long enough to scare me."

He sits up. "I'm sorry, I—"

I put my hand up. "No, *I'm* sorry—I should've been more clear about how you'd feel and tapping out. Listen, you have to let me buy you dinner sometime, make it up to you. I'm sure that was no fun."

"Actually, it kinda was, but I won't pass up dinner with you. How 'bout today?"

Wait—did I really just ask him out? "Yeah? You mean as in tonight?"

"If you don't have plans already," he says. "I don't—not to sound like a loser or anything…"

I hesitate: this is so weird, and it's happening so quickly. *I do feel bad about knocking him out.* "Um…OK, I guess I sound like a loser too, because I don't have anything going on tonight either."

"Well now you do," he says, standing up. He puts his hand out to me. "Here—help you up."

I take the offered hand and he pulls me to my feet. I end up standing close to him, my hand in his, looking up into his face. "Let's spar some more," I say, turning quickly away and taking my hand with me.

Eight

Mike stamps his feet on the sidewalk in front of a funky little Porter Square restaurant called Christopher's. He's not really cold—the thirty or so minute walk over from Inman Square warmed him up, but stamping his feet helps dispel some of the nervous energy he seems to be overflowing with. He's a little early for their date. *Would she call it a date? It's hard to tell what she's thinking.* For about the hundredth time he remembers how upset she was when she knocked him out, and how she slapped his chest—the first time he ever saw her really lose her composure. He hadn't intended to pass out; in fact, it was a little embarrassing, but it was worth it to see her drop her guard for once. He smiles a little to himself, and looks around at the twilit scene. The street lights have just come on, but there's still plenty of daylight left to see by. Bunches of cars stop and go at the direction of the traffic light, pedestrians wander or hurry by, pushing in and out of the storefronts in their winter coats and hats. *What the hell am I going to talk about with her tonight?* He decides to try again to get her to open up a little about herself, get her to do most of the talking. He'd been mostly unsuccessful when they met for coffee at Au Bon Pain, but maybe she's starting to loosen up around him now.

"I wish she'd hurry up—it's cold out here."

Mike's head snaps around at the familiar voice, and sees Shailene's face looking back at him, the little sweet smile on her face and in her eyes. All the bustle around him—the traffic noise, the conversations floating by—all of it vanishes for a long second, and there's only that face looking up at him.

"How'd I do? Did I read your mind or what?"

"Sorry, you may be skilled in knocking people out, but not so much at reading their minds. It's not that cold out; at least, I got warm walking over, so I'm not feeling it."

"You walked here? All the way from Inman Square?"

"It's only about twenty-five, thirty minutes. I didn't feel like dealing with parking, and there's no bus that runs from Inman to Porter."

"And if you'd walked to Harvard Square, you'd be halfway here already, so might as well walk the more direct route, and screw the bus."

"That's right—*screw* the bus," he says, smiling. "Not to mention the time waiting for and riding the bus. Anyway, I like walking."

"Yeah, I do too. That's one of the things I love about this city—it's so great for walking."

"Yeah." Mike realizes he's just looking at her dumbly. "So you want to go in?" he asks, gesturing toward the door.

"Yeah, probably a good idea," she replies, nodding with an exaggerated look of thoughtful consideration on her face, her brow furrowed and eyes narrowed.

Mike mimics her, then smiles and opens the door for her. As Shailene enters, it occurs to him maybe he should have made reservations, or at least gotten on a waiting list when he first arrived. Fortunately, it's early enough in the evening they don't have to wait for a table. "So have you ever eaten here?" he asks her as they take their seats at a small table next to a wall.

"Not yet." She makes the little smile quickly, then adds, "I don't eat out much. I like to cook, plus, you know, being a vegan, sometimes I have trouble finding stuff I can eat in restaurants."

Earlier, at the Y when she told him to pick a place for dinner, she'd told him she was a vegetarian. "Around here in the People's Republic of Cambridge you'd probably have a hard time finding a place that *doesn't* serve some vegetarian stuff," he says. "By the way, is it OK to ask why you're a vegetarian? Were you always that way, even as a kid?"

"Was I always that way?" He gets the crooked smile, but her eyes look amused. "What you're really asking is, 'were you always a pain in the ass'?"

Mike smiles. "No! No, no—that's not how I meant it. I'm just wondering if you were brought up a vegetarian, or if that's something you decided on your own."

"I know—I'm just teasing. I chose it."

"When? Why?"

She looks down.

"I'm sorry—if that's too personal—I'm just rea—"

She looks up and shakes her head. "No, it's OK. I, uh, when I was fifteen I decided I didn't want to hurt anything that can think if I don't have to. We don't need to eat other animals to be healthy—actually, the opposite can be better if you do it right."

A waiter stops by, introduces himself, hands them menus and takes their drink orders: unsweetened iced tea for Shailene and a Sam Adams for Mike.

Mike scans his menu, looking for stuff Shailene can order. He picked this place because he thought he remembered reading something somewhere about it being a good place for vegetarians, but he wasn't really sure, and now he feels a little anxious. "Oh look," he says, "you can get the vegetable lasagna."

"Yeah, no, I think I'm going to get the grilled portabella mushroom on rice. The lasagna has cheese, and I don't eat that. Once I learned what happens to animals used to produce food on an industrial scale, I decided I didn't want to have anything to do with that, so I don't eat dairy or eggs."

"Wow, really? Isn't that hard?"

"Sometimes—sometimes I have to be flexible. But I really like portabella mushrooms."

Mike wants to ask her more about her food ethics, but thinks it might be too heavy for first date conversation, so he goes back to scanning the menu.

"Do you still need a little more time?" the waiter asks, appearing alongside them and setting their glasses down.

"I'm ready, but I don't know about Mike," Shailene says, looking across at him with a trace of amusement on her face.

"Go ahead," Mike says, folding his menu.

She orders the portabella.

"I'll have the same."

"Are you sure?" Shailene asks.

"Yep."

The waiter takes the menus and goes.

"You know, you don't have to eat the way I do—I'm not easily offended."

Mike shrugs. "I like to try new stuff, and I've never had a mushroom as a main course before."

"Actually, I think you'll like it—I hope you do, anyway. Grilled portabella mushroom tastes kind of like grilled meat, or at least the way I remember grilled meat tasting."

"How long has it been?"

"About eleven years—a little more actually."

Mike does the math and figures she's about a year younger than him. "You weren't raised to be a vegetarian, so your parents must be...normal...or whatever a non-vegetarian is called. I'll bet they loved it the day you came home and told them about your decision," Mike says, smiling, giving her an opening to complain about her parents or tell a story about them.

Instead, Shailene looks down and bites her lip.

Oh shit. "I'm sorry—I just said something wrong, didn't I? You've never mentioned your folks—are you on the outs with them?"

Still looking down, she tilts her head slightly and slides her eyes so they're looking at some point in the middle distance between her and the floor.

Shit! You idiot—they're probably—

"My parents...they're, uh...they're dead." She looks up at him and her green eyes are shiny.

"Shit, I'm really, really sorry. I had no idea—I'm... really sorry." *Brilliant. Now what? Where do I go from here?* Irrationally, for a moment he's actually angry with her parents for dying and with her for missing them. *I'm such an idiot.* "I'm sor—"

She waves her hand at him and shakes her head as she looks down again. "It was a long time ago—years. But I still feel—I really miss them. I'm sorry, let's, uh, talk about something else, OK?"

Mike nods and looks down at the grain of the wooden table top, his mind completely empty except for the self-loathing.

"Losing them," she pauses and he looks up at her. Her eyes are cast down at the table, but there are no tears and her voice is steady. "Losing them made me realize how fragile and precious life is. I guess that's part of why I became a vegetarian. The odds are really stacked against life, so it's extremely rare. We take life for granted because it's all around us, but our planet is weird compared to most of the universe. So I think we should respect life and value it."

Mike continues looking at her, but she keeps her eyes down. "Yeah," he says, not knowing how else to respond and feeling ridiculously ineffectual.

"So how 'bout them Red Sox?" she says, looking up, one side of her mouth pulled up in her crooked smile.

Mike smiles back. "Um, they're not playing now."

Her brow wrinkles a little in confusion. "They're not— oh yeah, of course, it's freakin' March. I guess you can tell I'm not into sports." Crooked smile again.

Mike forces a smile, despite still feeling bad. "I like baseball. I used to like basketball, before the Celtics sucked so much." *She's not into sports—did you miss that part? Talk about something else.* "So, uh, what do you like?"

"I don't know—I'm pretty boring. I read a lot, go to the gym—I like to lift weights."

"Really?" he asks, trying to match up the petite woman in front of him with his mental image of a big sweaty guy in the Olympics lifting those sagging bars with the giant weights on the ends.

She nods. "Oh, and I'm trying to grow chile peppers in my apartment. I think I'd like to garden, but all I have is a porch. Still, the porch faces south and has no roof, so I think I might be able to grow stuff in pots out there, once the snow melts."

They talk some more about gardening, then the food arrives. Mike finds himself looking at the biggest mushroom he's ever seen, laid out like a steak, partially resting on a fluffy bed of seasoned rice, beside several asparagus spears. There's just the one mushroom cap, but it's easily the size of a large hamburger patty, and it glistens in the soft lighting. "Wow—I didn't know they made mushrooms this size."

"You've never seen a portabella before?"

"I guess not—this thing is massive." He lifts one side of it with his fork. "And heavy." He lets it drop, and thinks he hears a slapping sound when it hits the plate.

"Don't let it freak you out—"

"No—no, I wanted something different and new, and this is definitely all that." He lifts the edge of the mushroom again and drops it, listening to the splat.

"Just pretend it's a steak. It's known in veggie circles as 'the filet mignon of mushrooms.'"

He raises his eyes to her. "'Veggie circles'?"

She nods. "You know I'd never hang out with veggie squares." She's completely deadpan, looking down and slicing her mushroom.

"Was that a joke? Did you just make a funny?"

"Now you know why I don't do it often," she says conversationally. She looks over at his plate and gestures with her knife and fork. "So stop delaying and try it already."

Mike cuts off a small piece of the fungus and puts it in his mouth, not really knowing what to expect, and bracing himself for the worst. But... "It's not bad."

"There's a ringing endorsement if I ever heard one," Shailene replies flatly.

"Well, I wasn't sure what to expect, so I'm still processing it."

"I'm just kidding—you don't have to say you like it for my sake."

"I know. No, it's pretty good. Better than I'd expected. I like it."

She swallows. "Really?"

"Yeah. Yeah, it's pretty good."

"Would you order it again?"

"Maybe. I don't know—there's other stuff I like better. But I'd *consider* getting it again." He switches topics, eager to get Shailene to talk more. "So tell me more about the Army. What did you do? Were you like—I don't know—a commando or something?"

"What makes you think *that*?"

"Oh, I don't know—first, when we were sparring today, you got past my defenses and threw a punch that would have put my nose in my brain if you'd followed through. Then you went on to knock me out."

"I'm never gonna hear the end of that, am I?"

He smiles. "No, no—I don't mean it like that, but you've got skills, so I figure you must have learned them for your job in the Army, right?"

"I told you: I took close-quarters combat in PE"

He looks at her skeptically. "Yeah, right—you actually became that proficient in a couple PE classes." Mike actually isn't sure what to think, but enjoys trying to get a rise out of her.

She shrugs. "I took the classes pretty seriously; I think you get as much out of school as you want to get out of it. But anyway, no, I wasn't a commando, and by the way, in our Army they're called Rangers—'commando' is British, I think. Women aren't allowed to be Rangers—that's one club we feminine types haven't infiltrated yet. I flew helicopters."

"Really?" Mike asks, his fork paused midway from plate to mouth.

The waiter stops by to check on them, but they don't need anything.

"So you flew helicopters?" Mike prompts, eager to hear more.

Shailene nods. "Yeah, nothing fancy—just Hueys. You know, the ones you see in the Vietnam movies and photos, dropping guys off and picking them up."

"They still use those? I mean, aren't they kinda old?"

"Yeah, they are, but they're a good, solid aircraft, and they're a lot cheaper to fly and maintain than their successors, the Blackhawks, so they still get used for hauling around senior officers, VIP's, food, mail, and other light-duty stuff. We used to joke that a Huey would sling load—uh, that's 'carry'—the last Blackhawk to the scrap heap. Who knows?"

"So what was that like? Flying, I mean."

"It was fun, mostly. Well, there was a lot of paperwork and studying and crap like that surrounding it. And staying on top of the maintenance was a pain. But the actual flying itself was fun. I was stationed in Korea, in and around Seoul, and the only time I got out of the urban area was when I was flying. Seoul was—probably still is—an environmental disaster that made Los Angeles look like the Swiss Alps, but once you left the city, the scenery could be stunningly beautiful, especially up near the DMZ, because hardly anyone lives there. I flew over these high, jagged mountains, and looked down on perfectly blue rivers winding through the ravines. There were forests and grasslands, and hardly any human crap. Of course, eventually we always had to go back to Seoul. You could see this huge brown dome off in the distance, and as you got closer you'd see it was just the air around the city. Kinda sad, really. But the flying was usually cool—sometimes boring, but mostly pretty fun."

"Do you fly now?"

"Nah, flight time is too expensive—I don't like flying *that* much."

"Why don't you do it for a living?"

"To get hired as a pilot, most organizations want you to have at least a thousand flight hours under your belt—otherwise the insurance premiums are really high. I only have about five-hundred hours, so I'm a long way from what they want. Plus, like I was saying, the flying itself was fun, but all the studying and testing and bureaucracy I can do without."

"Do you miss the Army?"

She shakes her head, finishes chewing, swallows. "No. I didn't really fit in culturally. Most people in the Army really don't get the vegetarian animal-rights outlook or the people who embrace it. And I'm kind of an introvert—"

"No, c'mon—you're kidding me!" Mike says sarcastically, wishing he hadn't even as the words escape his mouth.

"Hard to believe, I know," she says, matching his irony. "The Army is really big on the group, and being outgoing and assertive, but I'm a hermit girl: I'd rather mind my own business and be left alone. So I wasn't their ideal, and they weren't perfect for me either. And sometimes, over in Korea, I felt sort of like a mercenary. Being there didn't seem to have much to do with defending the United States, and a lot of the

Koreans didn't want us there either. I felt like I was being paid to prop up a leader of questionable legitimacy in a quasi-democracy."

"How many people do we have over there?"

She shrugs. "I don't really know—twenty-, thirty-thousand—something like that. A bunch."

"And the Koreans don't want us there?"

"Well, mostly it's the younger people who don't want us. Most of the people old enough to remember the Korean war like having us around. One time my helicopter was parked near this farm field, and I was just standing around, waiting for my passengers to come back, when this old farmer walked up to me and the aircraft. He spoke maybe five words of English, and I don't speak much Korean, but he came up, pointed at the tail boom on the aircraft, and read off 'U-S-Army' and then turned to me, gave me a thumbs-up and said 'good!' Stuff like that made me feel better about being there.

"But I notice I'm doing a *lot* of talking tonight," she says suddenly. "What's up with that? I feel like I'm being interviewed or something."

This catches Mike off guard; he didn't think he was being so obvious. Besides, in his, admittedly not *that* extensive, experience, women liked to talk about themselves. And this one was definitely more unusual and interesting than the others had been. "Sorry, I'm just…you're really interesting. Half the things you say surprise me."

"I don't know why," she says, dropping her eyes. "But look—you're almost done with your food and I'm barely halfway. So you tell me something."

"Like what?"

"Why'd you become an architect?"

He nods, smiles. "I guess I wanted to stay a kid. When I was little my favorite thing to do was build stuff. I had Legos, wooden blocks, a giant Erector Set, and Lincoln Logs—you know what those are?"

"Yeah, I had those too—those wooden logs with the notches cut in them so you can build log cabins."

"Well, I had a *giant* set of those—it was pretty much all I got for Christmas one year, but it was maybe the best present I ever got. So, I always liked building stuff."

"But then wouldn't you want to be a builder?"

"Well, sure, there's that, but I realized what I really liked doing was designing the buildings. I never did much with a hammer and nails—except this birdhouse I built that let in so much water I don't think anything ever lived in it. The Legos and Lincoln Logs required no skill; they were really just a means of designing in three dimensions, of easily expressing the pictures I saw in my head. Now, instead of little pieces of plastic and wood, I create pictures on my computer screen, and build models out of cardboard and glue. It's the same thing, really, so I get to keep on doing something I did for fun when I was a child. Obviously it's more rigorous and detail-oriented now—I have to think about tensile strengths and material densities and all that, but I'm doing something I love. Getting paid to do what you'd want to do for free anyway is more rare than it should be, so I feel pretty lucky.

"And besides that, when a building is done and actually exists in the world, I can look at it and see my ideas made real. I can walk inside it, look around, and it's like walking into one of the little buildings I created as a kid. With those, when I was little, I used to press my face up to the doors and windows so I could see inside, and tried to imagine walking around in my creations. Now I can do that for real. Especially if it's a public building—then I can keep going back, and I can bring friends with me too."

"What are some of the buildings? Anything I'd have seen?"

"Maybe. I worked mostly on single-family houses early on, just because those are less complicated, and easier for more senior architects to take the time with young architects who are still learning the profession.   But our firm did a church in Medford, and I was on that team, and we did the addition to the library in Belmont—I had a bigger role on that one."

"That sounds really neat—let's go see it sometime."

Mike laughs a little. "Yeah, that'll be a great date—a trip to the library."

A troubled look comes over her face, and she looks down at her now mostly empty plate.

"Are you OK?" Mike asks.

"Huh?" she asks, looking up and appearing a little confused.

"Are you OK? It looks like you just ate something bad."

She shakes the unhappy expression off and replaces it with an almost exaggerated "who, me?" look. "No, no I think I'm just tired."

"See, that's why you should do most of the talking: you get me started talking about architecture, and it's snooze-city. Sorry, I—"

"No!" she says emphatically—so much it startles Mike. She seems to realize it too, because she continues in a more normal tone, "No, that's not it at all. I really like listening to you. It's just…I don't go out much, and I think this is…a lot for me. I'm just not used to it, that's all. But I really liked dinner and I like talking with you. You're a great guy, Mike."

Mike isn't sure how to interpret this; he senses he said something wrong, but can't figure out what it was. *What were we talking about? Oh yeah, visiting buildings I worked on— the library in Belmont. Does she have something against libraries?* "Well, anyway, we don't have to go to the library in Belmont—or the church in Medford, but if you change your mind, or want to see anything the firm has worked on, let me know. I'd be happy to take you there."

"Thanks."

There's an awkward silence and Mike tries to think of some new direction to head in with the conversation, when the waiter appears.

"Are you all set here? Can I interest you in dessert or coffee?"

Mike looks the question at Shailene.

"Would you like dessert?" she asks.

He shrugs, "If you do."

"Nah," she shakes her head, then looks at the waiter. "I'm pretty full—just the bill, thanks."

The waiter clears the plates, heads off to the kitchen.

"So any big plans for tomorrow?" Mike asks, sincerely wondering what she does with her free time.

She shrugs. "Go to the gym, do some reading, go to the library—the one in Arlington, though I really would be interested in going to the one in Belmont sometime. How 'bout you?"

"Goin' up to Lowell to visit my folks. I'll go to church with them in the morning, and try to convince them to let the manager they hired to run the pastry shop do his job while they stay home and have a leisurely Sunday dinner."

"Think you'll succeed?"

Mike nods. "Yeah, I'll guilt them into it—say how I drove all the way up just to spend time with them. It'll be good for them to take a break. Of course, they'll try to guilt me into quitting my job and replacing the manager they hired—always plenty of guilt to go around in a Mediterranean family."

"That's really cool—not the guilt part, but you spending time with them. I'm sure they'll be really glad to see you."

"You know, you're welcome to come if you like—there's always room for one more at my mom's table."

"Even for a non-church-going vegetarian?" She smiles the crooked smile.

"Well, it's true, they probably wouldn't be sure what to think of you, but they'd be nice to you, as a guest in their home, and as a friend of mine. My mom's a great cook, and she could whip up something meatless for you."

"Thanks, but I think you should give her a little more advance notice than just showing up with me. Besides, I really do have stuff to do at the library. I get a lot of my reading material there—books, magazines, newspapers. Public libraries are the best deal anywhere—totally free, and more books than anyone can read in a lifetime. So I'm going to return some books, check some out, like that."

The waiter returns with the bill, which he places between them, but more to Mike's side. Shailene reaches for it, but Mike takes it first.

"Hey—this is my treat," she protests.

Mike waves her off. "Allow me."

"Mike, the whole point of this was because I knocked you out."

"You're just gonna keep throwing that in my face, aren't you?" he asks, smiling.

"I'm the one who messed up. C'mon, seriously."

"You want to split it?"

"Just give it to me, Dorko."

"Such language," he says, sliding the bill across to her. He watches her read the paper, count out some cash, and put it all in a little pile. "By the way," he says quietly when she's finishing up, "uh, you don't really need to mention how you knocked me out to the people at work, OK? I've got my bad-ass architect street cred to maintain, you know."

"You've got nothing to worry about, tough guy. I've got my demure, sweet, helpless girl rep to protect too."

The air outside feels especially chill after the warmth of the restaurant.

"So thanks for teaching me karate stuff, and for having dinner with me," she says, turning to him on the sidewalk out front. The early evening crowd has thinned out now, and they can stand by the building without being jostled and glared at.

Mike realizes they're at that weird "how do we say good-bye" point, and he looks at her for a sign. There's nothing he'd like more right now than to lean in and kiss her—nothing overly intimate or wet—just to touch her lips with his. He takes a step toward her, holding her eyes.

She takes a step back and continues talking. "So I'll see you Monday. Have fun at your parents' tomorrow."

Damn. "OK. Have fun at the library."

And then it happens: she smiles full on at him. It's quick—just a flash of teeth, and then she turns and starts walking away, but his mind takes the picture and holds on to it. "Bye!"

She looks back at him over her shoulder. She's still smiling and, as she walks away, she waves.

Nine

The time display on Wayne's computer screen tells him it's four minutes before midnight—hopefully Bill and Tony have finished prepping the tables for tomorrow. Wayne makes a few clicks with his mouse to command his computer to shut down, then stands, stretches, and rubs his eyes. He walks across the small office, clicks off the sound system, takes his coat from the hook by the door and puts it over his arm, then turns out the light as he leaves, pulling the locked door closed behind him.

Standing between the office and the kitchen, in the little alcove where the employee punch clock is, he looks out across the main floor of the restaurant. It is almost empty now—just Tony carrying a tray of ketchup bottles and salt and pepper shakers. It's also strangely quiet with the sound system off. Since this quiet always accompanies leaving for the day, it automatically makes Wayne feel a little happy. He looks over at the entrance, but Dana, the usual evening hostess, is of course gone and her station by the door is vacant. He already knew this because he saw her punch out. He feels a squirm of mixed emotions: disappointment, self-recrimination, and relief. He turns and enters the kitchen.

It's still warm and humid in here, and awash with cooking smells, though a sharp current of cold air is cutting through the big room from the open back door. Andy—the new kid with the sandy hair and bad complexion—starts up one dishwasher, then turns to another and opens its door to a cloud of steam.

"Hey Wayne," Emily says, coming up behind him.

He turns to face her, but he already knows what she's going to ask. "Monday," he replies.

"Monday?! What about tomorrow?"

"Tomorrow's Sunday, Emily. Give me a break—it just broke yesterday, and now it's the weekend. Trenton Appliance will be by on Monday to fix it. I already talked to Rick about this earlier, told him to adjust the menu if he has to, but you guys seemed to manage OK today."

She rolls her eyes and does a little movement with her head, as if she were going to toss her long black hair indignantly, but of course her hair is up and tucked under her chef hat, so she just looks ridiculous. Emily is only a sous chef—*at a Reilly's*, Wayne reminds himself—but she acts like she's the freakin' exec chef at the Marriott or something.

"All right, let's wrap it up folks," Wayne says to the room. Charlie and Pablo help Andy unload the washer that just finished, gingerly handling the hot glasses, dishes, and pots, but not dropping anything. Emily pushes a cart loaded with various containers into the walk-in fridge. Tony comes in and sets down the tray with a couple ketchup bottles still on it. Wayne goes and stands by the front entrance, and puts on his coat. Soon the remaining staff starts filing out, all of them except Andy pulling on coats as they come across the dining room. Andy almost never wears a coat, but Wayne has given up wondering about that. At the door they say their see ya tomorrow's and goodnight's, and with a jingling of keys they head for their cars. The light in the kitchen winks out, there's a pause as she clocks out, and then Emily, her hair no longer concealed, crosses the room. "So have a good one, Wayne."

"You too, Emily."

Wayne activates the burglar alarm then steps outside. He has left the dining room lights on, and the sign lights too, which has always seemed wasteful to Wayne, but that's how corporate says to do it, and it's not his nickel. He locks the deadbolt on the main entrance, and turns in time to see Emily's Corolla's lights go on, and then she's pulling out, leaving only Wayne's Pathfinder in the lot. His keys in his right hand and the ring of restaurant keys in his left, he walks across the pavement.

He thinks of Dana again, wishing he'd said goodnight to her when she clocked out. Even at the end of a night of greeting customers and managing the wait staff, she almost always looks gracious and professional. She could easily work someplace better than a cheesy yuppie and college kid hangout like Reilly's, but he knows she's going to school in her spare time, and eventually, after she gets her masters, she'll be leaving them to work at some lucky library somewhere. It strikes him as ironic because he worked in a book store to put himself through college so he could work in a restaurant, and she's almost doing the reverse.

He thinks of her face, dominated by big hazel eyes, her lightly-freckled forehead framed by dark red hair, which she always has pulled back and put up when he sees her, since he only sees her at work. He thinks of her bright, cheerful smile. She has nice teeth, though he can tell she never had braces as a kid since her canines are a little forward of the other teeth, slightly out of line. For some reason this slight imperfection appeals to him, and he always looks for it when she smiles. She seems to have a nice body too, though it's a little hard to tell since she's always dressed conservatively for work.

Standing next to his Pathfinder, he uses his keys and gets in.

Dana's not an option for him. Neither is that other girl, "Sandi" according to her name tag, who works at the Shop Rite's deli counter. He used to try to time it so she would be the one to help him, but then she started talking to him. That was OK at first, but then she actually introduced herself and smiled at him. *What did I say to her then?* He thinks he told her his name too, but can't really remember *what* he said. Since then he's actually been afraid to go by the deli counter when she's there. Now, instead of trying to time it to get her, he avoids her. Sometimes he goes out of his way to visit a different supermarket. He would never date her because if she ever got to know him, she'd realize his secret.

His mind strays to the memory of Todd.

Wayne starts the engine, puts the vehicle in drive, and heads out.

It was the same with certain other women he encountered, going back to that girl Karen in high school, and Jennifer, the one he met at Mercer County Community College. In each case, thoughts of the woman kept popping into his head at odd times, and he felt anxious around her—actually avoided her sometimes because she made him so nervous.

Since Todd was, obviously, a guy, Wayne thought for a while maybe he should just forget about women and date guys. He went to gay bars a couple times, but no one at those places appealed to him. Outside of bars, Wayne isn't even sure how he would approach a guy, or how to tell if he's gay.

"My life sucks," he says under his breath as he makes a right on to Clinton Avenue, which is mostly deserted now.

His mind goes to the last time he was with someone. It seems like months ago, but really it's been about six weeks. He sees his face, sees the smile, hears his excited voice.

The red light he was braking for turns green; he moves his foot from the brake to the accelerator.

This solitude has got to change. His stomach squeezes a little at the thought of—

An electric blue sports car blasts through the intersection right in front of the Pathfinder; Wayne slams his brakes. "Holy shit!" He looks down State Street in the direction of the red light runner, but he's already just a couple of tail lights. "Fuckin' asshole," he says. He looks the other way and sees no other cars on State. He puts his foot on the gas again and continues home.

He parks on the street and walks back to his building. Up the front steps, he keys the lock, enters, and climbs the stairs. His place is only two flights up, but he's a little out of breath when he gets there. *I need to do something to get in shape*, he thinks, the way he almost always does after climbing these stairs. He should probably join a gym again; it's been over a year since he let his health club membership lapse.

Several minutes later, he's changed into a sweatshirt and jeans, and is sitting in front of the TV with reheated Chinese take-out from a couple nights ago. One of the downsides of getting off work in the middle of the night is there's usually shit on TV when he gets home. Often he watches something from his collection of videotapes: maybe one of the Star Wars or Indiana Jones movies, or he has an episode of *The X-Files* he set his VCR to record for him. But *The X-Files* was a rerun this week, and he doesn't feel like watching it again right now. He doesn't really want to commit to a movie either, so instead he flips through whatever happens to be on. Working the remote with his left hand and the fork with his right, Wayne bypasses basketball, pauses briefly on an exercise equipment infomercial, cruises through a shopping network selling shit jewelry, and skips over a get rich quick infomercial. He hesitates on a *Love Boat* rerun, watching for a couple minutes in morbid fascination, then passes on some boring-looking movie, before hitting CNN. More out of fatigue than interest, he leaves the TV on that and puts down the remote so he can use both hands to cut his sweet and sour chicken into smaller pieces.

One of the fluff pieces CNN mixes into its lineup comes on. A man wearing a baseball cap fitted with light-up red devil horns appears saying "If you can't take the heat, don't go *near* the kitchen!" At first, Wayne isn't sure *what* they're reporting about. The text along the bottom of the screen reads "Hotter Than Hell!" The next images are familiar: people sitting in a restaurant with big plates of food in front of them. Wayne's immediate reaction is a mix of repulsion and relief. First, it's as if the annoying but necessary customers from work have invaded his apartment. This is quickly followed by relief as he registers that these customers are behind the TV screen, and apparently in Cambridge, Massachusetts, and are therefore not his problem. Many of these customers are visibly sweating, and one says something about heat coming out the top of his head. There are some close-ups of the food—a big plate of pasta, a rack of lamb chops, a salad—and the reporter is saying something about hot peppers. There's a shot of a menu, and again Wayne experiences that sequence of aversion closely followed by relief, like when you wake up thinking you have to go to work and realize it's your day off.

The television shows more groups of diners laughing and talking, triggering another familiar feeling in Wayne. If he were to give the feeling a name, it'd be "the wolf." When he sees groups of happy people socializing he feels like a member of a different species, like a lone wolf looking in a window as he trots by in the night. Obviously the sight is familiar to him; he knows this is something people do, but it's outside of the wolf's experience. What do they talk about? Why are they laughing?

The guy with the devil horns is shouting and ringing a bell now, and then handing a popsicle to a red-faced middle-aged man who grabs the frozen dessert and puts it in his mouth. Then there are firemen, carrying axes and wearing the long tan coats and black helmets, pushing through the restaurant's door. One of them shouts "Did somebody report a fire?" and the whole place cheers. "Weird," Wayne mutters and takes another bite of sweet and sour chicken as the anchor comes back on and says something inane.

Wayne sits through a few commercials, not really paying attention, just glad to be having dinner since he was so hungry. He wonders if Dana is having dinner now too, and if so, what she's having, and if she's alone. Maybe she's watching TV too.

The news comes back on. This time it's real news—world events, national politics—but nothing sufficiently interesting to capture his attention. The movies he'd earlier decided against watching seem pretty good now, but he's tired and done eating. He stands and carries the empty take out cartons and beer bottle back to the apartment's narrow galley-style kitchen. The cartons go in the trash, and he rinses the bottle once and drops it in the plastic bin for recycling, then turns and goes back to the main room.

"…by a hiker in New Jersey's Wharton State Forest."

Wayne's ears perk up at the place name.

"The body was apparently partially uncovered by foraging area wildlife. Officials had been withholding the identity pending notification of the boy's family, but have now confirmed the body is that of Jimmy Turcotte of Trenton, who disappeared on his way home from school in January."

Wayne stands in his living room with his mouth hanging open, staring at the television and picturing the body of the boy lying in a clearing in the woods. *Foraging animals?* The thought of the boy being ripped apart by animals angers and saddens him.

"State police and personnel from the state coroner's office exhumed the bodies of three more children not far from where the first was found. State officials just about an hour ago identified one of these bodies as that of Sebastian Connelly, another boy from Trenton, who went missing last October. The identity of the other bodies has not been released yet, pending notification of the children's families."

Wayne feels dizzy, and leans on the back of his couch to steady himself.

"So far there has been no official word on causes of death or whether these four bodies might be linked, but the fact that both identified boys disappeared from the streets of Trenton in the past several months, and that at least one other Trenton boy has been reported missing during this same time period, has fueled speculation they may all be victims of the same serial predator. New Jersey Attorney General Frank

Pepperdine has scheduled a press conference for tomorrow afternoon to discuss the case and advise the public on possible threats to safety.

"From the State Police barracks in Red Lion, New Jersey, I'm Shirley Germaine for CNN."

Wayne turns away from the television and slides down the back of the couch until he is sitting on the floor. He closes his eyes. *"Foraging animals,"* he thinks, slowly shaking his head. He almost feels like crying, though he's not sure why the idea of animals digging up and eating— He scrunches his eyes more tightly shut, and feels his chin wrinkle involuntarily.

Ten

The door swings shut behind me as I cross the first floor apartment's rear porch and descend the three steps to the asphalt parking area. I look over the tops of the first and second floor tenants' cars at Stacey gleaming aqua blue in the sunlight, which feels warm on my face. It's a beautiful day, full of springtime promise. Of course, it's only the second day of March, so there will be more winter weather before spring, but today at least it's sunny and springy for my weekly walk to the library in Arlington Center.

The weekend trip to the library is a ritual I began almost two years ago, after the Florida incident. Before Florida, I had a theory about what the recurring pain of the old wound in my upper abdomen meant, but the idea was so bizarre I didn't really believe it. Since this weird sense is triggered so infrequently, it was easy to ignore, until I encountered that couple in, of all places, a shopping mall. Mostly out of curiosity, I tracked them from southern Alabama, where I was stationed at the time, to Panama City Beach, Florida. The night culminated in almost getting shot, beating the male half of the couple to death with a tire iron, gunning down the female half with the guy's weapon, and failing to save the woman I saw them pick up at a bar. She'd already bled out by the time I got to her. The whole evening is pretty unforgettable, but that last part, the young, dark-haired woman dead on the floor of the van, is what really sticks with me. That made me realize the responsibility implied in my ability to detect the near presence of recreational murderers. I tried to rationalize it away and convince myself I'd been through enough already, but nothing I came up with could change the simple reality of my situation: I was in a position to stop the

Bad from happening. I couldn't change my history, but I could prevent someone else—multiple someone elses—from having their own Bads. If only someone could have done that for my parents and me...

Understanding I have a moral duty and coming up with a plan to fulfill that duty are a long way from each other. I started out carrying a military dagger around under my clothing, so I'd be armed with something besides a tire iron if I found myself up against bad guys again. That was impractical, though. The knife—eleven inches long all together—was hard to conceal on my small body under a T-shirt and jeans or shorts, and it could be years—or never—before I'd need the thing. Plus, merely going around armed really wasn't doing much to stop bad guys. So I put the blade, which was a gift from some pals at the Military Academy and has a lot of sentimental value, back in my keepsake box. I didn't really want to use it anyway, and I definitely didn't like the chance it could get lost or stolen.

Not long after that I hit on the idea of scanning newspapers for reports of unsolved and apparently related strings of murders. The irony of this has not escaped me: My best guess about this sense I have is it's a survival adaptation my subconscious evolved in response to the Bad, so I could sense trouble coming and escape it. Instead, the *actual* effect of my sense is I go looking for trouble and put myself in its path. Both times I've done this it's almost gotten me killed. My last mission, in New Orleans a little over a year ago, put a bullet behind my right shoulder blade. So much for my survival adaptation.

I don't check papers anymore; now I run searches on the Internet, which is more efficient and faster. Actually, I haven't been super-diligent about this over the past year. In fairness to myself, my life has been in serious flux lately, with finishing grad school, traveling around the country, finding a place to live and a job, and even trivia like buying civilian clothing so I have more than a couple shirts to wear to work. But I've been back on track since I finished settling into my apartment last November, and I've been lucky—no news about anything that looks like the work of a homicidal sociopath.

I always carry at least a little dread with me when I make this weekly trip, but today it's minimal. Instead, I'm preoccupied with thinking about Mike. Well, mainly I've been thinking about what I think about Mike, more than Mike himself.

What? I shake my head at that.

I wouldn't say I'm attracted to him; even if I were, I wouldn't say it. That would feel wrong somehow. But I honestly don't think I'm interested in him physically. The idea of being naked with anyone is cringe-y. But there was that moment yesterday, when I was pressed up against him while I had him in the choke hold. I wouldn't have wanted, and still don't want, it to go any further than that, but there was something really...*good* about how that felt: the warmth and firmness of his body pressed against mine. It reminded me of how Miranda's body felt against mine the first few times we were intimate, before it stopped being exciting. That was before I started thinking about the specifics of what we were doing and getting grossed out at having someone else's tongue in my mouth, or having my tongue inside hers. Isn't there a happy midpoint, where I can touch someone, but not have to exchange fluids with him or her? Because the opposite extreme, the way I've been living since losing Miranda, makes me feel like someone sanded off my fingertips, or like I'm in a glass box. Before yesterday, besides shaking hands I hadn't touched anyone in two years. Well, except for that guy I tackled in New Orleans, but he shouldn't count since he was trying to kill me.

The touching thing can be confusing, and I'm not ready for the whole girl-guy thing, but it was an unmitigated good to have conversations with someone again. Miranda was also the last person in my life I could talk to for more than a couple minutes. That's what I miss most—talking to her. But she wanted more than a platonic relationship, and I don't blame her. It's natural. Maybe I'd be with some guy by now if my mental wiring for that hadn't been cut when I was fifteen.

Maybe it can be fixed?

Would that be OK? *"Because you're hot..."* Those fucking words. I killed *him*, but his fucking words...

I wait for the light to change at the corner of Pleasant Street and Mass Ave. The walk signal illuminates, accompanied by the coded bird chirping sound to tell blind people it's safe to cross now. I think that's a great idea, but the only place I've encountered it is here in Arlington. That's either saying something great about this town, or crappy about all the other ones I've been in.

I pass the Unitarian Church and the stone marker by the sidewalk telling how "the old men of Menotomy" captured a British supply wagon there during the first day of the American Revolution. Looking around peaceful, prosperous Arlington now, it's hard to imagine the running firefight that took place here, but I've noticed several markers like this one along Mass Ave. The best one is about Sam Whittemore who, at age 80, single-handedly ambushed a group of British troops, getting himself shot, bayoneted, beaten, and left for dead, but still managed to recover and live another twenty-eight years after that.

I turn down the driveway and ascend the broad stone steps. Arlington's public library is pretty amazing—the big marbled foyer looks like it belongs to a much larger city's library. Arlington only has about sixty-thousand residents, but we definitely have quite the impressive temple of literacy. I walk past the check out desks, past the big staircases, and into the older part of the building. This is where the computer terminals with Internet access are, and fortunately it's still early enough on Sunday that there are some stations open. I sit down at the nearest one, go to the search engine site, and type in the usual keywords: murder unsolved serial. I click on each of the first ten hits, but none are what I'm looking for and dreading. I get a lot of hits on book and movie synopses, and I get the same old, archival news stories week after week. That's fine with me.   As usual, I try more keyword combinations, mechanically clicking on the first ten hits for each. Click, scan, nothing, click on the Back button, click the next link. Click, nothing, click. I usually do this for half an hour, then call it good. I've done my bit, and I can go back to the life I'm building. Click,

Four Bodies Discovered in Wharton State Forest
By JOE HESTER
Staff Writer

Atsion, New Jersey—A local man hiking in Wharton State Forest Saturday morning made a grisly discovery when he found the body of a seven-year-old boy. The boy, subsequently identified as Jimmy Turcotte of Trenton, was reported missing in January.

State Police, working in conjunction with the state coroner's office, have since turned up three more bodies, one of which has been identified as six-year-old Sebastian Connolly, also of Trenton, who was reported missing last October.

The identity of the other two bodies has been withheld pending notification of next of kin, but an unidentified source in the coroner's office has stated one of the bodies is also that of a young male from Trenton, who has been missing since November.

"Fuck," I whisper. "This is it, isn't it?" Head swimming, I read the rest of the article. Either my search terms missed the news about the missing kids or the occasional missing kid isn't newsworthy because it happens too often. Could've been my search terms since I search for serial killings, and until the bodies were found, these boys were missing people, not murder victims. Now not only are they homicides, but the article goes on to state all four bodies were found in the same small clearing, which pretty much forces the conclusion these dead boys form a string of killings by the same person or group—most likely a person acting alone. I've done enough research to know the couple in Florida was unusual; most of these bastards are solitary.

Trenton. At least it's not so far away. I'm not sure, but I'd guess five or six hours from here by car. Driving is essential since I'll be taking the Glock—no way I'd get that through airport security. I guess I could take a train, but the car is easier and cheaper, and I'll have transportation when I get there.

"Crap in a hat," I whisper, but there's no point in whining about it. I search on some key terms from the article like "Trenton" and "child." I get a few more articles to read, and realize I forgot to bring paper and pen. Fortunately, someone left a ballpoint pen in my carrel, so I use it to take notes on my left forearm; I'll transcribe them when I get home.

About midway through the second article, it occurs to me I'll need to ask for the time off from work. I have yet to take any time off, and my employer just granted me ten more days of vacation on the first of the year, so I have the time to take, and theoretically I should be able to get it approved. *But what if it's not approved?* The idea of shrugging my shoulders and putting off the mission is appealing, but not acceptable. A kid gets killed because my employer wouldn't grant me time off? Not on my watch. Obviously I'm going to Trenton, no matter what, but I'd like to have a job to come back to after it's over.

I open another browser window and log in to the web interface for the firm's email server. I start to type the message, then pause. What am I going to say? I suddenly have an urgent need to go on vacation? No, this is a personal emergency. I don't like lying, but it is for a good cause, and it is an emergency, and it is sorta, kinda personal. OK, that last part is stretching it, but it is for a good cause, and it might well be an emergency, depending on the bad guy's timetable.

Is this going to work? I wonder if my unpaid "job" is even compatible with holding down the paying one. What if the mission runs long? I only get a couple weeks off each year. One mission could eat that—New Orleans took about two weeks, spread out over two trips. But then it's been almost a year and a half since; maybe I'll end up only needing a couple weeks a year—like one mission per year. Maybe.

I shrug, read the message through, then send it and log out of the email interface. I bring the article up again and resume taking notes.

Eleven

Lying on his back, Wayne stares up through the dimness of his bedroom at the shape of the light fixture. He wonders what time it is but forces himself to not check the clock again just yet. Outside on the street below a truck rumbles by, and Wayne shifts his eyes to the window. Even with the heavy drapes drawn, the bright border around them reveals it's fully day out, and sunny too. He rolls his head on his pillow and looks at the digital clock on the small table by his bed. The glowing red numerals spell out 10:23; he rolls his head back to center.

There's no way I'm falling back asleep now.

He got maybe three hours of sleep last night, adding up all the brief, restless periods of unconsciousness. Exhausted but not at all sleepy, his mind keeps coming back to the image of a little boy lying in the snow, being pulled at and eaten by animals. Maybe seagulls or crows pecked at him, as if he were garbage or road kill, and it's incredibly sad.

It's not what Wayne intended at all. He'd intended to give Jimmy and that puppy a decent burial, like the others. He'd meant to tuck Jimmy in under a blanket of dirt, with the puppy he liked so much, so they could be at peace together. But the ground had been frozen hard in January. Wayne hadn't expected that; maybe he should have, but he hadn't. The shovel he used wasn't much good for the task of breaking up the frozen soil. If he'd known, he'd have brought a pick axe. Actually, if he'd known, he might have waited before bringing a boy home, although waiting would have been harder than that frozen ground. Anyway, he'd ended up opening a small depression and wedging the lower half of Jimmy's body in there. Then he put the little puppy in close to the body, and placed Jimmy's right arm around it, as if they were napping together. Finally, he'd covered them both with the frozen clumps of dirt, pine needles, some fallen branches, and some sand he'd hauled from the trail in a plastic grocery bag he'd found in his car. For some reason the sand on the side trail had not frozen—too dry and loose, he'd guessed. He'd piled whatever was at hand on to Jimmy and the puppy until no trace of the bodies was visible. What else could he have done? He hadn't thought of animals—he'd never seen any animals there except squirrels, and everybody knows they only eat nuts, right? The birds—well, he hadn't really thought about them either, but if he had, he'd have figured if they couldn't see the body, they wouldn't know it was there.

"Shit," he says quietly, then sits up and swings his legs over the side of the bed. "There's nothing I can do about it now; I just gotta let it go." *At least now he'll get buried, him and the puppy.* He wonders if they'll be buried together. The news didn't even mention the puppy. Wayne's brow furrows as he wonders if the animals dragged the dog away, and he feels like he could cry again. Jimmy had really liked that puppy—couldn't take his eyes off it, even when Wayne was giving his love to Jimmy. "Just got to let it go," he whispers again.

He stands and walks to the bathroom. As he drains his bladder, he has a thought so disturbing it actually chokes off his urine stream for several seconds:

What about evidence?

He forces himself to relax down there so he can finish, reminding himself the news didn't report the police having any leads or suspects. The stream starts up again, then finishes naturally.

There're no leads or suspects, but they only found the bodies yesterday. He's going to have to watch the news and read the paper, see if they have any idea, any chance of coming close. *But how can they? There's nothing to point the finger at me.*   His mind replays what happened with Jimmy. Wayne doesn't know the specifics of DNA testing, but that's always getting play in the news. What Wayne does know is, just like fingerprints, the cops would need to compare his DNA with what they find on the victim to see if they match. But neither Wayne's fingerprints nor, certainly, his DNA, are on record anywhere, so they'd have to have some other evidence linking the boys to Wayne before they would even think to come to him for his DNA or his prints. Does that other evidence exist? Maybe there's stuff on the bodies from Wayne or Wayne's apartment—threads, dust, even some of Wayne's hair.   But like the fingerprints and DNA, there's nothing to single him out from all the thousands of people living in and around Trenton.   There's nothing to tell the police his name, to tell the police to come and look at his apartment, or his car. At least, he doesn't think there is.

At any rate, whatever the cops have, they have—there's nothing Wayne can do about that now. What he can and probably should do now is lay low. The thought is frustrating and disappointing; after all, just last night on the way home from work he'd decided to try for that boy he's had his eye on, the one with the red hair and freckles. Now it looks like he'll have to be alone for who knows how long, and not just because the cops will be looking for anyone interacting with kids at parks, in stores, and on the streets. The boys will be harder to approach too—at least some of them will. The boys most in need of Wayne's attention are the least likely to be coached by their parents or to be aware of what's been happening around them, but some of them will be on guard, and that shrinks the already too small pool of boys who are both interesting and open to him.

He's just going to have to be patient, and wait for people to get tired of being vigilant. It won't be easy, but he has to lay low until it's safe again.

Twelve

Mike stands in the office kitchen, pouring coffee into his Boston Society of Architects mug. He takes his time emptying a couple sugar packets into it and then stirring the black liquid. He lingers over these tasks, and even after they're done, hoping to be there when Shailene comes into the kitchen for her routine of filling her I *heart* Massachusetts mug with water from the tap, but even after rinsing the spoon and putting it in the dish drainer, she still hasn't appeared. Instead, Sam walks in.

"I don't suppose anyone brought donuts in," Sam asks, looking past Mike at the empty counter before stepping up to the coffee maker and grasping the handle on the pitcher.

"What made you think there'd be donuts today?"

"Nothing—I'm just really hungry. Got up late, didn't have time to stop at Dunkin', but I may have to go back out."

"OK, I'll have a chocolate glazed."

"Really? Cool—get me a couple of those Boston creams."

"Nice try pal. Looks like we're both going to be hungry," Mike says, stepping past him and heading back to his desk. He glances over at Shailene's desk on the other end of the room as he sits down, but although he saw her come in and drape her coat over the back of her chair, she's not there now. *Probably in the computer room.*

He takes a small sip from his mug—it's still too hot to drink, but the tiny shot of caffeine immediately makes him feel better. He'd interrupted the morning ritual of reading his email messages when he'd seen Shailene come in, so now he finishes reading through the list of assignments from Jeff, who's managing the project he's been working on. Next there's a message from Kate The Office Manager to complete timesheets, so he does that before opening the set of plans he was working on last Friday.

About a half hour later he hears the familiar voice he replayed in his head countless times yesterday as he mentally relived the time they spent together on Saturday.

"Hey Mike."

He looks up to see Shailene standing right in front of his desk. "Whoa—I didn't even notice you walk up! Freakin' commando girl."

"That's 'Ranger' girl; 'commando' is British, remember? But I think it has more to do with you being focused on what you're doing than any special stealthiness on my part."

"Oh yeah, I'm all about the drawings," he says ironically. "So how you doin'? How was the rest of your weekend?"

"Not so great; I have to leave town for about a week."

"Uh—really?"

"Yeah, Henry just approved it," she says nodding and looking away.

"Is everything all right?"

She meets his eyes and nods some more.

Mike focuses on her eyes, her right eye in particular, and really notices the bright moss green of the iris, like a sun-drenched forest seen from high above. Of course this isn't new to him, but he's still surprised by the intensity and singularity of the green in her eyes.

"...some stuff I have to take care of—it's kinda personal, and I can't really talk about it," Shailene is saying.

"Why not?" he asks, worried that she actually just said why, but he missed it somehow.

"Beee-cause...it's...personal?" she says slowly, as if listening to her own words to hear if she left anything out the first time.

Mike feels a bloom of frustration, like a dark puff of smoke, somewhere in his head, and wonders what could be so secret that she can't even hint at it. He wonders if she told Henry more when she asked for the time off. But then she's giving him that lopsided smile, and it's hard to stay irritated.

"Seriously, it's something I really can't talk about, but I need to ask you for a favor."

"She's plays all mysterio, then wants a favor—hmmm."

Shailene drops the smile and continues to stare at him.

"OK, OK, but you're all right? You yourself, I mean, not this thing you can't talk about."

The smile returns, barely. "Yes, I'm fine. Thanks," she replies quietly, sounding sincere.

"OK, what you need mang?" he says, doing his Scarface impersonation.

"Tomorrow and Wednesday I need someone to change the backup tape." She holds up a small square plastic box for Mike to see. "This tape—it's for the weekly backup—it goes in tomorrow, and Wednesday you put the daily tape back in."

"In where?"

"I'd better show you—can you come with me to the computer room now?"

Mike thinks he might go into the sewers with her if she asked him, but he shrugs. "Sure, OK." They walk across the room, through a short corridor, and down the back hallway. "So how was the library yesterday?" he asks.

She glances back at him, a startled look on her face. "The library?"

"Didn't you say after dinner on Saturday that you were going to the library yesterday? Return some books or something?"

"Oh," she says, sounding suddenly cheerful, which is a little weird coming out of Shailene. "It was fine—returned some books, surfed the web, got a couple new books. Good times." She unlocks and opens the door, admitting them into the loud white noise of the server room. She flips on the light.

It occurs to Mike that, if they closed the door and turned out the light, they'd have an enormous amount of privacy.

"So I'll just leave the tape here on the workbench for you. Tomorrow, you just push this button here to eject the tape." She presses it and after a few seconds the tape cartridge rolls out partway. Shailene pulls it completely out of the drive bay and shows it to Mike, pointing out which side goes in first. Then she hands it to him. "Just feed it in until you feel the motor take it from you."

Mike puts the tape in the slot, and when it's about three-fourths inside, a small force pulls the cartridge from his fingers. "Cool."

Shailene gestures toward the weekly cartridge sitting on the table. "So here's your tape: swap it in tomorrow, then swap the daily tape back in on Wednesday. Any questions?"

"No, it's pretty easy."

"Yeah, it's wicked easy. OK, come with me to my desk—I need to give you last week's tape—you'll keep that one offsite at your apartment, and then on Wednesday bring it in and keep it here, and take the one you record tomorrow night home with you. You'll record over the one I made *last* week if I'm not back *next* week."

"If you're not back?" he asks. "I thought you said you were only going for a week."

"I am—at least, that's the plan. But you never know—I could be in a car accident or something, and then you'll have to do this until they hire someone to replace me."

Mike stops walking. "Hold on a minute," he says to her quietly.

Shailene stops walking and turns to face him in the short corridor.

"What are you telling me?" he asks quietly.

"Mike, honestly, my plan is to just be gone the week—I should be back next Tuesday."

"But...?"

"But nothing. Except if something weird happens, like I'm in an accident or something. I really should have taught someone to do this stuff a while ago, so I wouldn't be a single point of failure for our information systems. Because, you know, anybody could get hit by a bus or something."

"Are you always this morbid?"

She makes a poor attempt at smiling, but it comes off as impatient and faked. "I'm not being morbid. C'mon." She turns and starts walking again. "Remember, I used to be a helicopter pilot, so I'm always thinking about what might go wrong," she says, punctuating the sentence with a crooked grin.

It occurs to him she could be up to almost anything on this mystery trip, but he suppresses the urge to ask again and follows her silently back across the big main room to her desk.

"So here's last week's tape," she says, handing him another plastic box like the one they left in the server room. "Sometime today I'll print out the notes I've been typing since I started here, and put them together in a binder—at least you'll have that as a reference. And here, let me give you my cell phone number," she says, turning and bending slightly to write on a Post-It note before peeling it off and handing it over. "If something urgent happens, or you have a question, you can call me. But take a look at the binder I'm going to give you before you call; there's more in my notes than I can remember off the top of my head, OK?"

Mike looks at the note, at her slightly curvy feminine handwriting, and he feels a tiny thrill, reminding him of when he got a note from a girl he liked back in seventh grade. "Wow, the phone number…"

"Uh, yeah…'the phone number,'" she says flatly. "It's not a big deal—Henry has it too. Call me if it's an emergency or you have a question."

Her tone is impatient, almost irritated, and Mike feels irritated back at her. Here he is helping her out, and she's acting like he's some kind of nuisance. But then he reminds himself she probably has a lot on her mind with whatever it is she has to do—her mystery trip out of town. "OK," he says, sighing. "So where are you going, anyway?"

She hesitates a moment, looking uncertain. "Uh, out of state…Pennsylvania."

"What's in Pennsylvania?"

"Mike, I appre—"

"All right, all right, I get it—it's personal, right?"

"Yes," she says, sounding a little hurt.

"OK, I'm sorry. I'm just, I dunno, I'm *worried* about you."

"Thanks Mike, that's really nice, but don't be, OK? I'm sorry I can't tell you more, but I can't, and I've got a lot to get done before I leave today."

Thirteen

I look at the gear laid out on the gray blanket covering my futon mattress, and try to imagine a typical day and what I'll need to get through it. Underwear, of course—several cotton underpants and snug-fitting cotton tank tops. Some are white, but the newer ones are all dark blue or green.

I have about as much cleavage as a dinner plate; even bending at the waist to get a gravity assist, I can't really fill out an A-cup, so instead of bras I wear these tank tops. They smooth out my lines and keep me discreet. When I was a girl, before the Bad, I used to feel a little weird about my lack of curves and wondered when I would start looking more grown-up. After the Bad, I hoped to stay like I was so guys wouldn't look at me. Now I know guys—straight guys, at least—will look at anything female. I'm still glad my body's the way it is. I think bigger breasts would just get in the way; I like being streamlined.

In addition to the underwear, there's an equal quantity of sock pairs and T-shirts. The socks are all white, but the T-shirts are a jumble of colors and associations: road races, high school teams, Army units, public radio shows, and leftover military-issue brown undershirts. What this assembly lacks in uniformity is compensated for by the neat squares they're all folded into, a legacy of my years as a cadet. There's three pairs of jeans too, and since it's March, some sweatshirts and sweaters. I take my suit out of the closet and check it to make sure it looks OK; I haven't worn it since I was job hunting months ago. I lay it out on the mattress. I might need to wear it to gain access somewhere; who knows what kind of guy the predator is. I stare at the collection a little longer, then turn my attention to the other gear.

I'll probably eat out at restaurants some, but that can get expensive. In New Orleans I ended up making peanut butter and jelly sandwiches in my hotel room for lunch every day, and sometimes for dinner too. This time, though, I'm bringing my little butane camping stove and three cans of fuel. The stove burns clean enough to cook indoors, and will enable me to have some hot meals on the cheap in my hotel room.

Obviously I'll need to find that hotel room, but I'll figure that out when I get there. Trenton can't be too busy with travelers this time of year. Before leaving work today I printed out MapQuest directions to the AAA office near Trenton. That'll be my first stop, and I'll be able to get maps and hotel listings there.

I put a couple cans of soup, lentil and vegetable, on the mattress next to the stove, along with peanut butter, a loaf of wheat bread, a jar of pre-sliced pickles, a spreading knife and spoon, an aluminum cook kit, and the Swiss army knife that has my can opener on it. I make a mental note to pack oatmeal, cold cereal, and wheat germ after I make breakfast tomorrow morning. Beyond that, I can go to a grocery store while I'm down there to get more supplies. I put this kitchen stuff in a paper grocery bag.

Hygiene stuff I'll take care of in the morning after I shower and brush my teeth.

I put the book I'm reading now, an Andrew Vachss novel, and the new issue of *National Geographic* on the mattress. There probably won't be a lot of downtime, but there might be some, and if I have trouble falling asleep, reading in bed usually helps.

My plan going into this mission is pretty much the same plan I had in New Orleans: try to figure out a pattern to the killings and the victims, and use that to formulate a guess about where the bad guy is and where he plans to find his next victim. Then I'll drive and walk around in those places, hoping to get within about a hundred meters—a city block, give or take—of him. Once that happens, I'll sense his presence, and I can use the pain in my upper abdomen to home in on him, sort of like warmer/colder hints for a masochist. It's not as thoughtful and smart an approach as I'd like to take, but given my lack of resources and what little I know, this is the best plan I can think of.

I'd rather work with the police—they could maybe help me narrow down my search area, and then I could lead them to a person to focus their investigation on. The problem is figuring out a way to explain my ability to them, to convince them it's real and I'm not crazy. But even I have a hard time accepting the reality of my situation, so I don't know how I'd convince someone else. No, I'm on my own. Ideally I'll find out who the bad guy is before he's close to hurting someone, assuming my sense works when the predator isn't hunting, which I can't confirm yet. If it does work, and I do find the bastard before anyone is in danger, then I can tip the cops anonymously, and maybe they'll follow up and catch the guy. That part of my plan is based on what I know about the arrest of David Berkowitz—the Son of Sam killer. In that case the police showed up to arrest him, and Berkowitz basically confessed even before any mention was made of the charges. It's nothing to count on, but it'd be great if I could get the police to knock on the killer's door and then he just gives himself up. Or maybe by taking a closer look at someone the cops can learn something about him that leads to an arrest.

I dread the other contingency, but my experience in New Orleans a year and a half ago taught me I have to be prepared for it. That consideration, the worst-case scenario, accounts for this last pile of equipment resting on the foot-end of the mattress. Most important is my "Baby Glock"—the compact Glock 26. It uses the same nine-millimeter ammo as the larger Glocks, but its size makes it perfect for my small hands and for carrying concealed. It also has no real safety beyond the trigger guard, which means it's always ready to go. I had the

Alabama gun vendor who sold it to me install a laser sight in its grip, making it easier to aim quickly, especially in low light. He also sold me some used 12-round magazines, enabling me to circumvent the federal prohibition on magazines holding more than ten rounds.

Along with the Glock goes the ammunition. I use hollow points both for their stopping power and their safety. The same characteristic which causes safety slugs to distort and expand on impact with bone, maximizing tissue damage inside the target, also causes the bullet to lose much of its lethality if it hits window panes, walls, doors, furniture, or whatever. This makes it less likely I'll accidentally shoot a bystander through a wall or through a bad guy, and minimizes the risk from ricochets. I consider leaving the Glock unloaded for now, but then what would be the point? If I'm going to have it with me, I might as well have it ready to do some good. I fill the magazine and insert it into the weapon, chamber a round, eject the magazine, push one more cartridge in and reinsert the magazine. Now I've got thirteen rounds ready to go. I load up my spare magazine.

Next I put the Glock and the spare magazine into the shoulder holster and then wriggle into the harness. It's still adjusted from the last time I wore it, so it fits fine.

I decide to take the box of ammunition along. That's almost certainly unnecessary, but what the heck.

I think about taking a backup weapon—my Fairbairn-Sykes British commando dagger. Even though it was a gift, an engraved memento from the guys I went through Ranger School preparation with at West Point, it's a real knife, not a prop. Its blackened double-edged blade is intensely sharp. But it also has a ton of sentimental value for me—I'd hate to lose it somehow. Besides, I have the small canister of pepper spray I always carry, and with a handgun everything else seems superfluous anyway. Plus the dagger, with its seven-inch blade, is pretty hard for me to carry concealed in a way that also makes it accessible, especially since I don't have a rig for it like I do for the gun. No, the dagger stays in its wooden box, which is inside a cardboard box with the other things I don't use much, in the back of my closet.

I pack my clothes and gear into a soft-sided suitcase and a garment bag, then take the shoulder holster off and lay it on the mattress by my pillow. Satisfied I'm ready, I go into the bathroom and brush my teeth, then turn out the light and slide between the sheets, which are wicked cold at first, but warm up quickly.

I lie awake in the darkness and feel bad about giving the people at work such short notice before taking off, and being so secretive about why. One thing I noticed immediately about the civilian workplace is how informal and friendly everyone is, so I really want to do right by them in return. I can't see any way around this situation, though, or anything I could have done better. I guess I always knew this could, and probably would, happen eventually, but it was easy to just not think about it while I was looking for work. Hopefully it won't take me long to find the bastard that killed those boys.

And put the police on him.

And see him arrested.

Yeah, right. Thinking about it now, it seems almost impossible that this will be done in just the week's vacation I got approved today. It was a week in New Orleans before I even found the guy.

And when I did find him, he shot me. My stomach twists at the memory. Even a year and a half later, my shoulder and upper back on that side are still stiff when I do certain movements; I guess the scar tissue in the muscle there isn't as flexible.

It was almost another week before I found him when I went back the second time. Almost got shot again, but that time I was armed too. Shooting back impaired his accuracy. *Shit I hate this stuff.*

All together, it took two weeks on the ground before that mission was complete. *I only have two weeks of vacation total.* Even if I do complete the mission in a week, if something else comes up later this year, I'll almost certainly run out of time off. Plus, how many "personal emergencies" can I have before Henry gets fed up and fires me? He's a nice guy, but he does have a business to run. *Is this job thing going to work? And if not, what will I do for a living?*

I guess I could go back to the phone bank. When I first arrived in Massachusetts after my big road trip, I took an hourly job making phone calls for a polling firm. It was easy, clean, safe work, and it paid OK—ten bucks an hour to start, but they raised it to twelve after I'd been there a month, shortly before the architects hired me to take care of their information systems. Another good thing about that job was I could pretty much set my own hours and it was clear I could take time off whenever I wanted. I didn't get paid when I didn't work, but I could be absent as much as I wanted as long as I gave some notice. And when I left, they told me I could come back and work any time.

Well, I'll deal with that if and when I need to. At this point all that matters is finding the son of a bitch in Trenton and stopping him, one way or another. The thing is—and this puts my problems in perspective—the thing is, there's some kid in Trenton who'll be abused and killed unless I find this fucker. That kid doesn't know it, but he's counting on me.

Fourteen

The window could use cleaning; actually the whole place could. Lunch—french fries and a grilled cheese sandwich—is OK, but I think it's good I don't know what the kitchen looks like. The diner was crowded when I came in, but luckily the two guys who had this table before me left just as I was looking around for an opening. It's a small table with room for two at the most and, even more lucky, it's by the window. No one has needed to sit across from me, so I've had it all to myself.

I watch the cars and pedestrians passing by on Trenton's Broad Street, and notice it's raining again. I actually like rainy days, but only when I can be inside, warm and dry, looking out at them. At West Point, part of the summer training between our first and second years was "infantry week." We spent eight days and seven nights living outside and doing things like walking patrol, digging foxholes, sitting up all night waiting for attacks, walking more patrols. It rained every day of my infantry week, and by the end I had no dry socks left and my feet were gray and wrinkled, the calluses on my soles accumulating in mushy rolls under my fingernails when I scratched at them.

I stare for several seconds at the chrome wire caddy with the salt, pepper, ketchup, and sugar, then lift my eyes back to the scene outside. Pawn shop, vacant store front, run-down apartment building, urban ministry—if I sat here long enough, staring across the street, would these sights start to have the familiarity of home? I guess any place would after a while, though that doesn't mean it would necessarily have the pleasant connotations normally associated with "home." Sometimes when I come to a place for the first time, I get a feeling about it right away. The town where I live now, Arlington, was like that: it immediately felt comfortable; I could tell right away it was a good place for me. Newburyport, up on Massachusetts' North Shore, is another place where I had that love at first sight reaction. Trenton is the opposite of that. It feels bad to me; it's a place I don't want to be.

The parade of strangers past the window continues, and I find myself thinking of Mike, wishing he were sitting across from me. He's called my cell phone a few times since I've been down here, asking how to grant someone rights to an electronic file, wanting to know where I keep the blank CD's, stuff like that. Sometimes I think he's just calling to talk, but then wonder if I'm flattering myself, or maybe just hopeful. The first time he called, I was surprised at how good it was to hear his voice—a familiar, friendly, normal voice. Not just that: it mattered too that it was *his* voice. I think about him, wondering if anything is possible for us. I'm pretty sure if it were just up to him we could have something together. I consider that, trying to gauge my reaction to the idea. In my mind I see the interior of the restaurant we had dinner in: the fire on the hearth across the room, the warm lighting, the old pictures of Cambridge's Porter Square, Mike laughing—*Did I say something to make him laugh? Do I have that ability?* I try to remember what I might have said, but I can't. It was just so good to talk to someone, to have a real conversation.

I think of Miranda's face—I can picture her laughing too. Even something as banal as hunting through used clothing stores for additions to her swing dancing wardrobe was fun when I was with her. The problem was sex. Because of her gender, I was able to mostly overcome my aversion to being touched, but her gender also meant physical intimacy quickly lost its appeal for me.

Maybe Mike doesn't want sex.

I suppress a shudder and push the now empty plate and my glass of water to the side.

I spread the partially-opened map of Trenton out, obscuring the gray Formica table top's gouges and cigarette burns. I look again at the three dots I circled, marking the locations of the schools each of the identified boys attended: one from Lincoln Elementary, one from Harris, and one from Robson. My first day in Trenton I found the public library and went through the last few issues of *The Trentonian*, the local sensationalistic rag. Three of the victims' schools were listed in the articles about the recovery of the bodies. They still haven't identified the fourth boy. He'd been in the ground a lot longer—since last spring the article said.

I spent yesterday systematically wandering around two of the schools' neighborhoods, and today I've been doing the same with the third. But like yesterday, my first full day in Trenton, my scar has been pain-free—not even an itch down there. My search methodology is desperately frustrating; I find myself wishing I could be everywhere in this city at once so I can just find this guy and move things along. Instead I'm tramping up and down one street at a time, systematically covering the blocks in an expanding pattern around each of the marks on my map.

I've thought about simply driving by all these areas; after all, I drive from my hotel to each area, but once I get there I park and walk. Partly this is because the streets here are unfamiliar to me, and it's easier to navigate them on foot than to watch traffic, look around, and do the occasional map check all at once. It's also easier to take longer in an area when I'm on foot, and I think being in a particular place longer increases the chances that I'll be there if my target passes through. This cold drizzle has made me reconsider that strategy, but I've been gutting it out—"sucking it up," as we used to say back in school.

The waitress comes by and asks me if I want anything else. She has light brown hair, freckles on her face, and a big smile. She's friendly and cheerful and looks like she's in her mid-twenties—about the same age as me or a little younger. I tell her I'm all set, and she tears a sheet off her pad and places it on the table, then takes the plate and glass and wishes me a good day, sounding like she means it. When I first sat down and she came over to give me my menu, she was so friendly and chatty I felt awkward. I was worried she'd want to talk with me, but fortunately she's been too busy for that.

I feel a little bad about being antisocial, but I'm accustomed to keeping to myself, and it's usually hard for me to step out of that—more so now than it was a few years ago. Plus, when I'm stressed, I pull in: loner normally, super hermit girl when I'm under pressure. Breaking my first rule, the imperative to keep safe, is really stressing me out.

At least I'm mostly warm again. After sitting in the diner's toasty atmosphere for the last half hour, my hair is dry, and so is the oversized denim work shirt I'm wearing to conceal the Glock. My coat, hanging over the back of the chair opposite me, is still darkened with wetness: normally a dark forest green, the shoulders are now almost black. But I figure it has to be at least dry-*er* than it was when I came in. *I should really look into some kind of waterproofing treatment for it.* It's supposed to be water resistant, but more than a sprinkle and it's not resisting anything wet. Fortunately the lunch crowd has thinned out considerably, so I feel like I can linger here a while longer and let my coat dry some more while I consider my next move.

I turn my attention back to the map and peer at the street names, matching some of them up with the pictures of street signs I have floating around in my head, checking my work and lightly shading the map with a pencil to show the searched areas. *Now what?* I study the map some more and notice, not far away, a couple elementary schools I haven't visited yet.

Maybe the guy is hunting new grounds to make himself harder to track? I find again my current location, and chart a course across town to the area of these other two schools. I'll drive there, and to make it easier I memorize the names of the streets I'll take. That done, I fold the map and tuck it under the work shirt and into the waistband of my jeans behind the small of my back. I had been keeping it in a coat pocket, but the rain eventually soaked through and began eroding the paper, so I'll carry it behind my back and a couple layers deeper for the rest of today.

I look at the bill and leave twenty percent on the table, then glance out the window. It's not obviously raining, but could still be drizzling—I can't really tell. I stand and shrug into my coat, still heavy with accumulated rain, then walk to the register and pay the bill.

I finish snapping shut my coat as I walk down the sidewalk, heading for where I left Stacey this morning. The neighborhood I'm headed to is a pretty good distance from here, and after I get done there I plan to go back to the hotel and call it a day. The drizzle is soft but steady as I walk the block and a half to where I parked, but tapers off soon after I pull into traffic. I leave the low-end commercial district behind and enter what looks like a solid middle class neighborhood made up mostly of Trenton's ubiquitous narrow three-story houses. Some are obviously, by the multiple mailboxes set into the fronts of many of them, split up into rental units, but a lot are single family too. Most of the buildings are in good repair and the street is tidy.

Across the street, going in the opposite direction, I see two adult women with about a dozen kids between them, walking in a line. The kids, who are all around four or five, are linked together by cords tied to their clothing, and are mostly laughing and chattering like little monkeys. The vibe here is safe—completely different from the blighted trash-strewn area I walked through yesterday where more houses were boarded up than not.

So the faint itching that appears just below my sternum surprises me. I remind myself it shouldn't; if there's anything I've learned from my research, it's that predatory sociopaths transcend all lines. They can be anyone in any place, from a middle-aged recluse in small-town Wisconsin, to a young, attractive attorney on the west coast, to a music promoter in Atlanta.

I slow the car and look around anxiously, wondering about the source's location. I immediately check for cars around me, but I don't see anyone ahead. In my mirrors I see one car moving away, and one car following. If the predator were in the receding car I would have felt pain as we passed each other, but I didn't. To check the car following behind, I pull over. The vehicle, a gray minivan, passes me by, but the itch remains constant. The bastard is stationary, or close to it, here on the ground. I switch off the engine, and swallow hard. Even though I've been seeking just this event all week, it still scares me. My experience tells me I'm now within about a hundred meters of the predator. *OK, here we go.* I get out and continue walking in the same direction I'd been driving, reminding myself as I go that I don't fit his victim profile and I'm only going to find out who he is and phone it in to the pro's—no interaction and no violence required. I scan the street and glance over both shoulders, but I don't see anyone around.

Heading down the street, the itching intensifies to a more painful scratch, like the jagged edge of a fingernail being pressed into and drawn along my skin, tracing the line of scar there. Two more houses and across a side street, and my scar feels hot, like a really bad sunburn. As I pass another house it feels like the skin there has burned through and is tearing open. The pain goes deeper: a sharp ache penetrating into the middle of my torso, toward my heart. I finally give in to my instinct, stopping and tearing my coat open, and pressing my fingertips against the layers of clothing between them and the scar. I push against the soft part of me in the bony upside-down V formed by the two halves of my rib cage. The flesh there is firm and intact, of course, and massaging it does nothing to reduce the pain. *Gotta suck it up and keep going, find the bastard.*

I know I'm close now; I'm between two houses, and he has to be in one of them, probably the one still ahead of me. A few more steps and I'm in front of it, but the pain—unless I'm imagining it, the hurt eases a tick. I stop and look around. There's still no one else in sight. I walk to the next house down and now I'm certain the pain has diminished. *OK, colder.* I stop and turn around, feeling a little ridiculous. I look across the street at the houses over there. I suppose he could be in one of those, but I don't think so. Given the intensity of the pain, and how quickly it varies, he's got to be very close, on this side of the road. I retrace my steps. The pain seems to peak when I'm between the houses—numbers 166 and 168. I stand on the end of the driveway running between the two buildings, hesitating. The driveway, which leads back to an old garage made of stone blocks, is empty. It's a dim day, but I see no lights on in either house. *Now what?*

I consider ringing the doorbells on the houses, using some ruse like I'm looking for Mike or Michelle, the opposite gender of whoever answers the door. If he were to answer the door, if I were standing just a few feet from him, I'd know because I'd feel like I was being stabbed—the Bad re-lived. It'd be hard to keep it from showing on my face, but I can do it; I've done it before. And then I'd have his face and his address, and maybe I could find out his name, either from a label on a mailbox, or by doing a reverse lookup through the phone company's website. Then I could phone—*OK, so ring the doorbells already.*

I go up to the building on my right—168. There are three doorbell buttons, presumably one for each unit, on a metal plate with a circular pattern of holes for the intercom speaker. I hadn't thought of that—I might not get a face to face, just a voice on an intercom. Still, if I only get one response, it's gotta be him—most likely, anyway. I press the first buzzer, and hear it muffled, but not so far away on the first floor. Wait several seconds, press it again, hear it from inside. But there's no other noise inside—no rustling or footsteps, no voices, TV, or radio. I try the next button up, and barely hear the buzz above me on the second floor. Wait, repeat, nothing. I go through the same routine for the last button and hear nothing. I turn, cross the porch, and take the three steps down to the sidewalk. *He's got to be here, somewhere. Got to be the other house.* I take a right on the sidewalk.

I'm crossing the driveway when I hear a cat screeching. I know the sound because I grew up with a cat and once, when I was maybe five or six, the sound of his fighting woke me from a sound sleep. I didn't know what the sound was, but it sounded like some kind of monster; if I'd known the words then, I'd have thought "banshee" or "demon." It scared the crap out of me—this was long before I found out the real monsters are human. I remember yelling for my dad; as a child, when I was hurt I always called for my mother, but when I was scared I shouted for my father. The sound had woken him up too, because I remember him answering me immediately from my parents' bedroom, which was right next to mine, and a second later he was in my room, explaining it was just Sammy, our cat. Together, we went downstairs to the kitchen and turned on the flood lights to illuminate the backyard. My father held me in his arms so I could see out the window over the sink, and he pointed to where Sammy, looking just like a Halloween cat with his back arched and fur puffed out, was facing off with some other cat from the neighborhood.   The flood light had distracted both of them, and their eyes shone green in the wash of illumination.

The emotional content—fear followed by comfort from my father and relief that the monster in the night was just Sammy—etched deep the memory of the incident, including the sound of an angry cat. The sound I just heard was enough like that so I immediately recognized it, but this time there was a panicked quality to the cat's voice that I don't remember in Sammy's. I stop in my tracks and turn my head in the direction it came from: down the driveway by the garage. I glance up at the windows in the two houses, see they're all still dark, then walk down the driveway, my sneakers making no noise on the clean pavement.

As I approach the garage, the pain in me intensifies. *The ghost of that bastard is penetrating me again, stabbing toward my heart.* I shut the thought down and refocus on my situation. The source is very close now—within a couple dozen feet of me. I slow my pace, and begin undoing the upper buttons on the oversize denim shirt, opening access to the Glock. With each step, lines of sight open up to the tiny back yards on either side of the garage, and to the right I notice a child—a boy, I think, given the short hair and dark blue jacket—squatting down, his back to me. He's young—prepubescent; even from behind I can tell that from his small size. His head, covered with neatly-trimmed, straight blonde hair, is canted forward. He seems intent on something in front of him on the ground.

The stabbing below my sternum tells me the target is close by, and I think he must be watching the same little boy I'm walking up to now. I wonder where the predator is—in the house? The garage? My eyes flick toward the row of small square windows set into the broad garage door. There's only blackness behind the windows, but that fits: the bad guy would have the lights off since he's looking out at the boy, not at anything inside the garage with him.

"Hey kid," I say intending to warn him, to tell him to get the hell away from here. But as soon as these two words reach the child's ears, his head spins around. I'm only about ten feet away now, and there's panic in his eyes. Then he's turning his whole body and launching into a sprint, all at once. His response surprises me, and the only reaction I manage is to step quickly out of his way. As he goes by his smooth young face is flushed bright red, and I glimpse something small and metallic in his right hand, which is stained a deeper, brighter red. *Blood.* Instinctively I say "hold on—" but he ignores me and I don't repeat myself; after all, a couple seconds ago I was going to tell him to get out of here. I watch him run down the driveway, turn the corner, and vanish behind the house. Then I remember the killer. I reach inside the denim shirt and touch the Glock, ready to draw it, and return my attention to the garage and the backyards.

The pain is abating rapidly.

What...? I look over my shoulder, down the driveway at the street. I listen hard, but except for the sound of a car passing by every few seconds, and the more distant low background hum and chatter of the city, it's quiet. I snap my head around again, back toward the garage, but I hear no movement there or in the houses, or in the outdoor space around me—no doors opening or closing, no more running feet now that the boy has disappeared down the street. The ghostly penetration of my body has reversed: the hurt has already diminished to sharp cramps, then moves out to my skin, where the tearing sensation eases to a hot line along the scar. After about ten seconds there's only an itch there, and even that is diminishing. The easing of pain was too slow for movement by car, but about right for a person running. *A child running?*

Confused, I glance behind me at the driveway again. *Cat...* I remember what I heard and turn once more, looking at where the boy had been squatting on the ground by the garage.   There's a white, red, and orange shape there on the light brown bed of dead grass. I walk over to it.

It's a mess. I feel my lips press together into a frown as I observe the spilled entrails and blood-matted fur.   Then I notice the slow, weak up and down movement of its flank. "Oh shit," I whisper. I squat down next to the animal and examine it. The cat's legs are pointed toward the wall of the garage, and its back is the part nearest me. The back looks wrong: instead of a smooth convex curve, there's a break in the spine, and the hind part of the cat seems somehow separate, yet still connected, to the front part.   "What happened to you?" I ask softly, turning toward the head as if I expected a response. There's blood on the fur there too. I shift my angle and feel my face contort reflexively at the sight of the rough, bloody hole where the eye should have been. "The little fuck," I say softly, thinking of the glimpse of metal I saw in the boy's bloody hand. The cat is unrestrained; there is nothing to bind its legs or its teeth, but the odd angle of its back and inertness of everything beyond that break tells me the spinal cord has been severed there. One of the front legs looks crooked too, and I wonder if the cat was a target of opportunity for the young predator, if he came across the cat after it had been hit by a car. Maybe the kid carried it back here so he could experiment on it. The alternative would be the kid somehow managed to break the cat's back and leg himself, when the cat was still whole and able to defend itself. "I'm sorry, little one," I say quietly. I want to comfort the animal—to stroke the fur on its head reassuringly, but probably the last thing the creature wants now is to be touched.

Now what? The cat looks pretty bad, and I wonder if the best thing I could do for it is kill it quickly. I glance around for a big rock or something similarly hard and heavy I can use to crush the cat's head instantly. I spot a baseball bat lying nearby, and start to go for it, but then I think how right after the Bad I looked pretty messed up too—cut open, covered in blood. I wasn't paralyzed, and most of the blood wasn't mine, but still, someone might have considered me pretty far gone, and here I am. The cat deserves a chance too. I need to at least get it to a veterinarian, and let the pro figure out what would be best. I stand up again and pull out my cell phone.

What about the kid? I pause for a second, considering this. He triggered my sense, and here at my feet is the corroborating evidence. The kid has already proven himself a predator. *But he's what? Like seven years old? And even if I find him, what would I do? Report him to the police? How would I prove he's the one who hurt the cat?* In all likelihood, the cat was already hurt, by someone driving by. Even if I could prove that kid, whose name I don't even know, tortured this cat, what are the chances I'm going to get the police sufficiently interested in this to arrest the kid? "This is crazy," I mutter. The only alternative that makes any sense at all is to try to find the kid again and—

And what? *Execute* him? "That's *really* crazy," I breathe, feeling a little dizzy. I've killed three people, but each of them was trying to kill me first. There's no way I could hunt someone down and coldly kill him, *especially* if he's a little kid.

"I'm wasting time," I mutter. I open my cell phone, dial 411, and ask the information operator for a listing of an animal hospital in Trenton.

"I have nine listings here—do you know which one you want?" the woman asks.

"Do any of them list emergency services?"

"All I have is names, numbers, and addresses."

"All right, fine—what's the first one?"

She gives me a name, which I promptly forget, and a number, which I begin repeating to myself as I end the call and dial again.

"Animal Hospital of Trenton, how may I help you?"

"I have a cat here who was hit by a car, I think. Can I bring him in—do you have any kind of an emergency room?"

There's a pause, then, "I think you want the ASPCA hospital on Fourth Street."

"Can you give me their number?"

"Just a minute."

I hear a keyboard clicking, then she gives me the number. By now I've gotten a pen out and I write the number on the palm of my left hand, then thank her and end the call. I key in the new number and press send. The staffer at the ASPCA gives me directions.

I hang up, take another look at the cat lying very still on the ground, then sprint to where I left Stacey. As I go, I wonder if I'll pick up on the kid again, but I don't. I get to Stacey, crank her engine, and drive back down the street, pulling into the driveway and all the way up to the garage. Leaving the engine running, I pop the rear hatch and jump out.

There's a hard, heavy-duty cardboard piece over the well that holds the spare tire. I flip the carpeting back, remove the board, and carry it over to the cat, figuring I should try to move its back as little as possible. I squat down and lay the board on the dead grass, its leading edge just under the cat's broken spine, then consider how to get the cat on the board. I imagine using the board as a spatula, but I'm afraid I'll just end up pushing the cat around and maybe causing it more pain, or further damaging its back. Putting my hands on the cat's underside, bracketing the break in its back, seems like the best plan, but that means my left hand will be immersed in the coils of intestines. I wonder again if trying to bring this animal to a hospital is the right thing to do. Touching the intestines is gross, but mainly I wonder if I'll be doing some further damage. Even as I think it, I realize how ridiculous that is.

I move forward and squat again, this time on the board. I put my right hand out and cup the cat's chest. The cat does

not react. In fact, I can detect no movement of its chest at all.
The fur feels like any cat I've touched, except there's nothing
going on under it—no movement, no tension. It's like the fur
is the fabric on a small cushion. The up and down motion of
the flank has ceased. I withdraw my hand and stare at the
cat's chest and side; the creature is completely inert. The
mouth is slack: the teeth partly visible and where they're not,
the lips, under gravity's influence, have taken on the shape of
the teeth. I go to my knees, then lower myself so I can put my
ear against its chest. I feel the fur against my cheek and ear
and, holding my breath, I listen. I hear nothing except the
other sounds around me. I block my right ear, the one not
against the cat, with my finger tip and hold my breath again.
Still nothing. After a while, maybe a minute, I raise up again
and look at the sad bundle of fur, bone, flesh, and viscera, and
think about Sammy again. He was run down by a car too. At
least he died immediately, without suffering; that's how I
remember it, anyway. Definitely no one tortured him before
he died.

Kneeling there, I think about the kid again, about trying to
track him down, but I run into the same problem as before:
what would I do when I found him? There's no evidence
tying him to the abuse of an animal, an animal which is now
dead. Besides, the police are a little preoccupied with the
killer I'm *supposed* to be tracking down, so they probably
wouldn't give a shit about a dead cat. No, that course is out. I
could…take matters into my own hands, but I know I really
couldn't hurt the kid so it's pointless even to consider.

Maybe the sense is wrong in this case. Maybe the sense
is just craziness—my craziness. That is, after all, why I
always look for corroborating evidence the person is actually
what the sense says he is. I don't want to be like the ones I
hunt: accusing, and possibly killing, on the basis of delusion.
But the cat is proof of what that kid is, right?

Can someone so young already be a predator? How is a psychopath made, anyway? When does a person become a monster? Some books I've read say the combination of genetics and experience we call personality is pretty well set by age seven. So does that mean a sadistic, conscienceless predator is a done deal when he's still a child? *I guess*, I think, mentally shrugging.

If that's true, if a person is shaped into a psychopath while still a child, the implication is he doesn't have a choice about what he is after that. And when you're just a kid, you're not really *choosing* your path so much as being directed by the forces around you—parents, other kids, health, nutrition—all of it. *So...if there's no choice, is there any moral responsibility? Can you really be called guilty if you had no choice in acting as you did?*

What about the rest of us? Aren't we all shaped into who we are while we're still kids, and doesn't that core personality direct our actions for the rest of our lives? Are any of us really *choosing*, choosing *freely* what we do?

I shake my head. *Whatever.* Morally responsible or not, I'm not going to chase down and kill a kid. I'm just not. As for the bastard that's raping and killing kids, morally responsible for his actions or not, he's a problem that needs solving. I'm going to find him, and then I'm going to help the police find him and stop him.

I look around. I'm apparently still alone, and my scar is pain- and itch-free. I look back at the dead cat and give it a moment of mental silence. Then I stand, pick up the board, and walk back to Stacey.

Fifteen

As Wayne turns down his street, he scans it, as he has every night this week, for police vehicles. He knows there won't be any; by now it's become a sort of mind game with himself: indulging the fear of discovery so he can enjoy the sweetness of relief when he sees his street dark and deserted. They haven't been to the restaurant, and they haven't been here at the apartment building because they don't know his name. And how would they? It was crazy, really, to be afraid. It's actually difficult now to play the mind game with himself because he knows in his heart they won't catch him. There's no connection the police—or even the FBI, who, according to the news, have been called in to help—no connection they can make to Wayne Lambert.

Which is why he's decided it's OK to be close to someone again: close to the one he's been watching. The boy has red hair and freckles, and wears jeans too big for him, so he rolls the cuffs up. Probably his mom got them used— Wayne remembers how that was, the clothes not fitting right, or being too big when he first got them so he could grow into them. The kid, "Red" is how Wayne thinks of him, walks to school with his mom every morning, and home alone every afternoon around three. Actually, Wayne's only watched Red walk home on Mondays and Tuesdays, but the boy has been alone on every afternoon Wayne has seen him. Wayne remembers how that was too: letting himself in to the empty apartment, fixing himself cereal for dinner, waiting for mom to get home, and then her being too tired to talk to him. "Why don't you go watch TV, Wayne honey?" she would say to him. "Mommy needs some time to herself."

He remembers too the year, give or take, that Todd was Mom's boyfriend and was living with them. Wayne was in third grade that year, and almost every day Todd walked him to school and back home again in the afternoon. That was great because Todd talked to him—*really* talked to him. Todd wanted to hear all about Wayne's day, what he did in school, what he was interested in. Even twenty-one years later he can still remember how great it felt to have someone to talk to.

It was in those afternoons together that Todd taught him about sex. By that time, they were close and comfortable with each other, and the things he and Todd did together were fun and exciting, and felt good in a way nothing else ever had before. But despite all that, Wayne sensed there was something wrong with what they were doing. Maybe it was because Todd swore him to secrecy. No. No, Wayne knew even before Todd made him promise not to tell. He just *knew*. It felt wrong, which was confusing, because it felt good too. Looking back now, it's easy to see he should have followed the little voice that told him not to take his clothes off with Todd. *What if I had said "no"? What would Todd have done? Would he have stopped talking to me?* It's easy now to say he shouldn't have done the sex stuff with Todd, but even twenty-one-years-older, adult Wayne knows how near impossible that would have been for eight-year-old Wayne. Still, sometimes he wonders how things might be different now.

Maybe he'd be dating Dana.

Doggy bag from Reilly's in hand, he gets out of his car and slams the door shut.

Fuck it. He picked his path. Now he was finally learning to live with it. Last spring he found a way to recapture what he had with Todd, only better.

He walks down the sidewalk, past the black metal mailboxes mounted next to the door, and uses the key to let himself into the stairwell.

He feels a little winded after climbing the three flights to his floor. *I really should join the gym again.* He drops the food bag on the kitchen counter, hangs his coat in the closet by the door, then heads into the bedroom to change into jeans and a sweatshirt. Back in the kitchen, he puts his dinner in the microwave for a couple minutes and gets himself a beer. While the food's nuking, he goes over to the TV and flips it on, then starts rewinding the video tape of today's—*well, technically yesterday's since it's now past midnight and officially Friday*—five and eleven o'clock news. While it's rewinding, he watches some late-late show where a host Wayne doesn't know interviews some celebrity Wayne's never heard of.

The microwave beeps, and he goes to the kitchen and gets his dinner: a box of garlic mashed potatoes and a box with an open face roast beef and gravy sandwich in it. He places the cardboard containers side-by-side on a bright orange plate, grabs a fork from the drawer, and heads back into the living room.

He takes a couple bites before using the remote to start the tape, then fast-forwards through five minutes of game show and commercials before the news comes on. Once again, his story leads. This time they go to a press conference from earlier in the day. The police chief speaks briefly, confirming what Wayne already knew: they have no clue. He doesn't actually say it, in so many words, definitely not in *those* words, but he pretty much admits it, actually appealing to the public for help as he introduces an FBI agent—Chief Patterson calls him a "behavioral analyst"—who has constructed a psychological profile of the killer.

"This should be good," Wayne says quietly, smiling a little.

Patterson yields the podium to a bald, clean-shaven black man with very dark skin. The smooth dome of his head shines in the light, reminding Wayne of Darth Vader's helmet, although obviously the guy isn't *that* dark. His name appears at the bottom of the screen: Special Agent Silas MacIlwane.

"Based on the evidence we have found so far and similar cases we have solved in the past, we know the person who killed these boys is very likely to have the following characteristics: He's a white male in his late twenties or early thirties, probably living here in Trenton itself. He's intelligent, and most likely has a white collar job. He might live with a parent, but it's more probable he lives alone. He is socially isolated: he doesn't have many friends and no intimate relationships—no dating, and not married. He may seem a little awkward in social situations."

Wayne lifts his beer toward the television. "Not bad, Lord Vader," he says. "But you've still got nothing connecting to me—that description probably matches thousands of guys."

"We think he also probably has at his home an inventory of items which would appeal to seven- and eight-year-old boys. He might have a collection of toys, video games, children's movies—things like that.

"Clearly," MacIlwane continues, "this description still matches a lot of men who are completely innocent, and do not feel the deep rage and hatred toward young boys that the killer feels."

"*What?*" Wayne gasps, standing up suddenly and almost dumping the boxes of food off his plate. "'Rage and hatred'? I don't—I don't *hate* my boys! I *love* them; I made them happy, and then saved them from the shit they'd gotten themselves into!"

"…not to report any and all men matching this profile. Rather, if you do know someone who resembles this description, we'd like you to be observant. If you notice this person spending time alone with a young boy, or in places where he's likely to encounter boys, or acting strangely in some way—perhaps exhibiting extreme, inexplicable mood swings—*that's* when you should call the tip line."

"How could they think I hate my boys when they saw how carefully I buried each of them with..." His voice trails off as he thinks of Jimmy, partially eaten by animals. "It was just so cold—the ground was hard..." he says under his breath while shaking his head at the memory and staring blankly at the television screen.

They must have seen how I buried him with the puppy? Maybe the puppy was eaten by animals—must have been. There was no mention of it in the news reports, so maybe it was carried off by an animal. Wayne feels tears welling up at the thought of the lost puppy. *I meant to do right by Jimmy, but the ground was frozen—I did the best I could.*

He didn't mean for Jimmy to be eaten by animals. He loved Jimmy. Sure, the boy was wrong to have sex with Wayne, just like it was a mistake for Wayne to choose that with Todd. But at least Wayne had made things right again by sparing Jimmy and the others all the shit that comes after the sex. That was more than Todd had done for him. That's an act of *love*, not *hate*. "Can't they see that?" he asks the room, his voice faltering on the last word because his throat is tight and the inside of his mouth is sticky.

I can tell them. He looks at the bottle of beer on the coffee table in front of him, then turns and walks to the kitchen, realizing on the way he's still holding the plate with his dinner on it. He puts the plate on a counter, takes a glass from the cupboard and fills it with tap water. He gulps the water down, nearly choking on it at first, but recovering. When the glass is empty he walks back into the living room, picks up the phone's cordless handset, and realizes he doesn't know the number for the tip line. He sits down on the couch and picks up the remote for the VCR. The recorded news show has moved on to another story now, so he rewinds until Special Agent Vader is on again, the toll-free number written on the screen beneath him. Wayne pauses the tape, turns the phone on again, and presses the numbered buttons.

In the pause before the first ring it suddenly occurs to him: *What if they have caller ID?* He takes the handset from his ear and quickly mashes the off button, hoping he cut the connection soon enough.

He sits staring at the frozen image of the FBI man on his screen, thinking about setting him straight. *I could write a letter to the editor.* He's never done that before, but isn't that what people do when they see something that's wrong, to set the record straight? He starts composing it in his head, considering whether to write as himself or as a disinterested observer: "Anyone who would take the trouble to so carefully—" No, that was stupid. How would anyone but the police, the guy who found the body, and himself know the bodies were "carefully buried" with the toys and, at one point at least, the puppy?

"Fuck 'em," he decides. It's none of their fucking business anyway. What he did, what he will *keep on doing* is between him and his boys. The police and the FBI obviously have no idea who he is or why he's doing what he does, so why shouldn't he keep loving? No one else *needs* to know he loves his boys, feels sorry for them, wants to make things right. They don't understand his love, don't know what it was like to come home to an empty house every day, to not have anyone to talk to, to have a mother too tired to listen and no—

Wayne's face contorts and he squeezes his eyes shut. A tear leaks out and rolls down his face. *They don't know what it's like to be so fuckin' alone.*

Sixteen

The growling emptiness in my stomach tells me it's close to six p.m. I've been driving pretty much all day, all around Trenton and its suburbs because, after four days of finding nothing, I decided to change tactics and cover as much ground as I can as quickly as possible. Really, this change was more an act of desperation and frustration than a considered change in approach. Unfortunately, this style of searching hasn't produced any better results than the more careful, focused tactic of walking every street in the killer's past areas of operation. *Maybe he left town after the bodies were discovered.* The guy who came after me when I was a kid moved after each attack he did, carrying his skills as a photographer from city to city across the country, taking a victim in each area, then moving on shortly afterwards.

But that's not this guy's style. His three identified victims were from right here in Trenton, and the fourth one probably was too. And since there was no evidence of an intruder or of the boys even returning to their homes right before their disappearance, the cops think he brings the kids back to his apartment. The police advisory said he probably uses some scheme to lure the kids to go with him, rather than taking them by force. So unlike the monster that came after me, who did what he did in the homes of his victims, this guy has a base of operations which is part of his method. Still, that doesn't mean he couldn't leave town once the bodies were discovered. Maybe he took a vacation—it could be that simple.

Or maybe he's decided his killing career is over. Maybe the switch that flipped in his head, making him want to kill, somehow got moved again, and now he's not looking to take any more victims. I've read that sometimes happens with predators. And my best guess about the sense I carry around is it's only triggered by *predatory* sociopaths, what some call psychopaths. While as much as four percent of the population are sociopaths—people without conscience who are unable to empathize with other humans—only a very small portion of that group tortures and kills for fun. It's apparently only this tiny sub-group that triggers the sense, given how rarely I'm aware of their presence. So it would figure that if a predator were to stop wanting to harm others, I would no longer be able to sense his nearness.

My stomach growls again. *Dinner.* I remember I ate my last can of soup last night so, while I still have oatmeal, peanut butter, and bread back at the hotel, I don't have anything different for dinner. I stop for a light on Olden Avenue and scan the shopping plazas alongside, looking for a grocery store. Up ahead in the fading light I see an illuminated sign for a Shop Rite; I put on my turn signal and shift over to the left lane.

As I'm pulling into the parking lot entrance, my scar starts to lightly itch. I keep driving, moving deeper into the parking lot and getting out of the way of the cars coming in behind me, meanwhile wondering if the itching, which is barely perceptible, is just my imagination, the result of focusing all day for five days on exactly how my scar feels. The itching stays constant after I scratch at it, providing a sort of confirmation. *Shit, where is he?* I think, feeling anxious I might lose him just as I finally found him. The Shop Rite is off to my right and, still mentally debating the whereabouts of what I'm sensing, I automatically turn for it.

The itch intensifies as I drive past the store, and becomes a scratch as I move past a CVS, Weight Watchers, and Radio Shack. By the time I'm in front of Staples my scar is beginning to feel hot. Staples is the last store in the row, so I follow a roadway which runs off to my left, past the far side of

Staples. The heat abates to more of a scratch again as I find myself in the loading dock area behind the strip mall. I stop Stacey and look back over my right shoulder. *The Staples? Or—aw shit! What if he was in the fucking parking lot, and now he's leaving?!* I quickly execute a three-point turn, desperately hanging on to the scratching in my scar, as if I can hold him in place by force of will.

My scar heats up again. I hang a right and pass in front of Staples. When the pain abates as I reach Radio Shack, I instinctively turn left down a parking aisle. My scar heats up and a sing-song voice appears in my thoughts: *Warmer, gettin' warmer...* "Fuckin' Easter egg hunt from hell," I mutter. There's a building ahead of me, and as I approach the burning intensifies.

Unlike the box stores behind me, this one-story building stands alone in its corner of the parking lot. The roof is steeply sloped around the edges, as if it were going to be peaked, but the slope stops after a few feet and the top is just flat. There's a sign with three retro-looking lamps suspended just above it. "Reilly's" is printed in relaxed, happy letters with rounded edges. A row of large windows set into the brownish brick walls show me the warmly-lit interior with large photos of athletes on the walls, people sitting at tables, and staff walking around busily. I've never heard of a Reilly's before, but this is obviously one of those chain restaurants that are supposed to be American versions of English pubs: friendly neighborhood eateries serving straightforward food and beer, with cluttered décor and cozy lighting. Ironically, they always seem to be located in that destroyer of neighborhoods, shopping plazas.

I drive a little way from the building again and put Stacey in a parking spot. When I'm this close, small changes in distance produce big changes in pain. At the parking space my scar is burning like a wicked sunburn, but by the time I walk the fifty feet up to the building, it feels like it's tearing open.   Based on my experiences with the sense, I figure another fifty feet will put me right next to the son of a bitch.

I wonder if I'm looking for an employee or a customer. I think about the profile that FBI guy talked about on TV the other night: white guy in his late twenties…white collar job… So if the profiler—what was his name? Silas something—if Agent Silas is right, the target probably isn't washing dishes or clearing tables. And he's probably not a waiter, but could he be a chef? Is that white collar? More likely he's eating here; I think this is a yuppie kind of place.

Two couples exit the building as a group, all laughing together. The four walk past me, mostly ignoring me, though one of the guys makes eye contact with me briefly before I look away, wondering how I'm going to figure out which person inside is my target.

The first of these missions began unwittingly at a shopping mall in Dothan, Alabama. I didn't know then what I was getting into; I barely understood what the sense meant or how it worked, but I quickly found I could use it to zero in on a person, or in that case, two people together. Two people don't double the pain of the sense; only proximity affects how much I hurt. They were in the mall's food court, so it was easy to not draw attention to myself while I followed the pain around the big room to them. But this place is different. I don't go out to eat much, but when I was stationed in Alabama I went with some other lieutenants to a similar place down south, a Shoney's, and there was a hostess at the door who greeted us and had a waiter escort us to a table. I'm sure this place has the same deal, so I can't go in and just start wandering around until I find the source of my pain. I could go in and, after being seated, pretend to go looking for the bathroom and walk around some. But then what if he leaves before me? I could just throw some money on the table and go, but I decide to first see what I can find out from circling on the outside. I've lost my appetite now anyway.

I turn left and start walking around the building. As soon as I turn the corner and move along the side away from Olden Avenue, the pain intensifies. I stop and catch my breath, reassuring myself the pain doesn't indicate a physical injury, even though the sharp cramps have gone deeper, and I feel the pain hard and sickening below my heart. I resume walking, past the end of the ribbon of window that wraps part-way around the structure. When it feels like I'm being stabbed just below my heart, I know I have to be no more than a few feet from him—effectively in the same room as him, except for maybe a foot or so of wall between us. I reach out and touch the cold, windowless brick, wondering what's on the other side—more seating for diners? The kitchen? I drop my hand. I can see from the roof line that the actual building ends just beyond this point, but the wall continues on without a roof— probably an enclosure for trash barrels. No windows and adjacent to the back trash area, I'm guessing this part of the building doesn't hold more seating, but rather the kitchen. Or the bathrooms—those have to be somewhere. If it's the bathrooms, if the target is using the can, then I should feel him move away after a few minutes. I turn my back to the wall and lean against it, hoping to be inconspicuous. I check my watch: 6:19.

While I'm waiting, it occurs to me there must surely be some kind of manager on the premises—someone to oversee the whole operation. Isn't that who people demand to talk to when they're really unhappy with something at a restaurant? *"I want to see the manager!"* Or is that in department stores? Probably both. If there is a manager, wouldn't he have an office—someplace he can sit and, I don't know, manage? Go over the books or something? Schedule staff? That sounds pretty white collar.

I think about that a while, then check my watch again: 6:27. Eight minutes seems a little long for the bathroom. The manager thing sounds good, but I could also have my back against a kitchen wall, which would imply he's a chef. I give it a few more minutes, but when the pain doesn't change, I start walking again, around the back of the building.

I breathe a little easier as the pain abates. I reach a tall wooden gate with spaces between the vertical planks. A sign on the gate tells deliveries to ring the bell on the front of the building. I peer through one of the spaces, and in the growing darkness I can see a glowing bar at the bottom of a doorway. That door has to lead to the kitchen, providing easy access for supplies coming in and garbage going out to the back enclosure. Plus, I can hear the roar of exhaust fans, and smell hot oil and grilling meat. Suddenly I'm feeling hungry again: over eleven years as a vegetarian, and the smell of cooking meat still makes my stomach growl.

Suddenly the back door of the building opens, and before I can even step back I see the silhouette of someone emerge carrying two big sacks. Leaving the door open, he angles off to my left, and I can hear the rustling of plastic bags and a couple soft grunts as he tosses the trash into what must be a dumpster behind another wooden gate to my left. Meanwhile I'm looking through the open door into the kitchen. A waiter goes by carrying a tray of food, and a young guy wearing an untucked white shirt—more like a jacket really—over jeans passes quickly by. The guy who took the trash out appears in my line of sight again. He goes back into the kitchen, closing the door behind him.

I resume my walk, continuing on around to the street side of the building, where the ribbon of windows starts up again. I don't linger, but I watch sideways as I pass by, looking in at all the people talking and laughing, eating and drinking together. The pain in my scar, though still burning, isn't so bad over on this side. I circle all the way back to the epicenter of hurt again and find nothing has changed. Based on all I've observed, I figure he's most likely working here, and he's also staying glued to one spot, probably sitting at a desk, which argues against him being a waiter or bus boy.

I'm hungry again, and if he works here he's probably not leaving any time soon, so I walk back to the front entrance. The hours are posted on the glass door—eleven to eleven every day.

Inside it's just what I expected. A hostess greets me at the door, asks me how many in my party and smoking or non. A young waiter, maybe a college student, takes me to a small table in the smoke-free section, which is fortunately located on the opposite side of the building from where the target is. I'm still hurting, but at least it doesn't feel like I'm being stabbed. I look around on my way to the table, and some more after I sit down. The back area of the building is clearly for staff, confirming my theory about the target working here. It takes less than a minute of watching the waiters to see the kitchen is on the street side of the building. There's a small, open area between the way into the kitchen and something else on the strip mall side—that's got to be the manager's office.

Satisfied, I turn my attention to the menu. Being a vegetarian eliminates most of the meal choices; even the salads all have meat in them. I was hoping to get a veggie burger, but surprisingly that's not on the menu. I thought they'd become pretty popular, but apparently not here. The closest I can get to something I'd eat is the cheese quesadilla appetizer, so I order that and, figuring it's going to be a long night, a cup of coffee.

While I'm waiting for the food, I wonder if there's some way to talk to the manager. Doing that would enable me to confirm he's the target while getting a good look at his face and maybe his name. But if I get a good look at him, he'll be getting a good look at *me*. I guess that doesn't matter...unless the police don't respond right away to the tip I'm going to call in. If they don't—and they probably won't—it'll be up to me to follow this guy around and make sure he doesn't hurt any more kids. The last time a target recognized me while I was following him around, he tried to ambush and kill me. Even if this guy doesn't do that, I might end up needing to catch him in the act of abducting a kid, and that'd be harder to do if he thinks I'm watching him. Better to stay under his radar.

The food arrives and I dig in hungrily. Despite my appetite, the quesadillas are pretty crummy. The cheese is too salty, and the bread—the tortillas or whatever—have almost no taste at all. At least the coffee is strong and bitter, and I let the waiter refill it once, but then worry about needing to pee. I linger a while after I finish the food and the second cup of coffee, then leave cash on the table and go to use the bathroom before I leave.

The bathrooms are located in the back, next to the corner with the manager's office. As I head back there, I'm able to see punch clocks in the short corridor between the office and the kitchen, but I can't see the door to the office or into the kitchen at all before I reach the entrance to the women's bathroom. He's definitely back here, though—the stabbing below my heart confirms that. For a second or two it's a struggle, but I'm able to suppress my nausea and avoid throwing up my crappy dinner. I empty my bladder, quickly wash my hands, and get out of there.

As I'm leaving, I take my time putting on my coat just inside the main entrance so I can look around for a name and maybe a picture of the manager. I remember seeing that at other restaurants I've been to, but there's nothing like that here.

Back out in the parking lot, I look around again, wondering if the staff parks somewhere special. There were no spaces behind the restaurant, but I notice a line of cars parked along the edge nearest Olden Avenue, and decide those cars are most likely the employees'. I walk back to Stacey and relocate her so she's facing the main entrance, but a few rows back, and not directly under any of the big lights illuminating the area. From this location I also have a good view of the employees' vehicles, or at least I will have a good view after the customers leave. I check my watch and see it's about half past seven.

Now I wait. When he leaves, I'll follow him, probably to his home. On the way, I'll get his license plate, and when he arrives I'll have his address and hopefully a name off a mailbox. Then I call the cops' tip line.

I recline my seat back and settle in. The public radio station out of Philly has gone over to a classical music program. Sometimes I like Mozart in the background when I'm reading, but I don't really appreciate classical music like I should, and that's not going to change now. I want something more fun and familiar to take my mind off the pain, which is holding at a constant level somewhere between burning and tearing. I put in one of my Radiators tapes.

I found out about the Radiators when I was in New Orleans and their sound pulled me in off the sidewalk. They were playing a club called Tipitina's and I was walking by, looking for a guy who was shooting couples in cars Son of Sam-style. Captivated, I wandered in and listened to the rest of their set before resuming the hunt. I've since bought all their albums except the first couple from the early eighties, which I can't find anywhere. Their music is hard to categorize, so the band actually created its own genre, calling it Fish Head music. I'm not an expert on music, but to me it sounds like they pulled a bunch of different influences together: rock, funk, zydeco, jazz. In that way, their music epitomizes their New Orleans hometown: a gumbo of diverse ingredients all cooked together to produce a feast for the ears.

Maybe it's the combination of the pain in my scar and the memory of when I first heard the Rads: I start thinking about that night in New Orleans. A couple hours after I left Tipitina's, James Lee Williams shot me. I'd found him, but then lost track of him while I was calling the police from a pay phone, which is why I carry a cell phone now. By the time I found him again, he was drawing his weapon on a parked car. What happened next is why I carry the Glock now. I was unarmed, so I did the only thing I could do: I shouted at him. Naturally he turned and shot me. He kept shooting while I was scrambling across the brick sidewalk for cover, so after I made it into an alley, I ran. By the time I came back to the scene with a couple cops who were cruising the area, Williams was gone, leaving behind two more dead bodies and a bullet lodged behind my right shoulder blade.

I spent the rest of that night, and the next one too, in a hospital thinking about what happened: about needing a weapon if I were going to keep doing this stuff, about the sense that got me into the situation in the first place, and about Harold.

When I was a little kid I thought God's name was Harold because of the prayer: "Our father who art in heaven, Harold be thy name…" Now when I think of God, which isn't often, I think of him as Harold to remind me I'm not his bitch anymore.

It's ironic that thinking about my ability to sense human monsters got me thinking about Harold again because the Bad, which as far as I can tell is what gave me this ability, is also what gave me my atheism. The Bad showed me God is either not the benevolent, loving, omnipotent being I believed in as a child, or he doesn't exist. No God at all is easier to swallow than some scary demon God making monsters like the one that came for my parents and me in the night.

But the reliability and consistency of my weird sense got me thinking about all the other order in the universe, from the laws of physics to the synapses in my brain. I understand and acknowledge the truth of scientific explanations like, for example, natural selection being the engine of design for creatures like me with their fat brains and intricate eyes. But the fact that there are explanations at all, or anything to explain in the first place, makes me wonder if random coincidence is really the most sensible view of the universe as a whole. And if the universe is not an accident, then is there some organizing creator?

Lying in the hospital bed in New Orleans, I fully intended to sort out what I really believe about Harold, but that hasn't happened. I've been too distracted by everything else in my life since then, starting with going back to New Orleans and literally running down Williams so the cops could arrest him. After that I decided to become a civilian before the government could send me overseas again so I'd be able to go after bad guys. Since then my focus has been on transitioning to my new life.

And now that new life is getting the shit kicked out of it by the legacy of my old one. *Crap.*

And I gotta pee. The pressure on my bladder isn't bad yet, but I'm guessing the target will be working here even after the place closes at eleven. I don't really know anything about running a restaurant, but it seems reasonable to think the customers don't all magically vanish at closing time, and there's probably also some clean up the staff has to do before it goes home. I look at my watch: it's a little before ten. That means I have at least another hour and a half to wait. I'm happy being a woman, but I wouldn't mind the convenience of being able to pee the way a guy does. In situations like this I could use an empty bottle or something to relieve myself without getting out of the car. I look to my left and across the expanse of parking lot at the Shop Rite. It looks like it's still open. Don't big grocery stores usually have public bathrooms in them? I lock Stacey and walk across the parking lot.

I have to ask a girl working in the produce section, but I find the bathroom. While I'm sitting on the can, in that moment of relief and inactivity, I suddenly imagine the target leaving. After all, I don't know if the manager stays all the way to closing time. *Well, he's probably not going to do anything bad tonight, and now that I know where he works, he'll be easy to find again tomorrow.* I finish up and wash my hands.

As I walk toward the store's exit it occurs to me today is Sunday, and he's working, which means his weekend *isn't* Saturday and Sunday. The hours on the door showed Reilly's is open every day, so who knows which days he takes off as his weekend? I start walking faster. His days off could even change from week to week. Outside I start running. Fortunately, I can still sense his presence, so I know he hasn't left yet, but I don't want to just miss following him because I'm separated from my vehicle when he leaves.

I make it back to Stacey and the target is apparently still inside. I'm glad I did the little sprint across the parking lot, though, because it got my blood flowing and now I feel more alert.

I think about the murdered boys: I have the dates of the identified boys' disappearances written in the notebook lying beside me on Stacey's passenger seat, but not the days of the week. I can't think of where I'd have a calendar to look up the dates, especially since three out of four of them were last year. Working backwards in my head, I figure out the most recent one was reported missing on a Tuesday.

I watch customers exit and cars drive off. Around eleven I watch a lone woman I think I recognize as the hostess walk quickly over to what I guessed is the employee parking area. She gets in a red sedan and leaves. A few minutes later a couple men also walk over to the line of employee cars, causing me to sit up a little straighter, but the pain of the sense remains constant, so I hold my position and watch them go. A group of about eight—five women and three men—step out, buttoning and zipping up coats and pulling on hats, but instead of going to cars, they congregate by the door. I count six cars remaining besides mine and the staff's, and figure this is the last group of customers. They remain in the light around the entrance, talking, laughing, occasionally taking little steps this way and that but not going anywhere. I expect them to leave after a minute or so; after all, it's pretty chilly out now. But they stay gathered there, voices rising and falling, occasionally laughing loudly and taking a step back, then moving closer again.

Through the windows I see the staff moving around inside, mostly taking things off tables or going around with trays full of items: what looks like a bunch of ketchup bottles, maybe salt and pepper shakers. They seem to be checking each table for a full complement of condiments, placemats, flatware, and the rest. I'd think that's something you'd have your staff come in early the next day to do, but that's me—I'm not a night person.

The pain in me amps up slightly, and I reach for the key in the ignition, then pause. No one leaves, so I drop my hand in my lap again and examine the windows and entrance to see what has changed. Besides the wait staff I've been watching, there's now a man I haven't seen before wearing a blue shirt with a red tie instead of the black shirts of the waiters. He's walking around, not carrying anything but apparently looking at the tables, turning his head one way, then another. I'm too far back to really see the details of his face, but I commit to memory the brown hair which is noticeably receding from his forehead, the slightly heavyset build, and the pale pink tint of his skin. He moves into another part of the seating area, and I can no longer see him, but I can sense him so I know when he returns to his office in the back.

The group by the entrance is still there. One of them breaks from the circle to go back to the restaurant's door. She must have rung the doorbell, because a few seconds later a waiter comes to the door and lets her in. Through the windows I see her walk quickly back to where the bathrooms are. A minute or so later she rejoins her friends outside. It seems odd to me that after having dinner together they would still be so interested in standing around in the cold so they can chat some more. I wonder what they're talking about.

I try to remember back when I was a teenager and before the Bad. I had friends then, and spent hours with them on the phone or in my dorm room at the boarding school I attended. I think of Becky, my best friend and confidant, and Derek, the guy who probably would have been my boyfriend eventually. We talked, but I'm having a hard time remembering what about. I know Becky and I talked about Derek, and about the guys she was interested in. We must have discussed things like music and movies too, I guess, and maybe classes.

Now, watching the group of friends, I feel like an anthropologist observing a foreign culture. I wonder if the guy I'm hunting feels this way too, like an outsider looking in, unable to relate to or truly understand what he's seeing in the lives of others.

Around 11:45 the friends finally break up and go to their cars, and about the same time the pain below my breastbone increases again. A group of five comes out the door. The lights inside are still on, but I watch as everyone moves off to cars, leaving behind one person, the heavyset guy with thinning brown hair, now wearing a dark-colored coat, who locks the door. As the other cars drive off, he walks over to the last car—some kind of mid-sized SUV—in what used to be the line of vehicles by the street. His headlights go on, and he drives off toward the parking lot exit, sending a shot of hurt through me as he passes thirty or so feet away.

A couple seconds after he's past me, I crank Stacey's engine, punch on the headlights, and drive off after him. A traffic light stops both of us, and I end up right behind him, but I'm pretty sure he won't be able to see my face with my headlights shining into his mirrors. Even so, I pull my stocking cap lower, so the edge of it covers my eyebrows, and I tilt my head down as much as I can while still keeping my eyes on the back of his car. I notice his right turn signal is blinking, but I don't put mine on. While we sit there, I grab the notebook and pen off the passenger seat and jot down his license plate and note the brown color, make, and model of his Nissan Pathfinder.   His brake lights go out and he starts to pull away. I lift my head and follow him into a right turn, but I take the left lane when he takes the right. I hang back a little, letting almost a block open up between us. This late on a Sunday in Trenton, there's not much traffic, so I can watch him from a ways back. Without much trouble, I follow him down Clinton Avenue until we're about in the center of Trenton.

Up ahead, his brake lights come on, then his backup lights. I stop, glancing at the rear view mirror and seeing no one behind me. It's a little risky, still being in the travel lane, basically double-parked, but I kill all my lights and watch him parallel park. The lights on his vehicle go dark, then the dome light comes on as he gets out. He walks around the front of his SUV, then continues a little further down the sidewalk before climbing a few steps and letting himself in to a brick building. I give him another second to close the door, then Stacey's lights are on again and I'm rolling. As I go by, I check out the front of his building, memorizing the look of its façade before moving on to find parking. I end up around the corner on Hamilton, then walk back.

There are four black metal mail boxes attached to the front of the building, next to the entrance the target used, but he didn't check any of them when he entered just now, so I don't know which is his. I step back and look up at the building, and notice lights on both the first and third floors, while the basement and the second floor are dark. I climb the three steps again and look closely at the mailboxes, barely illuminated in the light from the underpowered street lamps nearby. The boxes bear plastic strips from one of those handheld label makers you dial and squeeze to stamp letters into the plastic. The box with the "1ST FLOOR" strip bears the name "PATEL". The target didn't look south Asian; he was very anglo-looking. The "3RD FLOOR" box is labeled "LAMBERT". *Got to be.*

OK, so third floor, and it looks like one unit per floor, so his last name is Lambert and he's in number three, 499 South Clinton Avenue. Plus, I know he drives a brown Nissan Pathfinder, and I have the license plate written down in the car. I'm done here.

I turn and start walking back to where I left Stacey, but a thought occurs to me and I reluctantly slow to a stop as I reach the street corner. What I'm thinking of is something Sergeant Pike taught me: you don't really know the enemy's disposition until you "put eyes on the objective"—until you actually *look* at the enemy's position. Of course, this isn't always possible, but when we were patrolling we usually sent a couple people on ahead to check out the "bad guys" and report back to the rest of the patrol before we moved on them.

Likewise, I know the right thing for me to do now is to make sure about what I think I know, but I'm tired and already mentally half in my bed back at the hotel. I hesitate a couple seconds more, wavering between going to Stacey or going back to the apartment building. "Aw, what the fuck," I breathe, and turn myself around, feeling like I'm out patrolling in the middle of the night with Pike and the guys from school again.

I walk the short distance back up Clinton to the target's building, and try the door. It's locked of course, so I'm not getting in there to follow my sense around inside the building. I step back again and look up at the windows. The first floor's windows are only just above my eyes, but they're covered with curtains so I can't see in. The third floor windows don't have anything blocking them, but at my angle I can only see the ceiling, which isn't helpful. *So maybe I can't put eyes on...* I turn and start walking back, then pause in front of the narrow space between the target's building and the one next to it. It's only about six feet wide, and there's a little chain link gate between it and the sidewalk. In the dim glow from the lighted windows above, I can barely see trash barrels, a concrete path leading to what might be a back porch, and a fire escape running up the side of the building. I look left and right, see no one else on the street, then try the little gate.

The gate swings open easily and with barely a squeak. I step through, my foot catches on something, and suddenly I'm accelerating forward out of control. My arms fly out instinctively, and I get my other foot in front of me before I do a face plant or crash into anything. Looking over my shoulder, I see the concrete walkway I'm on sits a few inches above the sidewalk. *Nice going Sneakypants.*

I close the little gate behind me, then turn to look at the building. The fire escape has a ladder hanging down from the first platform. I can't reach the bottom rung from the ground, but I quietly pick up and move a battered metal trash barrel under the ladder. Planting both hands on the lid, I lean on it, gradually transferring my weight to it until I lift my feet off the ground. It holds and seems stable enough, so I carefully climb up on it. The lid flexes under my weight with a metallic *tok*, but then holds. I straighten up and now I can look in to the first floor windows; or I could if they weren't covered by flowery red and yellow curtains. I look up and see I can now easily grab the bottom rung.

I feel the sharp, crackly edges of peeling paint through the wool weave of my old Army gloves, as well as the coldness of the thin round rung. I flex my arms and back, and slowly lift myself off the top of the trash barrel. The ladder suddenly gives way as it takes my weight, causing my sneakers to impact the top of the garbage can. There's surprisingly little noise, mainly because the can stays upright, but the sudden drop scares me. *I'm a regular freakin' ninja, aren't I?* I should have anticipated the ladder moving like that. Theoretically it should slide most of the way to the ground so people can climb down it to safety. I debate about what to do, and decide to put my weight on it again. The bottom of the ladder is still no where near the top of the can, and now I'll be ready when it slides. I can work it down gradually and move the can if I need to. I flex my arms and back, but this time the ladder doesn't budge. I put my feet back on the can, then lift myself again more abruptly, but now the ladder feels stuck. Apparently the accumulated paint and corrosion, like what my hands are feeling on the rung, has bound it up.

OK, climbing...   I flex again and pull my chin over the first rung. "Shit," I grunt, looking up at the next rung. *I didn't really think this through, did I?* My feet swing slightly as I hang.

At the academy we were taught to climb ropes, and I was pretty good at it, but the techniques used both legs and arms. One day I saw the guys from the wrestling team climbing the ropes in the gym using only their arms; some of them could go the full twenty feet to the ceiling. I never made it that far using only arm strength, but after a couple years of working at it I was able to make it about ten feet to the suspended indoor track, one hand over the other in small increments. Of course, that was five years ago, and I don't think I've climbed anything other than stairs since.

Focusing on the next rung, I throw my right hand at it. My gloves are pretty thin, and the roughness of the old paint bites into my palm and makes my hold secure. Fortunately, doing my weight training without gloves has thickened and toughened the skin on my hands; otherwise this would be more painful and maybe bloody. Remembering technique, I flex hard with my right and move my left hand up to the same rung. Staying put is actually tiring, so I quickly transfer my weight to my left again and throw my right hand up. Flex right, throw left. The bottom rung is still too high for me to get my feet on it. I'm breathing hard now, the muscles in my upper back are burning, and the old bullet wound behind my right shoulder blade aches terribly. The roughness of the rungs makes for a secure grip, but everything is weakening— I'm running short on time. One deep breath, two, and I flex left, throw right. I pause another second. "Fuck!" I grunt, as I get my left hand to join my right.

I feel the bottom rung bump against my thighs. Flexing my body, I get my knees on the rung, mercifully taking the weight off my upper body. I kneel there until the burning in my arms and back subsides, then replace one knee at a time with the attached foot. I stand and, draping myself over a rung, I rest until my breathing is normal again. Then I climb the ladder normally until I'm over the railing, and ease myself down to the metal platform.

My hands are throbbing and feel raw, but I look down at the trash barrel and enjoy the feeling of accomplishment. Then I shift my gaze to the alley entrance and the street beyond—still no one around. I turn. The window at this level is completely dark. I cross the platform and climb the steep metal staircase to the third floor.

The pain has been increasing from burning my scar to ripping it open since I walked up to the building a few minutes ago, and now it's gone deeper: sharp, stabbing cramps in my upper abdomen. I'm much closer now, so he has to be up here. Still, *eyes on*... Before I come off the stairs, I glance over my shoulder and see the window at this level is dimly illuminated; that is, the room behind the window doesn't have any lights on, but light is filtering in from the rest of the apartment. Using the railing to steady myself, I step on the narrow part of the platform and move around the stairway opening toward the window. There's not much room; I compress myself so I can stand on the platform and against the brick side of the building without any of my body extending in front of the window. Across the alley is another brick wall, but the windows in that one have been bricked over. Feeling creepy and dirty, I turn my head and peek in to the window from the side. There are slatted blinds on the other side of the glass, but they're canted open, so I can peer through. Only dark shapes are visible against the lighter background of the walls. There's furniture, including something shaped like a bed. There are some big pictures, maybe posters, on the walls, but I can't make out any details. I lean forward some more and look at the doorway to the room. Through that I can see another, brightly-lit wall just beyond, but that wall is bare and a pretty neutral beige.

Since the lights are on in the other rooms, he must still be awake, and after all the work of climbing up here, I figure I might as well wait a little to see if he comes into the room, and maybe I can get a good look at his face. I quickly cross in front of the window to the other side of the platform where there's slightly more space, and sit down with my shoulder to the wall so I can extend my legs below the window sill. I absently knead my scar, as if I could massage away the hurt. I try to relax my body despite the pain, and stare down the small alley at the street beyond, then turn my head and look at the building next door again, noticing the slightly different color of the bricks which were added to close off the window openings. I close my eyes for a couple minutes, resting. It's uncomfortable enough, between the pain of the sense and the cold metal slats pressing into my butt, that I feel no risk of falling asleep, but it feels good to idle my brain and body.

A few minutes pass, then suddenly the pain ramps up dramatically, and it's like I'm being stabbed. I gasp and my eyes pop open. The light in the room is on, and spilling out across the fire escape beside me. It seems amazingly bright to my dark-adapted eyes: so bright I have to think anything on the fire escape would be visible on the other side of the window's glass, despite the usual reflectiveness of glass when it's bright on one side and dark on the other. I swallow hard and stay close to the wall, and just barely peek around the edge of the window. The stabbing is deep and about as bad as it gets without me actually touching the bad guy, so I know he must be just on the other side of the wall my shoulder is pressed against.

Peering into the room, the first thing I see is Darth Vader looking back out at me—it's a movie poster for *The Empire Strikes Back. What did the profiler say about the killer?* I remember him mentioning toys and video games, but nothing about posters or favorite movies. Still, how many adults have *Star Wars* posters hanging in their room? I can see the foot of the bed—I startle as a figure walks into view a couple feet from me, passing by just on the other side of the closed window, walking around the foot of the bed, and out the doorway, hitting the light switch as he leaves. I only had a couple seconds, but it was enough to see the same man as the one I saw locking up the Reilly's and then exiting his SUV and entering this building. He has the same brown, thinning hair and the same chunky build. *OK, good enough.*

I stand, take the steep metal stairs down to the next level, then the ladder down to the barrel. It's a little tricky when I finally have to uncoil my body at the bottom of the ladder and let my feet dangle free while I lower myself using only my arms, but it's easier than the climb up. I manage to stand on the barrel again and climb off it without knocking it over, and I put it back where I found it. Then I'm out of the little alley, closing the chain link gate behind me, and walking quickly back to Stacey, the pain mercifully subsiding.

Back inside Stacey, I write down the address and apartment number, and the name—Lambert—below his vehicle information. Then I head back to my hotel, which is actually a couple miles outside Trenton. On the way back, I consider the next step, which is to call the information in. The call needs to be anonymous, because if the cops know who I am, they might come around to ask me how I know this is the bad guy, and then what will I tell them? If I call from the hotel, will they have the number I called from and be able to follow it back to my room? The room I'm paying for with my credit card? I don't know for sure, but I don't think they have to trace calls anymore—isn't that instantaneous now? I mean, if you can hit *69 and call back a number that just called you, doesn't that imply that as soon as you call the police, they have your number? Which means my cell phone is definitely out too. I need a pay phone. *Where the hell is there a pay phone anymore?* In New Orleans, before I got my cell phone, I used one in a hotel lobby. I don't think there's one at my cheapo hotel though. This will just have to wait until tomorrow—there's some big hotel downtown, and if that doesn't have a phone then there's a train station and a couple hospitals I can try.

Seventeen

Julia checks her watch; it's already just about eight a.m. She's going to be late again. "C'mon Tommy, big steps," she urges. Tommy, her son, is already having a hard time keeping up; she can see that. But he's a good kid, and he lengthens his stride as much as he can with those little legs, so he actually looks kind of silly. If she weren't already so late, it'd be funny, and she'd do something goofy with the way she was walking, and they'd laugh about it together, but there just isn't time for it today, and the best she can do is not lose her temper. *There's never enough fuckin' time*, she thinks, and worries about Jeff, the owner, and Al, the line cook, and the other waitresses. She pictures them glancing at the diner's wall clock, sighing and shaking their heads. *Great way to start the week.* She opens her mouth to tell Tommy to walk faster, but she glances down again, sees the look of determination on his face and the exaggerated steps he's taking. Instead she says, "You're doin' great, Tiger."

Tommy looks up and smiles at her—one of those sweet, proud, completely happy little kid smiles.

Julia smiles back and wishes she could pick him up and tuck him under her arm, then run the rest of the way to the school, but, as small and skinny as he is, he's way too big and heavy for her to carry him any distance anymore. It's still amazing to her that at one point he actually fit *inside* her. Now here he is, walking around on his own, in second grade, growing up, even getting home on his own each night.

Julia doesn't like that last part, especially lately with the cops and everyone talking about those missing kids that turned up in the woods down south a week ago. But there's no way, *especially* after getting in late, she could leave the diner early enough to catch the bus, meet Tommy at school, walk him home, catch the bus *again* and get back to work—by then, it'd be time to go to her other job at the cleaning service anyway. Even if Jeff weren't such a hard ass, she and Tommy can't afford for her not to work that last hour at the diner and her evening job.

Anyway, Tommy knows to shout for help if anyone bothers him, and to just go straight home after school. "You're gonna walk with Charlie and those other boys on the way home tonight, right?"

Tommy hesitates a little.

"Right?" she asks more emphatically, not really asking, but telling in that mommy way her mom used to use with her.

"OK" he says, but doesn't look happy about it. "Last week Sam kept talking about how he and his dad were going fishing on Saturday."

"I know—you told me." *Here we go again.* "And I said he probably made that up—isn't it too cold to go fishing now?"

Tommy puts his hands, palms up, out at his sides in the clueless gesture. "I don't know. Can we go fishing sometime?"

"Baby, we've been over this before: I don't know how to fish, and neither do you. *And* we don't have a fishing pole." Julia says this, but she knows it won't do any good, and they still have a couple blocks to go before they get to the school.

"What about my dad? Does he know how to fish?"

She sighs. "Tommy, don't start this now—we don't have time this morning. And no, he didn't fish, and it doesn't matter because he's not coming back. So you're just stuck with me." She mentally kicks herself for that last sentence, which makes her feel immature like a kid and oddly, at the same time, manipulative like her own mother was with her. For maybe the millionth time, she wants to kill the stupid teenage boy who made her pregnant and then disappeared to

God knows where—Florida was the last she heard, and that was five years ago. And, maybe even more, she wants to dope-slap the teenage girl who believed him and took him inside her without makin' him wear a freakin' rubber.

She loves this kid walking next to her though, even if he is a pain in the ass sometimes. She just wishes she could have planned for him so she could give him a better life now, complete with a dad. The dad thing has been coming up more since around last Christmas. She guesses it makes sense, now that he's seven and in second grade. He's growing up, and trying to figure out how he fits in. And he's hearing kids talk about their dads. *Fuck it—it's done now.* She's doing the best she can for her and him. She wishes she had time to look for a decent guy to be husband and dad for them, but she doesn't, so fuck it.

"So look here we are." They stop at the edge of the paved area in front of the school's main entrance. Julia turns and squats down in front of Tommy. "Now promise me you're going to walk home with your friends, all right?"

"They're not my friends."

"Honey, it's just, whatever it is, six blocks. Just walk with them, OK?"

He nods. "OK Mom."

"OK," she says conclusively. "Give me quick kiss." Their lips touch briefly, then she finds and holds his eyes with hers. "I love you."

"I love you too, Mom."

"Can I get a smile?" she asks, making an exaggeratedly sad face, which almost always works with him, and this time is no different. "I'll see you at home. Don't forget to lock the door after you get home, all right?"

"All right."

"And don't open it for anyone but me or Gran."

"OK."

"And no cold cereal for dinner—nuke the Tupperware."

"OK."

"I mean it."

"OK Mom."

She kisses him again. "OK now, get going." She stands as he runs toward the school's door, and after he disappears inside she turns and speed walks to the bus stop, checking her watch as she goes. If she gets to the stop by 8:09, she should be at work by 8:30.

Eighteen

I don't wake up until seven and feel vaguely guilty about sleeping in, but last night was a late one. I smile as I remember I have what I came here for, and now I can phone it in to the tip line and get the hell out of Dodge. Tonight I'll be back home in my apartment, safe and comfy, and tomorrow— maybe I should look around and get Mike a T-shirt from here to thank him for covering my job for me. I actually haven't seen any Trenton T-shirts or postcards for sale, but I haven't been looking either. Maybe over by the capitol buildings—I saw a museum over there, so they'll probably sell tourist crap there too.

I roll out of bed and head for the shower. While I'm soaping up, I plan my day. I'll pack my stuff, check out, head over to the Marriott, call the cops, then look for a present for Mike before I get on the highway home. I should top off with fuel before I get on the road; that way I probably won't have to stop for gas again.

The hard part will be the call, but even that shouldn't be bad. I'll stay anonymous, just give the information and hang up.

And then...

And then I'm done. And Lambert's done.

Yeah?

I pause, bar of soap stopped mid-scrub on my left butt cheek. Sure, the police take the information and roll up on him at home, tell him—

Tell him what? That they got some mysterious phone message saying he's the killer?

The water drums down on my bowed head and slumped shoulders. The hand with the soap drifts to the outside of my leg and hangs there.

Even *I* really don't know if Lambert killed those kids. After all, there was that boy with the cat who triggered my sense, but he didn't kill the kids and haul them thirty-some miles south of here to bury them in the woods.

Sure, OK, but how many predatory psychopaths can there be in this little city? Lambert fits the FBI's profile; it's got to be him. No, I know he's the killer.

But even after I call the police, *they* still won't know. Will they even act on my information? What if they don't take my call seriously? Or what if they do, if they actually do go and question him, but he fakes them out, acts all innocent? What would the cops, or even the FBI, do then? Probably just forget about him. The most they *could* do is assign people to follow him. I really don't know much about how the police and FBI work, but they probably don't have the manpower to continue following suspects around indefinitely, especially if they've gotten other tips, pointing to other people. I can imagine people calling in names just to harass people they don't like. What if the police think that's what I'm doing? After all, if it were a legitimate tip, why would I call it in anonymously? I'd tell them who I am and how I know.

"Shit," I whisper. The soap slips from my hand, thuds against my ankle, and slides onto the drain. I lean against the smooth plastic wall of the shower stall and close my eyes.

If the police don't take my tip seriously, or if they do but Lambert acts innocent and claims ignorance, he could totally get away with it since neither I nor—guessing here—the police have any corroborating evidence on him, and they probably couldn't get a warrant based solely on an anonymous, baseless (from their perspective) accusation. I read the cops questioned John Gacy a few times over a span of a year or so before they finally figured out he was killing teenage boys. Meanwhile, Gacy kept adding to the collection of bodies in the crawlspace under his house. I can't let that happen here. I can't walk away from this until it's done, until Lambert is in custody or, I guess, dead.

Dead: there's an idea. But unless he gets hit by a bus or crushed by a falling anvil, which would be *really* convenient, I don't see how that's gonna happen. Because *I'm* not going after him. I mean, sure, the Glock could finish this pretty quickly, especially now that I know about the fire escape. But what if the sense is just craziness, and I'm all wrong about this? The sense is all I have to go on now; nothing I've seen tells me he kills little boys. And besides that, I'm just not doing it; I'm not assassinating someone. No way. I promised myself I'd avoid violence or, failing that, be ready to meet and end it as quickly and safely as possible. But hunting someone down and murdering him isn't exactly avoiding violence; it's *instigating* it.

Fine, so what's that leave you? "Shit," I say quietly again. That leaves me right here in fucking Trenton, until this is done, until he's arrested or deceased, which means there's pretty much no fuckin' way I'm going to be home tonight or at work tomorrow. "Bastard."

I'm gonna lose my job over this, aren't I? My head swims at the thought of messing up the little fledgling life I've started building. I do still have one more week of vacation left, but this could theoretically go on for weeks. I mean, what if he's laying low now? What if the police get nothing from him, and he goes to ground, and the whole thing just drags on, with no more victims and no leads in the investigation? How long am I going to be here? And what am I going to be doing? Following him around? I guess. After a while, though, he might notice me, which would make him even more cautious, which would make this go on *even longer*. What the hell am I going to do?

The thoughts about the Glock cross my mind again: something along the lines of *So I'm going to let him fuck up my life?* But I know I'm not serious. Maybe Henry will just give me the second week. Whatever. One thing's for sure: this mission *has* to take priority over my needs. The next victim's life is more important than my job. I'll just have to call work, see what they say.

"Crap in a hat." I bend, retrieve the soap, and finish washing and rinsing, my mind more or less blank and drained of all the energy I had a few minutes ago when I was heading home today.

* * *

I park on Lambert's street and walk over to the Marriott, the only large business-class hotel in Trenton's city limits. I find this surprising considering Trenton is the state capitol, but I guess that's all they need. The lobby is pretty standard stuff for this kind of place: it's well-lit but not glaring, clean, and spacious, and the polished wood front desk is wide enough for three or four people to work it at the same time. There's dark furniture and carpeting, all looking well-maintained. I'm comfortable finding my way around in hotels like this. When I go for long walks in Boston and Cambridge I use big hotels for making pit stops. As long as you look presentable and sober, and walk around like you know where you're going, the hotel staff doesn't bother you. I walk halfway down a side corridor and find a small bank of payphones across from the spacious rooms the hotel rents out for seminars and meetings.

I open my notebook on the little shelf below the phone and stand close so my abdomen blocks it from sliding off, then look at my notes and think. They'll ask for my name, but I'll just ignore that, tell them I know who killed those boys and then I'll read off the information. I debate again about an idea I had earlier, to try to lower my voice so they might think it's a man making the call.   I'm sure this is overkill, but if something happens and I have to act against the target on my own, I want it to be as difficult as possible for them to figure out Shailene Campbell had anything to do with it. I wonder if I can actually pull off sounding like a guy. I know my voice is on the low side of average for women, but it's not *that* low. If I pitch my tone down, though, maybe I can fool them or at least throw them off a little. It's worth a try anyway.

I pick up the receiver and put it to my ear, hear the dial tone, and punch in the toll-free tip line number. It rings a couple times, then:

"Trenton Police."

"Hi, I'm, uh," I hesitate because it feels so weird to be talking in this unnaturally deep voice. I feel ridiculous, and wonder if I just sound astoundingly stupid.   But I'm committed now, so I push on. "I have information about the man who killed those boys."

"OK…" The cop hesitates a beat. "OK…sir, let's start with your name, please."

"The man's name is Wayne Lambert—that's *his* name." I got the first name by looking him up in the phone book. There were several Lamberts—at least a dozen, but I scanned down until I found the address.

"Sir, I need *your* name first—what's *your* name?"

"*His* name is Wayne Lambert."   I spell the names out. "He lives at…" ignoring the cop, I slowly and deliberately recite all the information I have: address, phone number, license plate, place of work, job… I figure they have to be recording the call, so I don't worry about giving him time to write crap down or read it back to me.

"That's all I have. Bye."

"Sir, if—"

I hang up, pausing for a few seconds with my hand on the receiver, wondering what he was going to say and if I should have stayed on the line.   But no—they *had* to have been recording the call.

I close my notebook and turn to leave, then decide to use the bathroom before I go. I find the restrooms a little further down the corridor I'm in and empty my bladder. Then I leave and walk the several blocks back to Lambert's street, where I left Stacey. As I go, I consider my next move, which is calling Henry back in Cambridge and asking for another week off.

Henry seems like a really good guy. I wasn't sure what to expect when I got out of the Army because, besides a minimum wage summer job with a landscaping service when I was in high school, I'd never held a civilian job before. It took a while for me to get used to calling the two owners of the architecture firm "Henry" and "Rob," and not sir, though I still do that occasionally out of habit. This informality is probably part of what makes me appreciate Henry, but it's not just that.   He seems genuinely interested in how his employees, including me, are doing—not just professionally, but personally. And he has a certain soft-spoken, thoughtful way about him that doesn't compromise his authority as one of the firm's founding partners.

The fact that he *is* a good guy, and that I like him, makes me feel even worse about asking for another week off on such short notice. Part of me feels I should just quit so Henry and Rob can hire a more reliable computer geek who doesn't have a secret career hunting psychopaths, but I need to earn a living and no one is paying me to go after bad guys. And it's possible the cops will arrest Lambert by the end of the week and I'll be back at work by next Monday.

Shortly after I cross the tracks on Hamilton, my sense tells me Lambert is still at home. I turn the corner on to his street and walk past his building, setting my jaw against the rising pain, which dissipates as I continue another couple blocks down to where I left Stacey. I start her engine and move her to a new spot that's opened up, just on the edge of the sense's range, so there's only a slight itchiness to tell me Lambert is still at home. It's a little after nine now, so I take out my cell phone and call work.

"Kanter Mabry Architects."

"Hi Valerie, it's Shailene."

"Hey! How's your vacation going?"

I grimace and give the generic "fine" response.

"'Fine'? Sounds to me like you're having way too much fun."

"You don't know the half of it," I say truthfully. "Can I talk to Henry?"

"Since you're talking to me now, I'd guess you can."

Just as I'm going from *hunh?* to realizing she's being a smartass, she says, "Hold on," and there's a click and silence, followed several seconds later by another click.

"Hi Shailene, how're you doing?"

"Good morning Henry. I'm, uh, I'm fine, thanks. How are things there—is everything running OK?"

"As far as I know, but you should talk to Mike about that."

I grimace silently again. "I, uh," *I wish I'd rehearsed what I need to say before I called you.* "I'm calling because I need to ask for some more time off. Things are taking longer than I thought they would." I pause, wishing I could see him to know how this is going over.

After a couple seconds, he says, "Is everything all right?"

"Uh, well, it will be, but it's just...harder than I thought—more complicated, I mean."

"Mind if I ask what you're doing? Is there anything I can do to help?"

He's such a freakin' good guy. "Sorry, I—I'd rather not talk about it, but I really need to take my other week of vacation. I'm really sorry about the short notice, and if I can finish things up sooner, I'll be back early."

There's another pause. "OK," he begins. I hear the reluctance in his voice and know I'm pushing my limits with him, which I totally get. I mean, he's only known me for a few months, and he's probably aware that he's a good guy, so he's maybe worried I'm taking advantage and he really shouldn't allow that. "This really isn't how we normally do things here, Shailene. This would be easier for me if I had some idea of what your emergency is; I mean, has there been a death in your family?"

I consider agreeing to this, especially since technically, there *have* been deaths in my family, though not since I was a teenager. I've always tried to be an honest person, and my years at West Point really hammered that home with me. Plus it seems very wrong to lie to someone who's trying to help me. "I'm sorry, sir, I understand this is weird, but I really can't talk about it. I'm really sorry." I almost offer to quit, but hold back.

He sighs—not loudly or theatrically, but I can hear his frustration. "OK, take another week. So you'll be back a week from tomorrow, right?"

"Right," I say, but then the honesty thing kicks in. "I, uh, I hope so."

"Shailene, what's going on? Are you coming back?"

"I'm sorry." I notice I've closed my eyes and tilted my head down so I can hold it with my free hand. "I honestly can't guarantee I'll be back next week. I really want to be, hope to be, but at this point I just don't know. I know this is putting you in a bad position..." My inflection makes it clear I'm going to say something else, so he says nothing, waiting. Now I sigh. "Maybe you should start looking for someone to replace me." I'm surprised at the combination of nausea and relief I feel.

"Shailene, talk to me—just tell me what's going on."

"I—" *I was raped and almost killed when I was fifteen, and now I have this impossible ability to detect the presence of serial killers, so I'm trying to secretly help the police catch one.* "I really can't."

"So...are you quitting?"

"I..." I want to say something like "if you want me to," but that's really lame. "I...I don't want to—I really like working for you, but what I'm doing here has to come first, and that's not fair to you or everybody else there. And unfortunately, I can't talk about it, and I can't predict when I'll be done, or when I'll have to do something like this again. I'm sorry—I really hoped this could work out, but..." I let my voice trail off. What more was there to say?

The pause stretches a little, then, "Well, I'm sorry too. I think you were doing a great job here, but we really need to be able to count on you."

"I know. I do feel bad about this, and if I can get back soon, maybe I can do the job until you find a replacement? Maybe I can help get the new person up to speed."

"Sure...well, call when you're back in town and we'll see where we're at then."

"OK. Maybe I should talk to Mike, let him know what's going on, see if he has any questions."

"OK, hold on."

There's a click and silence. The silence drags on for maybe a minute, then Mike comes on. "Shailene?"

It's excellent hearing his friendly, familiar voice. "Hey Mike, how's it going?"

"I think I should be asking you that. Henry sounded, I don't know, kinda pissed off or bummed out—"

"Which?" I ask, not that it matters.

"I guess more bummed out—he said you're not coming back tomorrow?"

"Yeah, no, I'm not. This is taking longer than I thought it would. I shoulda just asked for two weeks off to begin with; I could've always come back early. But yeah, I'm staying down here for a while longer, maybe another week."

"When you get back you'd better tell me all about this trip—you really owe me now!"

"Yeah, yeah, whatever," I say, a little irritated at his persistent nosiness, but not wanting to let it show, especially since he *is* doing me a favor. "So listen, you'll have to change the backup tape again—use the one you didn't use last week, OK?"

"Sure, no prob, got you covered Kimosabe."

I smile despite, or because of, his extreme goofiness. "Thanks Tonto. And you're right, I do owe you, but I'm not sure how I'll make it up to you yet."

"I can think of a way."

"What?"

"Uh, you can take me to a play. Or something."

I know what he really said, and it's confusing, so I file it away to think about later. "We'll figure it out when I get back. So is everything else going OK?"

"Yeah, pretty much. Jennifer's having some trouble with the CAD software, but she's working around it for now. And the main printer was acting up, but Valerie called a service guy and he fixed it. Oh, and the email server crashed, but everybody's kind of glad for the vacation from email, so no big."

"Wha—when did the server crash?!" *Shit, no wonder Henry was pissed off.*

"Day after you left—didn't I mention that on any of the other calls?"

"No."

"Aaaah, probably because I'm just messin' with you. The servers are all fine. At least, as far as I can tell."

"Thanks Mike—your levity…what can I say?"

"It's a gift. So what are you doin' now?"

"Sitting in my car waiting."

"For what?"

"Bye Mike."

"Finish up your shit and come on back. We miss you."

I start to say something back, but realize he was just pausing a little long between sentences.

"I miss you," he says more quietly.

Weirdness... I think, not knowing what to reply. How can I at the same time completely like and not like what he's telling me? "I'm going as fast as I can," I say. "Thanks again."

"See ya, Shailene."

"Bye Mike." I press the end button on my phone and let out a long breath. "Well that was a hell of a phone call," I mutter. "Lost my job and got propositioned all in the space of a couple minutes." I look through the windshield and down the sunny street at the bare branches of a tree planted in the sidewalk and the brick faces of the buildings. "Well, fuck it." Maybe I can get my old job at the polling company back. I could pretty much set my own hours there. Probably I can supplement that with a couple other jobs that are also flexible on the hours and days off.

And Mike. He did make a pass at me, I'm pretty sure of that. But he's such a goof, it's hard to get too offended by it. *"Kimosabe."* I smile and shake my head. Just because I'm quitting my job doesn't mean I can't still be friends with Mike. Maybe it'll actually be better if we aren't co-workers. *What would be better?* Well, I *do* miss him. But... There's always that giant squid in the room, or at least in my head. Maybe we can just be friends... *"I can think of a way."* Shit, Mike, why'd you have to say something dumb like that? Why's it always come back to that?

Nineteen

Tommy follows the other kids out the door that leads from their classroom to the paved, fenced-in area where they have recess. He likes rainy days better, because on those days they stay inside and draw, or they can play with a toy they bring from home. On rainy days Tommy brings in the race car he got for Christmas, and drives it around on his desk. He makes ramps with his books and ruler. Sometimes the car goes flying off a cliff, sometimes it jumps over the bottle of glue and a box of colored pencils, and sometimes he just drives it crazy around the top of his desk. He would never play with the car outside because Charlie would probably take it. Inside the teacher is right there, but outside…

Today is sunny, so they're outside. Tommy goes out the door and walks a few steps into the paved area, which is surrounded by the school on three sides, and a fence on the other. He stops and looks around, not knowing what to do. Some girls are jumping rope or playing hopscotch. Most of the boys are just running around screaming. There's monkey bars and swings and a slide in the middle of the area, so he walks over to them. As he approaches, he sees Sam come down the slide. Sam's skin is the same color as Hershey bars, and his hair is really short, but otherwise he's a lot like Tommy—small and skinny. "Hey Sam!"

"Hey Tommy, what up?" Sam says, getting up from the bottom of the slide just as Akim comes sliding down behind him, screaming as he goes. Sam steps away from the slide just in time, and walks up to Tommy.

"So how was fishin'?"

"Cooooool!" Sam answers. "It took a long time, but I caught a good one. I caught a good one, but my dad caught two, and one of them was *huge*! We cooked them for dinner that night—fried them up in a pan. They were awesome!"

"You ate them?" Tommy hadn't thought about that, about what you would do with a fish if you caught it.

"Yeah, of course! What else? My dad catches fish all the time and we eat them. I guess some people hang them on the wall, but that's stupid and a waste."

"What did they taste like?"

"Like *fish*!" Sam says, looking at Tommy like he's crazy. "Haven't you ever had *fish*?"

"Fish *sticks*, and I hate them—they're gross."

"Yeah, I've had fish sticks—I put a lot of ketchup on them so I can't taste them. They *are* gross. But fish you catch is totally different. Like, they're not shaped like sticks— they're shaped like fish. And they taste good, not disgusting."

"I wish I could go fishing," Tommy says, looking across at the fence and the tree on the other side of it.

"Too bad your dad left, or maybe he'd take you."

"Yeah…" Tommy says, and wishes he'd never told anyone about his dad leaving.

"Hey losers," Charlie says, walking up with Joe and Billy. Charlie is a lot taller than pretty much everyone else in second grade—Tommy only comes up to his neck. He has curly blonde hair and usually smells bad.

"Hi Charlie," Tommy says quietly and turns to walk away, hoping Charlie will just let him go.

"Hey Tommy, where you goin'?"

"Nowhere."

"You got that right—stand here," he says, putting his hands on Tommy's shoulders so they're facing each other directly.

Charlie's blue eyes look at him; Tommy looks away and tries to see Sam, but Sam is staring at something else and seems to not be paying attention.

"You think you're tough yet?" Charlie asks.

He glances up at Charlie's dirty face again, then slides his eyes away and shrugs. Tommy knows what's coming, but doesn't know how to avoid it.

"My job is to toughen you up. Open your jacket."

Tommy does it. Charlie is bigger than everyone because he's actually s'posed to be in third grade, but instead he's doing second grade again. Tommy knows if he doesn't do what Charlie says, Charlie will beat him up, instead of just doing this.

"Ready?"

Tommy, still looking away, nods and shuts his eyes, waiting for the pain. Charlie told him how he should make his stomach muscles hard so the punch won't hurt as much, but he doesn't want to do anything Charlie told him to. If he doesn't stand here and let Charlie punch him he'll get beaten up, but he's not going to do more than he has to. The punch hurts like it always does. Tommy tries not to bend forward or move his face, but he can't help doing both those things a little.

"Still weak, Tommy!" Charlie says laughing. The other boys laugh too. "Sam, you punch him. You need the training."

"OK."

Tommy opens his eyes and sees Charlie step to the side and Sam move in. Tommy looks at Sam's face, but Sam is looking at Tommy's stomach, where Charlie is drawing a target with his finger tip.

"See, this is your bull's-eye. When I tell you to, punch right in the center of that as hard as you can."

Sam nods, looking serious.

Tommy closes his eyes. Now he tries to make his stomach hard, but he's really not sure how. He takes a deep breath and tries to hold the air down low, but it hurts.

"Three, two, one—punch!"

Sam's punch isn't as hard, but it still hurts, and it makes the air Tommy was holding in come shooting out his mouth all at once. That makes the guys laugh.

"All right, let's go take over the monkey bars," Charlie orders.

Tommy opens his eyes and is relieved to see they're done with him and everyone is turning away. He presses his fingers into his stomach and moves them around, trying to make it hurt less, and follows the guys over to the monkey bars.

Twenty

Wayne gives all his boys nicknames; he needs something to call them until he meets them. With this boy the name was obvious from the start, so he has been "Red" for weeks.

It's been so many weeks, in fact, that Wayne doesn't have to think about which street to take a left on. Every Monday and Tuesday morning he goes this way, and sees Red and his mother going to the school. Every Monday and Tuesday afternoon he goes the same way, sees Red walking home alone.

When Wayne was following Red all the way from the school, he noticed Red would sometimes start out tagging along behind a group of other kids his age headed in the same direction. But by the time they reach Monmouth Street, Red has always fallen well behind them. He walks to a squat box of an apartment building in the Euclid Avenue housing project and lets himself in with a key. Red is alone in the apartment throughout the afternoon and evening.

Wayne remembers how that feels.

Red is alone because his mother is working at a diner over on Broad Street. Wayne followed her too, taking her bus, watching where she got off, then waiting in that location the next day and following her, at a discrete distance, to the diner. She works there until five p.m., then works another four hours cleaning offices with a janitorial service. Meanwhile, there's no one home with Red. Wayne can't be absolutely certain of this, but he knows it in his gut.

His own experience allows him this knowledge. Wayne knows first-hand about coming home to a dark, empty apartment and waiting for Mom to get home. Wayne knew

Mom loved him, but she always got home late and too tired to talk. Usually when she got home, Wayne just rubbed her feet until she fell asleep. It was completely different for the year, give or take, when Wayne was seven and eight and Todd, his mom's boyfriend at the time, was living with them. Todd would wait for Wayne outside the school, and they'd walk home together. He was always interested in how Wayne's day was and what he was doing in school. During the day, Wayne would look for things to tell Todd about—a weird bug or piece of junk found in the schoolyard at recess, a fight between a couple other kids, or even an interesting fact he learned in class. When they got back to the apartment Todd would fix a snack, and they'd sit at the kitchen table together and talk about all kinds of things. Todd would help him with his homework, and fix dinner, putting Mom's aside in a container for when she got home. Todd did stuff with him on the weekend too, while Mom was busy working. For that year, those hours with Todd were the best part of Wayne's life. Wayne had hoped Todd would become his dad for real someday. God, how he'd loved that man.

He loved and trusted still when Todd began ending their horseplay and wrestling with kisses, and still when Todd began undressing both of them during the wrestling ("Aren't you hot? It's too hot to wrestle with our shirts on. Let's take our pants off too."). Young Wayne did think it was strange when Todd told him what they did had to be secret, but he just wanted to be a son to Todd. He chose to believe Todd when he said most fathers and sons did this together but kept it secret because it was so special—just between a father and his son. And why wouldn't Wayne believe him? After all, what did Wayne know about fathers? He just wanted to be a son to Todd.

As he remembers it now, what they did together those afternoons didn't feel bad; it definitely didn't hurt, and some of it felt really great, at least while it was happening. It's hard for him to recall exactly; it's difficult to sort out the feelings that came later from what it was like then. He thinks at the time he was glad for the attention, glad to be the center of someone else's focus, to know a father's love. Maybe if it had ended then it would have been all good, even if it was weird having to keep it secret, and even if he did know, deep down, that it wasn't *really* something fathers and sons did together.

The bad stuff mostly came later. As he got older and started noticing girls, he began to understand the full implications of his choice to be with Todd. He'd made his choice, and he knew anyone, a woman or even another man— maybe *especially* another man—who got close to him, especially sex close, would know the truth. And then what? As he got older he began to understand the jokes—*Hey little kid, wanna piece of candy?*—and he knew his instincts had been right. What he and Todd did was anything but normal for fathers and sons. It was the opposite of normal; it was disgusting. And it'd be one thing if it had been forced on him; after all, he was just a little kid when it happened. But he *liked* it. He'd *chosen* to go along with it.

It was strange beyond understanding that something which had started out so good, which had been so rewarding at the time, could be so completely wrong. But it was, and here he is, still alone, still lonely. But he's better than Todd because he's figured out how to fix it. *His* boys, they only have the love part—they never have to go through the shit that comes later. Only the father-son part, the love part, for *his* boys.

Today is a dress rehearsal, the key difference being Wayne is not carrying the radio-controlled Hummer. That's back home in his apartment. He wishes today were the day— no reason why it couldn't be, really, but better to give it one more day, do everything right, make sure everything still looks safe. This will be his first boy since the others were discovered in the woods, so it makes sense to be extra careful, even if it is hard to wait.

For the past four weeks, Wayne has made a point of passing Red when he's walking alone. Wayne checks his watch: right on schedule. He makes the left on to Monmouth Street. Up ahead, just like clockwork, he sees the group of kids Red starts out with. Then he sees his boy, crossing Monmouth down where it intersects with Tyler. The group of children coming toward him is taking up the entire width of the sidewalk, and the children are so busy chattering and laughing they seem not to notice his approach. Wayne is about to step off the curb to avoid them, but then the two on his half of the sidewalk merge in with the other four, and Wayne passes them. His boy—red hair over a pale face, and the usual puffy dark blue jacket—is trailing a block behind them.

Wayne wonders again what his name might be—Joey maybe—then he looks away before their eyes meet. Wayne casts his gaze into the street, registering the occasional passing car while focusing his attention on the boy in his peripheral vision. When they're about five paces apart, he moves his eyes back to Red, and before they pass Wayne smiles and nods a little greeting, as he has so many times before, and says "hi." When he first did this weeks ago his boy looked confused, but gradually he has grown accustomed to this greeting, and now, Wayne can sense, he likes it. Now when Wayne looks at him, his boy is almost always already looking back and smiling. When Wayne smiles at him, his boy says "hi" first. Wayne is not a stranger anymore—that barrier has been eroded. Today is no exception, and Wayne gets a thrill when he sees the smile and hears the soprano voice.

He wishes again today were the day. Now that he's here, in the neighborhood, and can still see no increased police presence on this street—no changes at all, really—he knows today could have been the day.   So tomorrow will be; until then they'll both just have to be lonely a little longer.

Twenty-One

*O*K, *what the hell is he doing?*
          After a long, boring day of waiting outside Lambert's building, he finally came out around three p.m., for the first time wearing a dark blue baseball cap. Expecting him to get in his vehicle, I was surprised when he just kept walking and took a left on Hamilton. I've followed him for several blocks and a few left turns, as if he's making a big loop. I'm starting to wonder if he's aware of me and is trying to confirm his suspicions by leading me on a nonsensical route, when I see the kids coming toward us, walking home from school. *Oh shit, here we go.*

And then he just passes them by.

He's gotta know I'm following him. "Crap," I whisper, wondering how this is going to work, and how long I'm going to have to live in this depressing town, bored out of my mind and scared, waiting for the police or Lambert to do something to bring this to an end.

I see another kid, a little red-haired boy, coming up the street. Suddenly, he smiles at Lambert. *Huhn?* I think the kid says something to Lambert, but it's hard to tell, and neither one breaks stride. They both just keep walking, but the smile lingers on the boy's face for several more steps.

Now I'm really confused. Does the kid know Lambert? And if so, why such a brief exchange between them? And if he doesn't know Lambert, why any greeting at all? Is Lambert hunting? Or maybe he's messing with me; I have not a clue.

Lambert reaches Hamilton again and takes a right before crossing to a good-sized park. I think it's called Columbus Park, and I've passed by it a few times over the past week.

It's nothing remarkable, but it's certainly a respectable park with some big old trees and grass which has worn thin in places, and a few paved walks crisscrossing the whole thing. I don't cross Hamilton, but instead walk down to the next cross street and go a few feet in from the corner, turn, and lean casually against a wall. From here I can still observe and sense Lambert as he walks deeper into the park. I lose sight of him behind a low building, but I can still sense him, barely now that he's gotten so far from me. I walk up to the curb to cross Hamilton, and as I'm looking for a break in traffic I see Lambert emerge from behind that building, heading back toward the avenue. Then he continues down Hamilton and I follow about a block behind him. Three blocks later he crosses, continues down his street, and goes back into his building.

I go back to waiting in my car.

It's pretty clear whatever he was doing when he went out was somehow related to the kids, maybe specifically that boy who spoke to him. I guess he was looking for targets, but I'm not sure how the park fits in with that—maybe he was looking for kids there too. I probably should have followed him into the park, but it's such an open area it would have been hard for him not to notice me following. If he were looking for a victim, I don't understand why nothing happened with that boy. *Maybe he wasn't Lambert's type.* "Ugh," I say quietly and shudder.

After a couple hours I call it quits, figuring if he were going to make a move on a kid he would have done it earlier.

Back at the hotel I take a shower, then heat up a can of vegetable soup for dinner. I think about calling the cops again, but what would be the point? It's not like I have any new information to give them. Plus I'd have to go find a payphone somewhere, and I'm beat. No, either they're going to act on the call I made yesterday or they're not.

Still...What I saw this afternoon was pretty clearly Lambert reconning his objective. I don't understand what the interaction with that little boy was, but something is up. If Lambert makes a move on the kid tomorrow, *someone* will have to stop him—either the cops or I. My mouth goes dry and, as hungry as I am, the soup I'm heating has suddenly lost its appeal. "Crap." I decide I'll call the tip line first thing in the morning, give all his information again and tell them I've seen him scoping out kids in his neighborhood. Maybe that'll get their attention. If they're clever, maybe they'll follow him like I did today and catch him in the act.

And then I can go home. Who knows, maybe I could even get my job back—cancel my quitting.

I close my eyes and shake my head, trying to avoid getting my hopes up. Things are bad enough already without setting myself up for disappointment. I once heard happiness equated to reality minus expectations. By that calculation, expectations always end up being a negative, a counterweight to my eventual happiness with whatever outcomes become my reality. If I expect and prepare for the worst and it doesn't happen, I'll be relieved and pleasantly surprised. And if the worst *does* happen, I'll be ready.

It takes some effort, but I push these concerns aside and open my eyes. The soup has begun to simmer, so I stir it and cut the flame. I go over to the TV and get the remote. Sitting down again, I click on the set and flip through the channels. I never bothered to get a TV for my apartment, so the set in my hotel room is kind of a novelty for me. By now, though, the newness of it is starting to wear thin as I realize I haven't been missing much. I settle on a *Star Trek* rerun. It's one of the newer Star Trek series—not the original, which I never really liked the few times I saw it as a kid. I've seen this version before. We had a TV in my unit's offices at the airbase in Alabama where I was stationed, and a couple of my pilots watched the show before it was time to go out for our night missions.   The writing and acting are actually pretty good, though I find some of the details confusing because I don't know much about the characters or back story, and no longer have my pilots handy to explain it to me.

This particular episode is set on a planet where same-sex relationships are standard and heterosexuality is illegal.   The point is obvious, but not at the expense of the story, which of course involves one of the Enterprise's male crew members falling in love with a female resident of the planet, getting everyone in trouble.

I've never understood our society's problem with homosexuality.   I mean, why would anyone care whether someone else is interested in sex and romance with her own gender or not?   I definitely don't get how it's any business of the government, but there's still laws on the books in some states regarding what kinds of sex consenting adults can have in the privacy of their homes.   Some people argue gay relationships "go against God's plan" because they can't make babies.   So does that mean sterile people shouldn't be allowed to have sex—even with the opposite gender?   What it really comes down to is some people trying to impose their superstitions on everyone, but the whole point of this country and its Constitution is to protect us from each other's tyrannies.

"God's plan"—Really.   I wonder if God's plan includes putting so many humans on this planet there isn't room for anything else, and then have people live in squalor and die from epidemic and famine.

After I clean the aluminum bowl from my camping cook kit, I pick up the shoulder holster, which I'd tossed on the bed when I got in.   I take out the Glock, eject the magazine, and pull the slide back, ejecting the round from the chamber onto the mattress.   I press the catch to hold the slide back, and carefully look the weapon over, holding it close to the one table lamp in the room.   There's no need to clean it; I haven't fired it in the month since I last had it at the range, and I cleaned it right after that. Too much cleaning—leaving the weapon dry—is no good. I can see there's still a light film of Breakfree oil on the moving parts, as there should be. I insert the magazine into the grip and release the slide, chambering a round. Then I eject the magazine and press the extra round into the top, and return the magazine to the cavity in the grip. The Glock goes back in the shoulder holster, and I go to the bathroom to brush my teeth.

Twenty-Two

"**M**ake it so, Mr. Laforge!"

"Aye, Captain!" Tommy says at the same time as Geordi Laforge on the TV. Tommy is wearing one of his mom's plastic hair bands across his eyes and peering out through the slit in it. When Tommy wears the hair band this way it's a VISOR, just like Geordi on *Star Trek* wears so he can see even though he's blind. In fact, with the VISOR, Geordi can see *better* than the others. He's smarter than the others too, which is why he's in charge of the *Enterprise*'s engines. Actually, Data might be smarter, but he's a robot, so he has a computer for a brain, and Tommy doesn't know if that really counts as being smart. Like, is a bulldozer strong?

The phone rings. Tommy wishes the show weren't at its best part, but it might be Mom calling—most likely *is* Mom—so he jumps up, runs into the kitchen, and grabs the phone off its hanger on the wall. "Hello?"

"Hi Tommy."

"Hi Mom." In the background on her side he can hear a vacuum cleaner running.

"How you doin', honey?"

"Good. Are you coming home now?"

She sighs. "I wish. No, I'll be home at the usual time. Did you have your dinner?"

Tommy thinks of the Choco Crunchies he had. He knows he was supposed to eat the stuff in the Tupperware, but he likes the Choco Crunchies because they turn the milk into chocolate milk while he eats them, so then he can drink the milk when he's done. "Um-hmm."

"Have you done your homework yet?"

She won't be home until after ten, so he has plenty of time to do his homework before she gets home. "Yeah," he says quietly. It's not really a lie, since he *will* do it.

"Really?"

"Well, not yet, but I'm going to do it now."

"Tommy," she says, her voice going up at the end of his name—her warning tone.

"OK, I'm going to do it right after *Star Trek*!"

"You'd better—I'm going to check it when I get home."

Tommy's not worried—she's said this before, but she's never actually done this. Well, maybe once. Anyway, he really is going to do it, after *Star Trek*.

"Hey Julia," someone says in the background on her side.

"Oops, gotta go honey. Love you!"

"Bye Mom—I love you too."

Her side of the line is quiet, and he realizes she's already gone. He reaches up and hangs up the phone, then runs back into the living room in time to see the *Enterprise* taking off through space, and then there's a commercial. Tommy watches the commercials, watches the show come back on, but now it's just Captain Picard talking about something, and then the show's over.

Tommy leaves the TV on because it's too quiet without it, but he opens his backpack and dumps out his books from school. He does the problems in his math workbook first because they're easy, and he can pretend he's Geordi, calculating stuff about the engine on the Enterprise. Then he reads the pages in his science book during boring parts in the monster movie that's on. At some point he ends up just watching TV until, during a part where everyone's standing around talking, he packs his books back into his bag, then goes into the kitchen and pulls a chair over to the counter.

He climbs from the chair to the counter, then opens the cupboard and goes to the top shelf where mom keeps the candy bars. He knows he's not supposed to have candy like this during the week, but she doesn't notice if he only takes one or two candy bars the whole week. He climbs down, puts the chair back, and returns to the living room. While watching commercials, he bites into the candy and chews the sweet, smooth, crunchy mash in his mouth. Sometimes he likes to fill his mouth as completely as possible with the stuff, but that means finishing the candy sooner. Today he just takes normal bites and swallows before taking another. Even doing it this way, though, the candy is finished too soon. He thinks about going for another, but instead stretches out on the carpet with a cushion from the couch under his head, and stares up at the flickering images.

Tommy wakes up when he hears the key in the lock. He looks at the TV, where the people are finally fighting with the monster in some dark place, then looks over his shoulder at the door in time to see it open. His mom looks at him over the chain.

"It's just me, honey," she says, then closes the door.

Tommy jumps up, starts to run for the door, then remembers the candy bar wrapper, dashes back to where he was lying on the floor, grabs it, and stuffs it in his pocket. Then he's back and reaches up to slide the chain out before opening the door. "Hi Mom!"

"Hey honey," she says, smiling her home from work smile that looks tired and happy at the same time. She walks slowly into the room, and Tommy closes the door behind her and locks it while she takes her coat off and hangs it in the closet.

Tommy goes to the kitchen and gets a can of beer out of the fridge and brings it to the couch where she's sitting, staring at the TV but not really watching it. Tommy hands her the can.

"Thanks baby," she says, popping the tab on it and drinking. He can hear the rapid liquid sound of the beer going from the can into her mouth.

He kneels down and unties her sneakers. After he loosens the laces on each one she holds her foot up so he can pull the sneaker off. When they're both off, she puts her feet up on the coffee table and Tommy sits pressed against her on the couch. She puts her arm around him and he leans into her more, taking in the familiar smells: hamburgers and onions from the diner, the sharp scent of cleaning stuff, and beer.

"What are you watching?" she asks.

He shrugs. "I dunno—some kind of monster movie."

"Did you have a good day at school?"

Tommy thinks about getting punched in the stomach but doesn't want to talk about that. He nods, then tilts his head so he can look up at her. "It was OK. The teacher did this cool thing in science where she burned sugar to show there was carbon inside it. It was neat."

"Um-hmm," she says, sipping from the can. "Sounds like she cooks like I do," she adds, smiling a little.

"Is that why Dad left?" Tommy asks, still looking up at her.

Little wrinkles appear between her eyebrows for a second, but then vanish and she just looks tired again. "Maybe honey," she says, still staring at the TV. "Baby, if I lay down, would your rub my head?"

"Sure Mom," he says eagerly.

He slides down to the end of the couch while his mom puts down the beer and pivots so she can lie back with her head in his lap. Her long hair falls across his legs. He brushes it back from her forehead with his fingers and then gently rubs her temples with little circular motions. After a while, he can tell she's fallen asleep. Tommy can't reach the remote, which he left on the floor where he'd been before she got home, so he has to watch the news show that comes on after the movie.

Twenty-Three

I turn off the music, listen to the street noises around me for almost half a minute, think about turning on Public Radio, but don't want to listen to a lot of talk. I sit a while, following each vehicle that comes down the street with my eyes, wonder what the tapping sound is, and realize I'm tapping my pen against the steering wheel. I stop myself, but a minute later I'm doing it again, so I put the pen in the glove box and fold my arms under my breasts. The fingertips of my right hand rest on the shape of the Glock's grip, touching it through the over-sized denim shirt.

The itchiness below my sternum and my view of his front door tell me he's still at home, up there in his apartment, doing who knows what. *Probably whacking off to kiddie porn.* "Ugh!" I blurt out and shudder, wondering where these thoughts come from.

I should just take him out; I know what he is. Earlier this morning, after I called the police tip line to tell them about yesterday afternoon and the little boy, I came over here in time to follow Lambert on foot again. The route was a little different this morning, a little longer, and involved a couple minutes of waiting around during which I tried hard to look like I was waiting for a bus. When Lambert started moving again, I realized he had begun following a boy and a woman, maintaining about a block between him and them. I followed him at about the same interval. It was hard to tell from my distance, but the boy could have been the same one who smiled at Lambert yesterday. Today, though, Lambert stayed well behind them, and they didn't seem to notice they were being followed. They walked to the school on Tyler Street, but Lambert broke off before he got there, and I followed him back to his building. Since then he's been inside and I've been here in my car. I look at my watch again: coming up on four hours now.

I think about climbing the fire escape, busting into his bedroom, and—*and what?* Shoot him? For following a kid around? Sure, it's creepy, but he's not hurting anyone. It certainly doesn't prove he's the killer. What if *I'm* the crazy one?

I'm not. Florida, New Orleans, even that time in Seoul, all proved the reality of the sense.

But to murder someone? To plan and carry out an execution? Based on little more than something I don't understand and have a hard time believing? To *murder* someone?

"Fuuuuck," I moan quietly, and notice my foot is tapping. I stop it.

"I'm going to have lunch soon," I announce to Stacey and myself. I eye the plastic bag containing a peanut butter and pickle sandwich, an apple, and a banana, and decide to wait a little longer, to give myself something to look forward to.

A UPS truck goes by, followed a few seconds later by a dark sedan. The car slows, passes a parking space by the curb, stops, and the backup lights come on. I idly watch the vehicle park, disappearing from my view in the line of cars along the block. After a few seconds I see two heads—a black guy and a white guy—appear above the car roofs and move toward Lambert's building. Both men are wearing dark trench coats.

"Could this be…?"

They hesitate on the sidewalk, looking first at the door to Lambert's building, then up at the windows, then at the door again.

Looks like cops, I think, a ray of sun breaking through the thick overcast of my mood.

The white guy steps forward and presses the button by Lambert's mailbox. They stand a few seconds, then they turn to each other and I can see them speaking.

"He's there!" I whisper, then slouch down a little as I realize I might look a little suspicious just sitting here watching. I grab the newspaper off the passenger seat and open it to the middle somewhere while keeping my eyes on the police.

They both look up, and I do too. One of Lambert's windows is open now, and then he leans out and looks down at them. He says something, but I can't tell what since I'm sitting almost a block away behind closed windows. The black guy says something back. I look up again, but Lambert's window is closing. I look down: the men are standing by the door, talking to each other and looking around.

I scootch down in my seat some more and look at the newspaper. After a couple seconds I peer over at them again. More standing around, then the door opens. The men each hold up something small—has to be badges. There's some talking, then the cops go inside and the door closes. I feel like I should be psyched at this point, but instead I feel uneasy.

Twenty-Four

"OK, remain calm," Wayne tells himself quietly after shutting the window. "Who knows why they're here, but if you act guilty, they're gonna start to know, and if they start to know, you're gonna act more nervous, and you're gonna incriminate yourself." He stops whispering to himself, stands up straight, takes a deep breath, holds it, lets it out. "I don't know why you want to talk to *me*, but if there's anything I can do to help, I'm happy to do it," he rehearses quietly, making himself believe his words: He really has no idea why they're here. He doesn't have much contact with kids, but he doesn't want them to get killed, so he's happy to lend any assistance he can.

He turns, walks quickly to the apartment's door, then pauses and looks back over his shoulder. Everything—the Nintendo, the comics, the toys, the radio-controlled Hummer—everything is neatly put away out of sight as usual. Except for the toys on the display shelves, obviously—those are still on display. But lots of guys collect toys and display their collections. He'll just have to make sure the cops understand that, but only if they seem to be paying attention to the toys. No point in making a big deal about something they otherwise wouldn't pay any attention to.

Satisfied, he turns his head back to the front and descends the two and a half flights of stairs. One more deep inhalation, mostly to slow his breathing, which has become a little rapid and labored, and he opens the door.

The cops turn and look at him, and he knows they've come to arrest him. His guts turn to water and his face feels numb, and he knows, he *knows*, and he can't say a thing to stop it.

"Good afternoon, Mr. Lambert. I'm Detective Jackson, and this is Detective Mulligan," the black cop says.

He opens his mouth to reply, then closes it and clears his throat. "Sorry—" he clears his throat again, this time for effect. "Sorry about that. Good afternoon, detectives."

"We'd like to ask you a few questions about the murders of four young boys from Trenton." Jackson pauses, looking right at Wayne's face.

Wayne feels like the cop is looking right through him, right through his face and into his brain, and he knows they know.

"I heard about those on the news. I'm happy to help in any way I can, but I really don't know anything about those kids. Besides what I saw on the news, I mean."

The voice surprises Wayne at first, and even more a moment later when he realizes it's his own. Then, just as surely as he knew they had him a few seconds earlier, he is now certain they've got nothing and they'll get nothing today. *Ask me a few questions—if they were going to arrest me, wouldn't they just start reading me my rights?*

"Well, we're following up on some tips and we thought you might know something that will help with the case. May we come in and talk with you for a few minutes?" Jackson asks.

"Sure. Hope you don't mind stairs," he says turning and leading the way back up.

"No problem, sir," says Jackson.

"So how do you think I might be able to help with this?" he asks between breaths.

There's a pause. "Sir, we'd rather not talk about this until we're in your apartment so there's less chance of our conversation being overheard and compromising the investigation."

Breath. "Oh, OK," he replies, and wonders what *that* means. "Well," breath, "here we are." He leads the way into his apartment. "Would you like to sit down?" He gestures at the table with its four chairs to the left of the door.

The detectives take their time getting to their chairs, looking around as they do. "You have a lot of toys," the white cop—Mulligan—says.

Wayne feels a moment of twinge, but there can be no second-guessing now. "I'm a collector—*Star Wars* stuff especially. Love those movies. Except for being off the card, all my stuff is mint. My friends think I'm crazy for taking them off the cards, but I really like to display them. I spend hours getting them just right.

"So can I get you gentlemen some water? I'd offer coffee, but I don't have any."

"No thanks," Mulligan says. "Mind if I look around?"

"Uh," Wayne hesitates. Besides his boys, no one ever comes in here. Just having them at his table feels like a violation; the idea of them walking around in his space, maybe touching his stuff... On the other hand, would refusing them seem suspicious? "Uh, that's fine, it's just—I have things set up a certain way, so please don't touch anything. Especially the toys, OK?"

"Sure, no problem," Mulligan says.

Wayne turns to Jackson. "For you detective? A glass of water?"

"Thanks but no. So for the record, you are Wayne Lambert, correct?" Jackson asks, taking out a notebook and flipping it open.

"That's right," Wayne says, standing awkwardly between the kitchen and dining area, resenting them for making him feel uncomfortable in his own place.

"And you live here alone, is that correct?"

"Yes sir, just me. So what is this about? How can I help the investigation?"

"You're already helping us, by taking the time to answer these questions with me now. Why don't you sit down, Mr. Lambert?"

Don't tell me what to do in my own place, he thinks through gritted teeth, and keeps his feet. "Sure, but what makes you think I would know—that I'd have helpful information? I mean, like I said, I don't know anything about this except what I've seen on the news."

"Sometimes you know something and you don't even realize it. Now, if I may, what is your marital status?"

"Single."

"Never married?"

"Not yet," Wayne says, forcing a little laugh.

"So you're seeing someone." The sentence is at once statement and question.

"Officer—detective—I really don't," it suddenly occurs to him to wonder where Mulligan has gotten to. He looks around and doesn't see him. "OK, hold on," he says to Jackson, then turns toward his bedroom. "Detective Mulligan—sir, would you come out here please."

Mulligan appears in the doorway.

"Officers, I'm not accustomed to having people here in my apartment. I don't normally have guests, and I'm not comfortable with the way you've come in and taken over. Now I'm happy to answer your questions, and then I'm happy to show you around, but can we please do this one part at a time?"

"Sure, sure," Mulligan says, walking over and taking a seat at the table.

Wayne, worried that he is now officially suspicious, takes a seat too. "OK, thanks. Sorry to be like that, but I'm really not comfortable with—"

"No need to explain, Mr. Lambert," Detective Mulligan says, holding up a hand in the stop gesture.

"OK, so what would you like to know?"

Jackson speaks up: "I was just asking if you're seeing someone—dating right now?"

"No, no I'm not, but what's that got to do with these kids? I really want to help, but these questions—I just don't see the connection."

Mulligan this time: "Mr. Lambert, we received a tip that you are the one who killed those boys."

The statement hangs in the air, and Wayne can feel both sets of eyes on him. He's not as surprised as he thought he'd be—the questions were too personal for it to be anything else, and at some level he already knew that. He also becomes immediately aware that what he does next will make all the difference. He thinks it, he believes it, he does it: Blank incomprehension is first: "What?" followed by studied puzzlement; he feels his brows draw together and his mouth frown. "Are you saying—someone—*what?*" Then, and he thinks this is the key, he relaxes his face into a broad smile. "Ooooh, why didn't you say so? You think...?" He laughs.

"I don't see that this is funny, Mr. Lambert," Jackson says. "Four little boys are dead."

Wayne quickly composes himself, puts on a suitably chastened and sober expression. "You're right; I'm sorry. It's just—well, I really didn't know *what* this was about. So you were, what? Seeing if I seemed guilty or something?" Suddenly he looks surprised and a little alarmed; at least, he hopes he does. "Oh shi—uh, damn, I uh, hope I didn't seem that way. I wasn't scared, just confused, but now I get it. Look, here's the thing," Wayne continues, the words flowing easily now. "I manage a Reilly's Restaurant; you know, the one on Olden Ave? Anyway, sometimes when someone we hire doesn't work out, I'm the one to fire him—or her, but it's usually guys I have to fire. So sometimes the person getting fired doesn't take it so well, and maybe resents or blames me. Who accused me?"

"We can't say," Jackson replies.

"Look, I'm not gonna do anything to the guy, but I understand: you have rules you gotta follow. But I'll bet you a dollar to a donut the guy who dimed me out is a guy I fired." Wayne really does believe this, and he feels the tension melting away. Now not only does this visit all make sense, but it confirms they have nothing on him, because if they did, they wouldn't be fucking around with all these questions. "If you want, tell me the name—it'll stay between us and end here, but I can save you a lot of trouble when you find out the only reason I've been accused is because of some ex-employee's attempt at petty revenge."

"Actually, Mr. Lambert, we can't say because the tip was anonymous."

"Anonymous? Well see—there you go. He didn't want to get in trouble for making a false accusation. He just wanted to make trouble for me. And, incidentally, for you. But OK, if you have more questions, ask away. I'll answer anything."

"Do you find young boys sexually attractive Mr. Lambert?" Mulligan asks.

Wayne turns his head and regards the detective calmly. "No. No I don't."

Jackson: "Did you know any of the victims personally?"

"No, I didn't. I don't know any children."

Jackson turns to Mulligan. "You got anything else?"

Mulligan looks at Wayne for another beat, then looks at Jackson. "No, I'm good."

Jackson looks back at Wayne. "Could we get that tour of your apartment now?"

"Sure," Wayne says. "Right this way." He takes them around the living room and makes them listen while he goes on about his toy collection. He takes them in the bedroom, shows them the framed posters, gives them time to notice the copies of *Time* and *Entertainment Weekly* on the bedside table. He waits outside while they both go in the bathroom and stand in the little open floor space while gazing around. Finally, he shows them the kitchen, and then shows them the door. By now they're ready to go, and he wishes them both a nice day.

Twenty-Five

The day's light is fading, so I lay the book I've been reading—*Watership Down*—on the passenger seat and gaze out the windshield, between some other cars, across the parking lot at the Reilly's. I've been reading since I followed the target here around three p.m. At least the three hours have passed relatively quickly, thanks to the book, which is excellent. I picked it up because I enjoyed another book by Richard Adams called *The Plague Dogs*, and this one is even better.

Still, I wish I were reading back home in my apartment, instead of sitting in this parking lot. I can't believe nothing has happened to Lambert since those cops visited him on Tuesday. I mean, what more can I do? I *handed* them the bad guy, and they've apparently just walked away from him.

I wonder if they're following him around, waiting for some kind of evidence; after all, I'm waiting around too, and he hasn't actually done anything wrong. Well, he did follow that kid and his mom from their apartment house almost to the school; that was kind of creepy, but that was before the cops visited him. If the cops are suspicious of Lambert and following him, you'd think I'd have noticed by now, given how I'm locked on to him and have done almost nothing for the past four days but sit around waiting for him to come out of places.

Not surprisingly, he's also been looking for people following him. On Wednesday he noticed me when he came out of the restaurant and took a walk around the parking lot. I was reading a newspaper at the time, and I used my peripheral vision to watch him stop and really look at me. I pretended not to notice, but shifted around so he'd have a harder time

seeing my face.   Hopefully he also got a look at how I'm
dressed—informal coat, stocking cap, denim work shirt—very
non-cop-like, I think.   Plus Stacey, being the aqua Geo Metro
that she is, doesn't look anything like a car a cop would drive,
so I'm hoping he just wrote me off as someone on a road trip
who was taking a break.   I do have the out-of-state plates, after
all.   To be safe, though, I've really backed off since then,
relying on my knowledge of his vehicle and his usual patterns
and destinations to follow him at a greater distance.   I thought
about renting a car, and even doing something like dying my
hair, so he doesn't recognize me as the same person, but
renting a car costs money, which I'm already running through
pretty quickly, especially for someone with no job.   Plus, who
knows how long I'm going to have to keep this up, paying for
the hotel room and, well, the main expense is the room, but
it's a big one.   Anyway, I don't think he's seen me since.

But as far as I can tell, it's just the two of us—no cops.
Like the target, I've started taking little walks too, while
waiting.   I've walked up and down his street and the
surrounding blocks, and around this parking lot, but I haven't
seen anyone besides me who seemed to be staking him out.   I
don't know what happened inside his apartment on Tuesday,
but he seems to have convinced them he's not their guy.

Maybe he's not.

I don't know how many times this thought has passed
across my synapses in the past few days.   But come on, what
are the chances?   What are the freakin' odds that this guy lives
here in Trenton where these boys went missing, that he
triggers the sense, and that he does some weird kind of stalky
thing with this boy, and yet he's not the one killing little boys?
What are the chances of *that*?   None chances, that's what—it's
gotta be him.

So kill him already.

I shake my head in the gathering darkness of the car
interior.   I just can't...can't bring myself to coldly execute

someone. Plus, there is a *chance* I'm wrong, slight though it may be.

Who am I kidding? I just don't want to do it. I want the police to take care of this. I don't want anything to do with this guy, any more than I wanted what happened in Florida or New Orleans. "I just want to be left alone," I say quietly and deliberately. "Safe and alone. Is that so much to ask?"

I don't even know who the fuck I'm asking.

Twenty-Six

There she is again. At least, that looks like her car, doesn't it? He squints across the parking lot at a small swatch of blue-green metal shining in the late afternoon sun. The color is somewhat distinctive. The woman inside was distinctive too. He didn't get a great look at her, but she seemed pretty despite the boyish way she wore the blonde hair he saw peeking out around the bottom of her stocking cap. He considers walking over to see if it is the same car and if the woman is inside it again, but it's way over by the Shop Rite. He'd noticed the car three days ago on Wednesday when he started looking for cops in unmarked cars, to see if they were watching him. He hadn't seen any dark sedans containing guys in rumpled suits, but he'd seen her sitting in her car reading a newspaper, and the sight struck him as odd. At the time he wondered if she could be a cop, if the police were actually more clever about disguising tails than the movies made them out to be, but then he noticed the Massachusetts license plates. He doubted the Trenton police or even, if they were involved to that extent, the FBI would go so far as to not only buy an underpowered, brightly-colored little economy car for surveillance, but would also go to Massachusetts, of all places, to register it. Plus, he realized, cops wouldn't be alone like her. In the end he decided she was just passing through on a road trip and decided to take a break. Seeing her here again kills that theory, though. Maybe she's visiting on business—checking out real estate or maybe scouting locations for a movie. That doesn't explain her hanging out by the Shop Rite, though, unless maybe she goes there for food on her breaks.

Whatever. It doesn't matter; she's nothing to do with him, but he's pleased with himself that he's noticing her, so he'd certainly notice cops if they were following him. Instead, he's seen no sign of them since they left his apartment on Tuesday. And *that* means he convinced them. By the time they left him, they must have realized the anonymous tip about him had no credibility, and now they've moved on to other suspects. Has to be.

Wayne even knows who probably gave the cops that tip: Roger Bascomb. He was a waiter with an ego the size of Philadelphia—a walking, talking attitude. Which would have been fine; everybody is a little weird in some way. We all have our weird points. Wayne was even willing to put up with the rolled eyes and smart-ass remarks, and so were Rodney, the manager, and Liza, the other assistant manager. But when Roger started getting sarcastic with the customers, specifically that prima donna yuppie couple with their sense of entitlement, Wayne fired him. Wayne didn't like those douche bag yuppie assholes either, but he liked less having to apologize to them on behalf of Reilly's, and bring comp drinks to them himself. That alone was sufficient cause, as far as Wayne was concerned, for firing Bascomb. But personal issues aside, pissing off customers is one of the unpardonable sins; it's essentially biting the hand that feeds you. Hey, we've all *wanted* to be sarcastic to the occasional asshole customer, and we've said the remarks in our head or to each other back in the kitchen or after the clientele has all left. But never directly to the customer. Dislike them as we do, we need their money.

Of course Roger Bascomb couldn't fathom how he really was responsible for his own firing. He made all kinds of threats, from bad publicity to lawsuits, but nothing ever happened. Until now. Roger must have seen his opportunity in that tip line and called it in, just to freak Wayne out, maybe embarrass him, generally make his life difficult. Wayne pauses in his walk around the building and stares out across the lot at the Staples, shaking his head. It takes a special kind of selfish pettiness to interfere with something as serious as a murder investigation—for children, no less—just so you can further your own personal revenge agenda. "What a prick," he says quietly.

Anyway, except for freaking Wayne out on Tuesday, no real harm was done. He *had* been freaked, he remembers, smiling a little now. Not only did he postpone his plans with Red, but he didn't even get to *see* Red. Wayne actually stayed in the rest of the day, not coming out again until Wednesday afternoon when it was time to go to work. Maybe that was good, though; maybe the police *were* watching him after the interview, and seeing he did nothing suspicious sealed his innocence for them.

Now it's more obvious than ever the police have no clue about him. After all, they looked *right at him—questioned* him even, and moved on. Why should they suspect him? There's no evidence connecting him, and he was the picture of friendly helpfulness when they visited. Even the tip that sent them to him was easy to account for. "Suckers," he says quietly through a smile and resumes his walk.

Twenty-Seven

Tommy is carried along by the stream of other kids flowing out the main doors to the school, and finds himself outside in a cool, sunny afternoon that smells a little like spring. As the flow hits the sidewalk, the crowd divides, with some kids going to waiting cars, others turning right, and Tommy, surrounded by bright-colored jackets and backpacks, going left. It's easier to walk now, with fewer people pressed around him, and he slows down. There's no need to hurry home—there aren't even any good TV shows on for a while, and it feels nice to be outside now that the air is getting warmer and smelling so good. The group around him thins out as some turn down the side street with the big green house on the corner, and some more when he gets to the next street where he has to wait for the crossing guard to walk him across.

A little while after that he realizes he's walking alone. Although this happens almost every day, he still feels bad because every morning Mom makes him promise to walk home with Charlie and those guys. But to do that he'd have to push and shove his way through the crowded hall like they do, and he doesn't like doing that. Anyway, it doesn't matter. A left turn, a few more blocks, and a right turn, and he'll be home. Once he's at home, he'll be inside until tomorrow morning, so he might as well take his time while he's still outside.

Down the street he sees the Monday-Tuesday Guy. Tommy's not sure when this guy started appearing; it was sometime during the winter. Tommy doesn't think about him much except on Monday and Tuesday afternoons, when he appears, always on this street, looking big and friendly, like a big friendly talking bear from a cartoon. He always has a baseball cap on, a Yankees cap, so Tommy thinks he probably really likes the Yankees, and maybe goes to their games sometimes. Tommy decided to be a Yankees fan too. He's never been to a baseball game, but thinks it'd be really cool, especially if the Yankees were playing. He's seen games on TV and the stadium looks huge, and filled with so many people.

Tommy's never even been to New York. He went to Philadelphia once, before Dad left, but he doesn't remember much about it, or about Dad—not even what he looked like. Tommy wonders if he looked anything like Monday-Tuesday Guy, or if he liked baseball. He really can't remember.

It's Tuesday, so there's the Monday-Tuesday Guy. But today he's carrying something under his arm. That's new; he's never seen the guy carrying anything before. It's big and yellow, and looks kind of like a box. Tommy stares at it, and as they get closer he can see it looks like a truck: he can make out a windshield, headlights, and a row of short, straight lines on the front part. As they get closer he watches the truck. The sunlight bounces off it as the guy moves it a little while he's walking. It's pretty big, too—big enough he could maybe stand on it without breaking it. He wonders why the guy has such a cool toy. Tommy has never heard of grown-ups having toys, but he thinks it'd be great to be a grown-up because then you could get anything you want. The truck looks new. None of Tommy's toys are new. Even when he first gets them, they're usually not new. It'd be *so cool* to be an adult and have new toys, any new toy you want, even a big, shiny, yellow truck.

"You like my Hummer?"

Tommy looks up, suddenly realizing the Monday-Tuesday Guy is right in front of him. Tommy smiles back up at him. Obviously the truck is called a "Hummer." "Yeah," he says.

Twenty-Eight

"You like my Hummer?" Wayne asks needlessly. Red's infatuation was obvious from fifty yards back. He can barely take his eyes off its bright yellow body, and Wayne can barely take his eyes off him.

Red looks up and seems startled for a moment. Their eyes meet, and his boy smiles up at him. "Yeah," he says, his voice a little awestruck.

"It's radio-controlled," Wayne offers, pulling out all the stops to hold the kid's attention. Wayne half lifts the black control set in his left hand, as if to corroborate his own information.

"Really?" Red asks, looking at the control set briefly and uncomprehendingly before looking back at the miniature vehicle.

"Yeah, I just got it. I'm taking it to the park to try it out, see what it can do. Wanna see?" Wayne has only been fishing a couple times in his life, but he knows he has to set the hook before the fish swims on.

The boy hesitates. It's obvious he wants to go to the park, but equally clear he's wrestling with directives from his mom and maybe his teachers to go straight home and not talk to, and certainly not go anywhere with, someone you don't know. This is where Wayne hopes the weeks of smiling and greeting his boy will pay off with him seeing Wayne not as a stranger, but as someone familiar and safe.

"Have you ever used radio control?" he tries again, keeping his voice casual, friendly.

Tommy shakes his head and looks at the toy Hummer again.

One last attempt, and then he'll have to let things go, maybe try again next week. This is crucial: if he pushes too hard he'll lose him, or worse. "I'll let you try it out if you want. I'm taking it to the park." Red looks up at his face again, and Wayne meets those innocent, trusting, beautiful gray eyes. He smiles down at him sincerely.

"You mean the park over there?" Red asks, pointing over his shoulder with his thumb. There's an awkwardness to the gesture; it's out of synch with the rest of the boy's manner, and now Wayne hesitates.

Time to go. "Yeah, Columbus Park—just down at the end of this street." He starts to walk again, moving past his boy. "You're welcome to come if you like. Go home and get your parents if you want—I'll probably be over there for a while, getting the hang of this. It's my first radio-controlled car." He walks without looking back.

Twenty-Nine

"You mean the park over there?" Tommy asks, pointing over his shoulder with his thumb. He saw someone do this in a movie once, and thinks it looks pretty cool, but hasn't gotten to do it himself before.

"Yeah, Columbus Park—just down at the end of this street." He starts to walk again, moving past Tommy. "You're welcome to come if you like. Go home and get your parents if you want—I'll probably be over there for a while, getting the hang of this. It's my first radio-controlled car."

Tommy turns in place and watches him go. Across the back of the truck there's the word HUMMER in black letters on the yellow background. "So does that drive by itself?"

The guy, still walking, turns around so he's walking backward and holds up the black box again. "You use this— steer it with this, make it do whatever you want. See ya!" He turns and continues walking away.

Tommy knows Mom wouldn't want him to go to the park with the Monday-Tuesday Guy, even if she knew about him and how friendly he seems, and how he's been around for a long time. But Mom's like that—she just wants him at school or at home, and doesn't really care about what he wants. Besides, the guy obviously doesn't care if Tommy goes to the park with him or not, so he can't be some creepy guy. He's just going to the park to play with his way cool truck—his Hummer. Tommy thinks once more of turning and walking the rest of the way home, but then he can almost see himself sitting in front of the TV watching some stupid show, waiting for something good to come on and for Mom to call, when he could have been making the Hummer drive around crazy, like when he plays with his little cars, only he won't be touching it—it'll be going around on its own. "Hey, wait up!" Tommy says and starts running, his books and stuff bouncing inside his backpack as he goes.

The Monday-Tuesday Guy keeps walking for a few more steps, then slows and half-turns, smiling under his baseball cap, looking more like a big kid than a grown-up.

Tommy reaches him and stops running, and his books immediately stop bouncing around.

"Here, you can carry the control unit," the guy says, handing Tommy the black box, which has a couple levers and some buttons on it.

Tommy takes the box and looks at it. In big yellow letters across the top is the word HUMMER. "Why's it called Hummer?" he asks, then looks up at the guy.

A puzzled expression comes across his face. "I really don't know. I think it started out as an Army vehicle—maybe that's what they called it, but I don't know why they would. Maybe because it 'hums along.'" He smiles down at Tommy.

Tommy doesn't think that sounds right, but thinks it's really neat that this is also an Army truck, even if it isn't green. It kind of looks like it could be an Army truck.

The guy starts walking again, and so does Tommy.

"By the way, my name's Todd," the guy says.

"Hi Todd," Tommy says, looking up into that big, round, smiling face.

"What's your name?" the guy asks.

"I'm Tommy," he replies.

"So Tommy, did you say you've operated a radio-controlled car before?"

"Me?" Tommy asks, surprised, wondering where he got *that* idea. "No way!"

"I thought you were supposed to show me how this works! That's why I gave you the controls to carry!" Todd says all this with a big smile, so Tommy knows he's kidding.

"No *way!*" Tommy says, laughing. "*You'll* have to show *me!*"

"I've never done this before either! Well, I guess we're just going to have to figure it out together. Pretty cool truck, though, isn't it?"

"Yeah, *way* cool," Tommy says.

"So when we get there, I'm going to take the controls first, and figure out how it works, OK? Then I'll show you how, and you can drive for a while. Sound good?"

Tommy likes the way Todd talks to him, like they're friends instead of grown-up and kid.

"How was school today?"

Tommy shrugs, not really sure what to say about Charlie punching him in the stomach again. "It was OK."

"Just OK?"

"These guys, they're sort of like my friends, but they're kind of jerks, you know?"

"Ooooh yeah, believe me, I know *just* how that is. I knew some guys like that. Let me tell you, Tommy, they're not really friends. Friends don't treat each other like crap. You know how you can tell a true friend?"

Tommy looks up at him, sees he's really waiting for an answer. "How?"

"The way they treat you. It's simple, really—if a person treats you right, if a person acts like a friend, then he *is* a friend. If he doesn't, he's just another jerk, and you should just forget about him—you're better off without him. It's pretty simple, really, don't you think?"

Tommy figures he's right. It *is* pretty simple, after all. People who act like friends *are* friends.

"See, friends do stuff for each other. Like I'm sharing my Hummer with you 'cause I want to be your friend."

They can see the park now, just across the street from them.

"Here, give me your hand, Tommy, and we'll cross together when it's safe."

Tommy reaches up and puts his hand in Todd's big, soft palm, and thinks of a cartoon bear again. They wait until a car passes, and then there's a break in traffic and they cross.

They walk a ways into the park, so they're in a big open area without any other people. Todd lets go of Tommy's hand, and puts the Hummer on the ground. "All right, let me see the controls…"

Tommy hands him the black box, which Todd fiddles with a little before saying "OK, here we go!" The truck starts making a noise like a big engine coming to life, but there's no smoke, so Tommy knows it's fake. Still, it's pretty cool. Suddenly the truck zips off across the mostly dead grass, and Tommy feels his face smile big. Todd drives it in a big circle around them, eventually bringing it close again, then stops and backs it up. When it's at their feet, he beeps the horn and hands the control box to Tommy.

"Cool! I didn't know you could beep the horn!"

Todd squats down close beside him and shows him how to use the controls: the lever for steering, the lever for speed and brake, the button for the horn, and the rest. "Here, at first let's control it together—you steer and I'll control the speed." Todd goes around to Tommy's other side and kneels on the ground. He puts one hand on Tommy's back, and the other on the speed lever. "OK, whenever you're ready, let me know and I'll start it moving and you can take it wherever you want to go."

"OK, go 'head!" Tommy says, anxious to try it. At first he just lets it go straight, then he moves the lever to the left, then the right, then the left, taking it on a zig-zagging path. There's a branch lying on the ground and he steers right for it. "Faster!" he tells Todd, and the truck speeds up a little, though not as fast as Tommy would have liked, and then it hits the branch and goes through the air a little before hitting again and almost flipping over. "Cool!" Tommy shouts. He looks at Todd, who is smiling too.

"You want to control the speed too?"

"Yeah!"

Todd takes his hand off the box and stands up.

With both hands on it, Tommy holds the control box near the center of his body and drives the Hummer all around, drives it crazy so it flips over. Todd runs out and sets it on its wheels again each time that happens, and lets Tommy drive it wherever he wants as long as he doesn't get too close to the street. He even crashes it into a tree once, but Todd doesn't seem to mind. "You want to drive it for a while?" Tommy asks, only to be polite and not really wanting to give it to Todd, but it *is* Todd's truck after all.

"Only if you need a break. You want to take a break?"

Tommy shakes his head.

"Then it's all yours! You're doing great!"

Tommy drives for a while longer, but then it seems like it can't go as fast, and the sound it makes changes. After that it really slows down. Tommy looks up at Todd. "I don't know what's wrong—it can't go as fast now."

"The batteries are probably running down and it needs to be recharged—we've been driving it for about twenty minutes or so, and I think that's how long the batteries are supposed to last, especially with a maniac driver controlling it!"

Todd smiles at him and Tommy knows it's OK and takes the "maniac driver" part as a compliment.

"Why don't you drive it back to us before it totally runs out of power."

Tommy turns it around and brings it back to them. He honks the horn again when it's at their feet, but he can hear how the sound has changed because the batteries are low.

Todd shows Tommy how to turn the Hummer off using the control box, and then he picks it up. "Yeah, I just wish the batteries lasted longer—it's still early and I want to do something fun," Todd says, staring off across the park before looking down at Tommy. "I think I'm going back to my apartment to play with my new Nintendo. Want to come?"

"You have a Nintendo?" Tommy asks, thinking again how much he wants to be grown up so he can buy all the toys he wants.

"Sure—I got it when it first came out. It's really cool. Mostly I play the new Super Mario on it. You're welcome to come back with me if you like—I'll let you try it out. I'm going to make hot chocolate too."

Tommy feels like his brain is driving around in his head like the Hummer. He really, *really* wants to play with the Nintendo. Sam just got one, and he was talking about how he and his dad play with it together. Tommy doesn't know any other way *he* would ever get to play with a Nintendo. He's not even exactly sure what it is or how you play with it, but Sam said it's like having an arcade game in your TV. Tommy played Super Mario in an arcade once—Mom put in the quarters for one game, but it was over pretty quickly because he didn't really know how to play it. Still, he knows he's supposed to go home—was supposed to *be* home a while ago, not here in the park playing with the coolest toy he's ever touched.

"I live really close to here—just three blocks down the street. That's why I walked. Sure would appreciate the help carrying this stuff home, and in return I'll show you the Nintendo. After that, I'll *drive* you home in my car, so you'll be home quick. It'll take twenty, thirty minutes tops. You can even call your folks from my place and let them know you're on your way—or have them pick you up. I can give them directions."

Tommy knows Todd can't call his parents because Mom's at work and no one knows where his dad is, but Todd saying he *would* call them makes Tommy feel like Todd is a good guy. And he'll drive him home, so that'll be quick, right? And after playing with his toy, Tommy should help Todd carry the stuff home—that's fair. Mainly, though, he really wants to play with the Nintendo. Then he can tell Sam and Charlie that he played with it—practically has one of his own. He nods his head and looks up at Todd. "OK."

"Great," Todd says, smiling. "Thanks, I really appreciate the help with this stuff!" He hands Tommy the control box, tugs the bill of his cap, and turns. "It's this way—just three blocks."

Thirty

I sit on a bench by the sidewalk, facing Hamilton Avenue. The sense tells me he's behind me in the park somewhere, about a hundred meters distant. Every so often I glance over my shoulder and see the two of them—man and boy, predator and prey—driving that yellow radio-controlled civilian humvee around. It seems extraordinary that he would be so bold to spend time with his victim in a public park, but he seems to know what he's doing. They're so comfortable together, they actually look like they're related or something—uncle and nephew, or maybe participants in a Big Brother program. Even the initial contact, which I watched from across the street and about a block back, looked completely innocuous. In fact, Lambert seemed to want to be on his way, and it looked like the boy was the one who had the idea of going with him to the park to play with the toy.

I hadn't really thought about it before, but getting boys who don't know him to go someplace private with him would be a challenge. If he tried to just grab them off the street, there'd probably be all kinds of yelling and screaming and carrying on. Even if there weren't, anyone glancing out a window and seeing the kid being abducted would realize something was wrong. But the way Lambert's doing it, everything seems fine, even to the kid. So to most people, they'd be invisible—just part of the background. I'd guess even if the cops showed up now and questioned him, the situation would *still* seem innocent. He could just tell them the truth; well, part of the truth: He was on his way to the park when the boy noticed his toy truck and asked if he could come along. Lambert, trying to be a good guy, maybe even to protect the kid from the bad guy who's been abducting boys like him, said sure, fine.   There's certainly no coercion involved, and the kid would back up this version of things because, as far as the kid knows, that's exactly what's happening.

All this poses a problem for me, because I apparently still have nothing incriminating to show the cops.   In truth, all *I* have to go on now is the weird sense.   If I didn't know otherwise, I'd have to guess their interaction is completely innocent.   But I do know otherwise.

Right?

Shit.   This is much harder than I originally thought it'd be.   I came up with the idea of finding bad guys and reporting their identities to the cops almost two years ago, after I realized what the sense means and how it works.   What I should have anticipated, but didn't, is because I find the bad guys first, I'm dealing with the threat by myself for a while.   Even after the police get involved, they aren't as helpful as I thought they'd be.   This time I actually get the cops to follow up, and I'm *still* on my own.   Lambert must have been really convincing; at least more convincing than my anonymous tip.

It'd be easier if the police knew me and believed me.   I tried to tell the detective in New Orleans about the sense, but he looked at me like I was crazy.   And that was *after* I'd helped him catch the bad guy.

So here I am, alone with the threat again, and shit looks like it might start happening.

So maybe I should call the cops now…

And tell them what?   Well, OK, tell them he's in the park with a boy who doesn't really know him.   Maybe they could at least scare him into not doing anything to the boy.

Oh yeah—good plan there.   Then what?   Wait another month or two before he makes another move?   You should just fuckin' take him out next chance you get.

What would that make me?   Killing someone—with cold premeditation, no less—killing someone because I have a bad feeling about him. That'd make me as fucked up as these guys I sense. Like the one in New Orleans who went around shooting women, me included, because he thought we deserved it. I sigh and stare across the street at a dry cleaning shop. Even if I were going to call the police, I don't know where there's a pay phone around here. There just aren't many of them any more; cell phones made them dinosaurs. I could call with my cell phone, but then they'll know it's me that called, and then if Lambert turns up dead by some violent means, I'll be at the top of the suspects list—or at least the persons of interest list. That's no good. No, I gave the cops their chance.

Then what? *What's the fuckin' plan?*

My stomach sinks and my head feels like it's going to float up off my neck. I cross my arms and touch the Glock with the fingertips of my right hand. "Oh fuck," I breathe. "I don't want to do this anymore; I don't want to be here."

A vibration passes through the top of my leg and my whole body flinches. I realize it's just the cell phone in my pants pocket, and my first thought is it's the police calling me. But that can't be true. I pull the phone from my jeans, flip it open, and put it to the side of my head. "Hello?"

"Shailene! Hi, it's Mike."

"Oh—" *Huh?* "Hey Mike," I say, trying to wrap my head around the surreality of this. "Uh, what's up?"

"I'm calling to ask you the same thing. Henry just—Hey, are you OK? Your voice sounds weird."

"Weird?" I force a more neutral tone. "Um, I'm fine. Kinda busy right now, but—"

"Well, Henry just told me you quit last week. I don't know why he waited until now to tell me, but they're running an ad for your job. Why didn't you tell me you quit?"

"I dunno...I was sort of hoping I could wrap things up here and maybe go back and un-quit. But that's not going to happen."

"I can't believe you're leaving! You're the best...the best IT person we've ever had. Now they're going to hire someone new, and who's going to train him? Me, probably, if you can imagine..."

I tune Mike out when I notice the hard scratching on my scar. *Oh shit.* Since Lambert saw me sitting in my car that time, I don't want to chance looking around because he might recognize me. I'm wearing a baseball cap I picked up locally, and my sunglasses, but if I turn around and he recognizes my face, it could spook him and drag this whole shitfest on even longer. I get up off the bench and, hoping my arm, hand, and the phone I'm holding will obscure my face, I start walking away down the sidewalk in the direction of Lambert's building, figuring if he's leaving the park he's going to be headed that way.

"Hello? Shailene?"

I become aware of the questioning voice and the ensuing silence in the phone. "Yeah, Mike, this is a *really* bad time. I'm gonna have to go now. I'll call you later, OK?"

"But what about—"

"Really sorry Mike, gotta go." I take the phone down and look at it so I can press the end button. Still walking fast, I flip it closed and pocket it. I take a left down the next side street and pause in front of the second house down. My scar is barely registering anything, and I think about backtracking. I can't afford to lose contact now; what if I'm wrong about him going back to his apartment with the kid? I go back up to the sidewalk, look back the way I came, but don't see them. I pan across the street: still no sign of them. I wonder if I'm imagining the slight itch I feel on my scar and reach up to scratch it while shifting my eyes back toward the edge of the park. I'm about to start walking back so the sense can pick up Lambert again, when I see them step onto the sidewalk. I shrink back a little, putting the house on the corner almost between us. They're looking to cross the street, which is good because now I can stay on this side and follow without being as obvious about it. They make it, jogging the last several feet to the opposite sidewalk and then turning toward Lambert's place. I back down the side street and pretend to be fiddling with my phone while facing away from Hamilton. Pretty soon the pain hikes up noticeably, peaking somewhere around a hot wire on my skin before backing off again. I give them a few more seconds, then slowly turn and walk back up to the avenue, looking at their backs and the yellow humvee under Lambert's arm. I let them go another block before I resume my pursuit. Predictably, they take a right on Clinton. They'll be inside by the time I get there, but I'm not worried since I know where they're headed. I cross the street and quickly cover the remaining distance.

Thirty-One

They cross together then turn left on the sidewalk and head down the street. Something about this seems wrong to Tommy—he'd been expecting to go a different way for some reason, though he's not sure why since he doesn't know where Todd lives. He starts to feel like something isn't right, and a little afraid, but then Todd asks him if he likes baseball. Tommy looks at Todd and, thinking of the cap Todd always wears, says "I'm a Yankees fan."

"Really? Me too. Best team in baseball. Maybe we can go to a game together sometime. Have you ever been to Yankee Stadium?"

"No, but I really want to. I've never even been to New York."

"Wow! Well, maybe we can go sometime. I'll give you my phone number when we get to my place, and you can have your parents call me. It'd be great if we could work something out where we all go to the game together."

"It'll really be up to my mom—I don't know where my dad is. He went on a trip when I was a baby and got lost or something." Tommy always feels sad when he tells people this, but he doesn't want Todd to dislike him because of that. People don't like you when you're sad, so he says "but I bet my mom would like to go. You'd like my mom—she's great! She works really hard, so she's tired a lot, but she's a great person."

"Sure! So are you cold? I'm a little chilly. When we get to my place, I can make some hot chocolate—would you like that?"

"Um, OK, but I can't stay too long. If I'm not home when my mom calls, she'll be really mad at me."

"OK, we'll be really quick. Mainly I want to show you my Nintendo. So what do you like to do in your spare time?"

"What do you mean?"

"You know, like when you get home from school—what do you like to do?"

Tommy tells him about how he mostly watches TV, and how he really likes *Star Trek* and, even though he's not supposed to watch it, *Buffy the Vampire Slayer*. He really likes shows with monsters and vampires in them, so *Buffy* is pretty much his favorite show.

"*Buffy the Vampire Slayer*? Wasn't that a movie a while back?"

Tommy's never heard of that. He shrugs. "Beats me."

"OK, this is my street," Todd says, taking Tommy's hand as they cross the side street and then turn right and head down its sidewalk. "And here's my building," he says after they've gone just a short ways down. "See? I told you it wasn't far." Todd uses a key to open the front door, and they go inside and up two and a half flights of stairs. By the time they get to the top, Tommy can hear Todd's breathing. "Whew!" Todd says. "Those stairs never get any easier."

Tommy nods his head, though he's not sure what that means.

Todd uses another key to unlock the door to his apartment.

The first thing Tommy notices is the TV. "Whoa," he says quietly. The TV is the biggest he's ever seen, and takes up a whole corner of the living room.

"What?" Todd says, then, "Oh, you like the TV? Pretty big, isn't it? It's great for playing Nintendo—wait 'til you see it. Here, give me your backpack and your jacket—I'll put them here by the door. Oh, and take your sneakers off too," he says as he sits in a chair by the door and takes his off.

Thirty-Two

As usual, the first thing the boy notices is the TV. "Whoa," he says quietly.

Wayne is expecting this and uses the opportunity provided by the distraction. "What?" Wayne asks as he slides home the simple, strong bolt he installed high up on the door, then, "Oh, you like the TV?" while twisting the standard deadbolt just above the door's knob. "Pretty big, isn't it? It's great for playing Nintendo—wait 'til you see it. Here, give me your backpack and your jacket—I'll put them here by the door. Oh, and take your sneakers off too," he says as he sits in a chair by the door and takes his off. "I don't like to clean much, so I take my shoes off when I first come in; that way the floor stays clean longer."

Tommy sits on the floor and pulls open the Velcro closures on his sneakers with quick ripping sounds, then kicks them off. Then he's up and walking over to the television set. "How do you turn it on?"

Wayne finishes taking his shoes off, then comes up quietly behind Tommy, enjoying the sweet, breathless anticipation of what is about to happen. "First let me give you the tour," he says. "Obviously, this is the TV, and this is my living room." He places his hand on Tommy's shoulder and gently turns him away from the expanse of darkened screen. "My Star Wars toys are on those shelves. Sometime we'll have to watch those movies together—you'll really like them." Wayne is sad this isn't actually true, and wishes there were some way around it. It's conceivable Tommy will forget all about going home after a while, but this has never happened with any of his other boys, and he knows it likely won't happen this time either. "So over here is the kitchen—I'll make us some hot chocolate while you're playing Super Mario." That part is true. The hot chocolate is how Tommy will avoid the shitty life Wayne had; the hot chocolate is Wayne's last gift to his boys. "Here's the bathroom—do you need to use it?" He looks down at Tommy, reading his face to know how to handle what comes next.

Tommy looks up at him and shakes his head. Wayne can see he really just wants to get back into the living room to play, but is working really hard to be polite. This is good.

"And here's my bedroom. These posters are obviously for the Star Wars movies. And this is my bed." With Wayne's first boy, Alex, they played video games first. To Wayne that seemed the best way, the idea being to get him comfortable and happy before moving on to showing affection for each other. What Wayne hadn't counted on was Alex getting impatient and anxious to go home. That time didn't go as well, and Wayne learned to use the video games as a carrot, and do the love stuff first. When Wayne used this approach, each boy was eager to establish his credentials as Wayne's best friend *before* he got to play Wayne's video games. Wayne sits on the edge of the bed and pats a space next to him on the mattress. "Have a seat, Tommy. There's something we need to talk about before I set you up with the Nintendo."

Tommy backs up to the bed and boosts himself up and backwards with his arms, until he's perched on the edge of the bedspread-covered mattress. He looks quickly at Wayne, then past him at the posters on the wall.

"So here's the thing," Wayne says, carefully putting his hand on Tommy's shoulder. "I only let my very best friends play with my Nintendo. These days that means no one but me plays with it because I don't have any friends, except maybe for you."

Tommy looks at him again, a surprised expression on his face.

"Yeah, that's right—you're about the only friend I have right now. At least, I think you are. We've been seeing each other around for a while, but we only *really* met today, so how do I know? You seem like a really cool guy, and I think we could be best friends, but do you think you'd like to be best friends with me?"

Tommy nods tentatively at first, but then enthusiastically, and smiles.

"OK, me too," Wayne says, feeling his stomach clench a little with excitement, and his penis stirring in his pants at the sight of Tommy's smiling, nodding face. "But if we're going to be best friends, we have to show each other how we feel. We have to do something to join us together, show we have no secrets between us, and prove we'd do anything for each other. Do you think you can do that?"

Tommy nods a little uncertainly, but looks very serious and intent on understanding and doing what he needs to do.

"All right, first, I kiss you," he leans forward and kisses Tommy's cheek, feeling the soft smoothness of it on his lips. "Then you kiss me." He leans sideways and offers his cheek to Tommy. He feels his boy's lips on his cheek, then he turns and, before Tommy leans back again, he kisses his boy squarely on the mouth, their lips compressing against each other.

Tommy's eyes are big and round when Wayne breaks off the kiss and leans back to look at him, but he doesn't run away.

"You passed the first test. Best friends have to kiss each other to show they're not just faking to play with the other person's toys. But remember what I said about no secrets between us?"

Tommy nods, very attentive.

"That means we have to take our shirts off so it's just us, man to man, with nothing to hide behind. Think you can handle that?"

Tommy's brow furrows.

Oh shit, I've lost him.

Tommy nods slowly. "OK, I get it." He reaches behind his head and pulls his sweatshirt off by its collar.

"T-shirts too," Wayne says as he finishes unbuttoning his shirt.

Tommy takes his T-shirt off too, exposing his pale, skinny, hairless chest.

Wayne feels his heart beating harder and faster now. He takes his shirt off.

Thirty-Three

I stand looking at the front of Lambert's building. *OK, now what?* Call the police? After all, he's got the kid in his apartment. But there are too many what if's with that plan: What if the cops take too long to get here? What if they get here and find Lambert and the kid just having milk and cookies? And once again, there's no pay phone around—if *I* end up doing anything, I don't want the police to have my cell phone number.

Meanwhile, as she stands in the street wringing her hands, another kid is getting molested. My mouth is dry and I suddenly need to pee; this is happening now, and I'm it for that kid. There's a tightness in my chest, making it hard to breathe and tugging at the back of my throat, and my fucking scar feels like it's starting to tear open. I clutch at the scar uselessly and try to swallow, but there's no wet in my mouth. *OK, let's do it.* I look up and down the street, see no one, then head for the narrow passage beside the building, touching the Glock as I go.

I open the gate, and remember to step up the few inches onto the concrete walkway to avoid tripping. The trash cans are still here, of course. I close the gate behind me and quietly lift one of the cans that has a lid on it and move it a few feet so it's under the fire escape's ladder. This feels much more conspicuous in the daylight; I glance over my shoulder and see no one. I know from all the hours I spent staking out Lambert's place that there's not a lot of foot traffic going by here, and the opening to the alley is so narrow that people driving by are unlikely to notice anything that's happening in the alley. I climb on top of the can. As I straighten up, I'm already breathing hard. I try to swallow again, with a little more success, and take a couple deep breaths. My heart is thudding, the hurt has moved deeper into me now, and I think I'm going to be sick. I look at the ground and the gate, seeing myself jumping off the can and running away.

I look up and see the bottom rung of the ladder, its peeling black paint and the rust beneath obvious in the daylight. My gloved hands grasp the rough, corroded metal and I lift my weight off the can. The ladder doesn't budge at all; it's still stuck by its corrosion and thick paint. Remembering how I did it before, I chin the bar then throw my right hand, grasp the next rung, then throw my left to even out. As I climb the next two rungs the same way, my arms and back burn like before, and I'm breathing hard, but all this is just background to the loud static of fear blasting in my head. I flex my body, get my knees and then my feet on the bottom rung, and climb the rest of the way to the platform at the second floor level. I hesitate a moment before crossing in front of the window here. Probably the resident is still at work since it's not even five yet. At any rate, I don't have much choice. I cross quickly, keeping my face turned away from the window as I pass by it, and ascend the stairs on the other side.

I hesitate just short of the third floor platform, and lean out away from the building to look at Lambert's bedroom window. The blinds are canted shut now—a good thing since, given the daylight, anything outside would be obvious to someone inside. On the other hand, I have no way of telling where he is in the apartment, or what he's doing. Even if the blinds were up, the relative darkness on the other side of the glass would prevent me from seeing anything unless I pressed my face to the window and cupped my hands around my eyes, which would be pretty stupid. I quietly ascend the last few treads and step onto the platform.

Blind and deaf—not the best way to plan my next move, but I realize if I try to press my ear against the glass I might create a silhouette on the blinds and unintentionally announce myself. I remove my sunglasses and snap them into a coat pocket, then crouch on the metal slats and look at the window. The last of the mental evasion has to end now; I can't put off any longer accepting what I'm here to do. My throat goes through the motions of swallowing, and I reach for the Glock. Instead of drawing it, I stop with my hand wrapped around the grip. *OK OK I'm gonna do this, but let's just think for a second about getting through that window.*

The window is a double-hung model, but each sash has just one big piece of glass in it, not all the little divided panes you see in older or more traditionally-styled houses. You'd think there'd be a storm window, but instead there's only a screen, and the window is just a single layer of glass, so there's that to be thankful for at least. Still, I figure my best chance of success lies in using surprise to my advantage, and in order for that to work, I need to be through the screen, glass, and blinds fast, without any noises beforehand to give me away. *How hard is it to break through window glass?* I also wonder how to avoid cutting something important on me as I do this. I let go of the holstered Glock and turn up the collar on my coat while judging the size of the lower half of the window. It's pretty tall—about three feet, and maybe two feet wide, with the sill about a foot above the fire escape's floor; should be big enough for me to fit through if I'm doubled-over. Probably best to go through backward, as scary as that seems. I don't know how else I can break the glass and enter all at once, especially without slicing open my wrists. I turn the ball cap around on my head, and cant it so the brim overlaps my coat's collar, covering the back of my neck. "This is fucked," I breathe, as a short film of me smashing ass-first into the window plays in my head. "Totally fucked."

As she stands wringing her hands, another kid is getting molested and killed. I turn my back to the window, then decide to take my fuzzy, loose-fitting old gloves off, in case I need that extra manual dexterity. I draw the Glock, and squat down, taking hold of one of the upright railing supports with my left hand. It's cold and rough against my skin, and I realize I'm going to have to wipe this bar off before I leave in case the surface, as uneven and corroded as it is, has my prints on it. *Worry about that later.* I look over my shoulder at my butt's target just about three feet away. "OK, wait— contingency plan:" I whisper to myself, looking down again. "If I don't break through, I take up a position just to the side of the window and wait to see if he opens it. If he does—" Suddenly, it occurs to me. Maybe I don't have to kill him. Maybe I can just sort of take him prisoner at gunpoint, call the cops, and hold him and the kid in place 'til the police arrive. I nod, look over my shoulder again, start to think about whether I should try to take him prisoner if I succeed in getting through the window, then stop the thinking and blank my mind.

I turn my head to the front and tuck it down, and tense my legs against my left hand's grip on the upright bar. "Three two one," I whisper and release my grip while pumping my legs, propelling myself backward.

Next is a blur. I perceive the moment of resistance followed by the shattering and giving way, a hot line appearing on the crown of my head while the blinds flap and slide over me. There's a brief fall, then the hard impact on my ass, and some barrier behind me, trapping me, preventing me from standing up. My mind screams *Open yer fuckin' eyes!* I tip my head back and look up, while kicking my legs and pushing against the thing behind me—*the bed*—my feet slipping on piled shards of glass. I get my legs under me, jump up, and turn, bringing the gun level.

Thirty-Four

"I thought we were going to be best friends," Wayne says gently, with a trace of hurt in his voice. "Don't you want to be best friends?"

Tommy nods his head, his look very serious and a little anxious.

"And what did I say about best friends? They trust each other, right? Because they know the other person would never do anything to hurt him."

Tommy nods again.

"And they have no secrets from each other, right?" More assent. "And they make each other feel really good. So I promise you, as your best friend, that if you trust me, I'll make you feel better than you ever have before, and you'll make me feel great too. That's what love is. Does anything I'm saying sound wrong to you?"

"No," Tommy says quietly.

"So," Wayne says gently, "take your pants off, and just lie here next to me," Wayne says, reclining back on top of the bedspread and patting the place between him and the edge of the bed where Tommy is sitting.

"OK, but then can we play Super Mario?"

"Sure—whatever you want. But this first—friendship first, right?"

Tommy unsnaps the waste band on his jeans, then pulls down the zipper and lets the pants fall to the floor. He stands looking at Wayne for a moment, and Wayne smiles encouragingly and smoothes the bedspread next to him. Tommy steps out of his pants, then flinches, and there's an enormous crashing and ringing of glass hitting glass, followed immediately by a loud thud which shakes the whole bed.

It takes a full two seconds for Wayne to mentally shift gears and redirect his attention to what's happening behind him, and in that time he thinks of a huge rock breaking through his bedroom window. He turns his head and sits up to look.

Instead of a rock, there's a person—short blonde hair, wearing a coat—on the floor between his bed and the wall. He's kicking his legs and twists his head to look back at Wayne, only it's a woman—a young woman raising something in her hands as she starts to stand. *Gun.* Wayne finally snaps to the situation at hand: someone with a gun has invaded his bedroom while he is with his boy. It doesn't make any sense, but it's happening. He rolls to his knees and throws himself at her, reaching for the gun as he does.

She's small and goes down easily under him, landing hard on the floor and absorbing his impact as well. The hand with the gun is outstretched on the floor, and Wayne scrambles over her and grabs the arm, but before he gets his hand on the weapon she flicks her wrist and flings it away. The gun bounces off the wall and lands in the corner, and Wayne crawls after it. His hand is on it; he's about to pick it up when his body is slammed to the floor, a weight—her weight—on top of him, seemingly all on his right shoulder, driving it into the carpet, and then there's an arm around his neck, and a hand pressing his face into the floor, into the encircling arm. Instinctively he grabs at the arm with his left hand, trying to pull it off, and bucks his body, trying to throw her off, to get up from the floor, but he is unable to do either. His face is starting to feel strange—swollen; he has to get her off his neck. He flails, remembers his right hand has the gun, and blindly tries to point it back at her, but the weight on his shoulder prevents him from moving that arm much. He tears at the arm around his neck again, then grabs behind his head and gets a handful of hair, and pulls as hard as he can, but he's starting to feel weak and dizzy. It's getting darker; his vision tunnels. He tries again to raise the gun, but he's not sure if his body is really doing what he wants. He can't see; he lets go of the hair and

Thirty-Five

I see him in my peripheral vision first, then he's slamming into me, knocking me to the floor. I hit hard, harder thanks to his weight on top of me. He squashes my right breast under his rib cage, adding a new center of intense pain to the knifelike stabbing behind my scar. I manage to keep hold of the weapon, but he's climbing over me, pinning my gun arm to the floor. He's going to take the Glock from me—take it and kill me with my own fucking weapon. My arm is already pinned down, so flexing and extending only my wrist, I toss the Glock as hard as I can, sending it somewhere away from us. He climbs over me, moving after it. As soon as most of his weight is off me I sit up, twist around, and leap on to his back. His hand is already on the Glock, so I get up on my toes and angle my body down, putting as much weight as possible on my right elbow, which I drive into the back of the shoulder belonging to his gun hand. His right arm is extended, so that corner of him is without support and I'm able to collapse and pin it to the floor. At the same time I snake my left arm around his neck and grab my right forearm. My right hand is on the back of his head, and my left hand pulls on the right forearm, levering his face into the carpet and his neck into the crook of my left arm.

I bring my knees up and place them on the backs of his shoulders so I can use all my weight to pin him. Bent forward, I maintain my lock on his neck and squeeze my arms as hard as I can, tensing my left biceps and forearm as I do. He struggles violently beneath me, bucking his body and grabbing at the arm around his neck with his left hand while trying to bend his right arm back to aim the gun clenched in his hand. I bear down on his right shoulder even more and squeeze my arms harder. My right hand keeps his face pressed into the floor. Then he's grabbing the front part of my hair and pulling it, rolling some of my weight off his right shoulder. The Glock raises higher and I press myself as close as I can to the back of his neck while maintaining the head lock and keeping my knees planted on his upper back. The arm holding the weapon drops halfway, tries to rally, then drops to the floor, and the grip on my hair relaxes. I feel the tension go out of the body beneath me.

I maintain the hold out of fear, too scared to do anything else. As the seconds tick by, though, I realize he really is out. I'm not sure when I'll start doing permanent damage, but the longer I hold on this way, the more likely it is I'm killing off neurons. If I kill enough of them, he'll never wake up. I should maybe let go—

A scream jerks my head around. The kid—I'd actually forgotten about the boy, the victim, but now he's leaping off the bed at me.

Thirty-Six

He's killed him. That's all Tommy can think. He's never seen a dead person before, and now he just saw someone—his best friend Todd—get killed, right in front of him. At first he thought Todd would beat up the guy who crashed through the window; Todd is a lot bigger than him, but then the guy jumped on Todd and strangled him or something, and now Todd isn't moving at all.

Tommy screams, leaps onto the bed, and springs right off it again. He lands on the bad guy, then pounds him as hard as he can with his fists, punching the bad guy all over his neck, shoulders, and head.

"Hey! Hey, what the fu—knock it off! Stop it! What the—!?"

The guy lets go of Todd and jumps up, throwing Tommy back as he does, but Tommy bounces off the bed and comes right back at him, fists flying.

The guy bends down and grabs Tommy, hugs him, pinning his arms down, but Tommy starts kicking him. When he jams his toe on the guy's leg, the pain reminds him he doesn't have any shoes on. Then he bites the guy's neck, just like the vampires on *Buffy* do.

"Ow! Shit! You little fucker!" The guy pushes him away, knocking him against the bed and steps back holding his neck.

Tommy is about to come at him again when he sees he's not a guy at all, but a lady.

"Hold it! Just hold it, ya little bastard!" she shouts, holding her left arm out and pointing her palm at him while holding her neck with her right hand. "Listen kid, I know this is really scary, but just *listen* for a sec, OK? That guy—

Wayne Lambert? He isn't your friend; he's a bad guy who was trying to hurt you, just like those other boys they found in the woods. You heard about them, right?"

"His name isn't Wayne! His name isn't Wayne!" Tommy shouts. She obviously thought Todd was someone else.

The lady's face is surprised, and she turns to look at Todd lying on the floor.

Tommy runs at her, but she grabs him and pins his arms down again. Tommy struggles, but can't break free even a little, and she's holding him back so he can't bite her again, except on her arms, which are covered by a coat.

"Stop it! Stop it!" she yells. "What did he tell you his name was?"

"His name's Todd! You got the wrong guy! Todd's really nice—he'd never hurt anyone!"

"Listen to me—he was already hurting you by making you take your clothes off in front of him. Didn't anyone tell you to not let adults do that with you? And his name is Wayne Lambert—not Todd. Look, I'll show you his driver's license if you promise not to attack me again, all right? We'll see what name is on it, and then you'll know I'm telling the truth. OK? If I let go, you won't attack me, right?"

Tommy feels mixed up *and* scared now. No adult has ever lied to him before, but either Todd or this lady is trying to trick him, and he can't tell which. But she has a good idea about the license, and she has pretty green eyes that look right into his, so he nods and stops trying to break free of her hold on him.

She lets go of him and turns toward Todd, quickly looks back once at Tommy, then reaches down and takes the wallet out of Todd's back pocket. Then she takes a couple more steps and takes the gun from Todd's hand.

Tommy turns and runs for the door.

"Hold it, kid!"

Tommy's already through the door and keeps running. If he can get out of the apartment he can go for help.

"Kid, stop! I put the gun away—I'm not going to hurt you!"

Tommy grabs the knob on the door to the stairway, but it won't turn. Tommy turns the little circle in the center of the knob to unlock it, then tries the knob again. Now the knob works, but the door still doesn't budge.

"Look—he's locked you in," the lady says quietly from close behind him.

Tommy yanks on the door as hard as he can.

"There's two more locks, and one of them is too high for you to reach. Now turn around—I've put the gun away, and I'm gonna show you his name isn't Todd—he lied to you."

Her voice is quiet and sounds safe, and Tommy can see the other locks on the door and knows she's right about him being locked in. He turns around and looks up at her.

She opens the wallet, and looks at it for a second before pulling out a piece of plastic and handing it to Tommy. "Can you read?"

Tommy looks at her, surprised by such a stupid question. "Of course!"

"Fine—read this," she says, pointing at the name on a credit card.

Tommy studies it. The letters are almost the same color as the rest of the card, so they're hard to make out. The first letter in his name is W. Todd doesn't start with W, but Wayne—the name the lady said—does.

"Here's his license—see, that's him in the picture, but look at the name."

Tommy takes the plastic card from her and looks. The picture is of Todd's face, but the name is Wayne. *She's right.*

"See? I told you true, right? *Right?*"

Tommy looks up at her and nods.

She squats down so she's about the same height as Tommy. "So you know he lied to you."

He looks at her eyes, which are really green—he's never seen eyes like hers before.

"He's a bad man, but he's not going to hurt you or anyone else any more."

Thirty-Seven

"He's a bad man, but he's not going to hurt you or anyone else any more." As I say this, I know it's true; I know what I'm going to do. And that means these smooth plastic cards bearing our fingerprints need to be gone when the police come to investigate, whenever that ends up being. I hold out my hand. "Give me back his cards."

The boy hands them over. He's a sweet-looking kid, with big gray eyes and a patch of freckles running from cheekbone to cheekbone across his nose. That plus the scrawny paleness of his body makes him look so vulnerable it's freaking me out, and making what that bastard in the other room was going to do even less comprehensible.

"OK, you need to go home now. Put on your clothes, all right?"

The kid nods, but doesn't move to comply. He seems dazed, which I get. I'm feeling overwhelmed myself, but I've got to get him out of here so I can finish and get my own ass out. "Now: Put them on now—you need to get home quick, understand? You don't want your mom and dad to be worried, do you?"

"My clothes are in there," the child says, pointing back at the bedroom.

I stand up. "OK, let's go then and get you dressed."

When we walk back into the room, there's a grunting exhalation of breath from the corner. Lambert is still on the floor, but he coughs once softly and his eyes pop open. I step quickly over to him. *I need to put him down again*, I think, kneeling beside him so I can cut off the oxygen. Lambert's arm moves back, hitting my knee. *Shit!* I lean down and put the hold on his neck again. He struggles to get free, but he's weak and I have no trouble hanging on. After several seconds his body goes limp again, but I keep the hold. I glance over my shoulder and see the fucking kid staring at me. "Move it, kid!" I tell him, letting tone rather than volume do the shouting.

He seems to snap out of his trance, looks down at the floor, then takes a couple steps, bending as he goes to pick something up.

I look back at the monster, his head sagging over my elbow. It's heavy so I lean forward slightly and rest his forehead on the floor, but keep the lock on his neck. I glance over my shoulder at the kid, who's fastening the waistband on his jeans. It occurs to me I'm sending him back out onto the streets, which is maybe irresponsible of me, but I don't know what else to do. I don't want him here when I finish this; I don't want him in the room now. "Do you know how to get home from here?" I ask.

The boy stops moving and rolls his eyes up, like the answer is somewhere high on the wall.

"Do you know your way home from the park?"

He looks back at me and nods slowly.

"Do you know how to get to the park from here?"

He stops nodding and the eyes go up again. "I'm not sure."

Fuckin' great. But it'd be a bad idea to just send him across town on his own anyway. Who knows what could happen to him, and the later he is getting home, the more questions he'll get asked, and the more likely it is he'll talk about me. *No, I've got to drive him home myself. He walks home from school, so he must know his way from where he met up with Lambert, even if not from the park.* "OK, finish getting dressed, then go out to the living room and wait there for me. I'm gonna drive you home, but I have to finish up in here first."

The kid nods. "OK," he says, and turns to go.

Lambert is inert, but I keep the hold. I've made the decision; I'll deal with my conscience later. Now I'm thinking about what I need to do before I get the fuck out of here. Two things: Lambert has to be unequivocally dead. There can be no chance of him coming to: no recovering so he can take more kids or, more likely, coming to in some kind of brain-damaged, vegetative state, which would just be sadistic on my part. The other thing is there can be no trace of me left here, especially fingerprint-wise. The credit card, license, and wallet in my pocket I'll take with me and burn somewhere. What else did I touch with my hands? I mentally retrace my steps from the fire escape when I took my gloves off. I held on to one of those upright supports on the fire escape—I'll have to wipe several of 'em to make sure I get the right one. Then I went through the window, but I didn't touch the glass with my fingers. Then there was the fight with Lambert— only touched the Glock, the carpet, and Lambert's clothes and skin. The struggle with the kid: touched him and the cards, which are in my pocket. That's it. OK, so I'll get a pillow case from the bed and wipe down the fire escape's railing supports.

Then I need to make sure he's dead. I swallow hard. *OK, the Glock?* But that'd be noisy—scare the kid, and there could be other people in the building who'd call the cops if they heard a gunshot upstairs. *Maybe I can just hold on like this for a while.* But I don't know how long it'd take to be sure he's dead. The screaming pain behind my scar tells me he's still alive for now. Knocking someone out is quick, but it might take a while to kill all the deep structures in the brain that keep the heart beating and the lungs working. I just want to get this done and get the kid and me home.

I feel dizzy and disconnected from myself, like I'm watching a bad dream unfold.

I need him dead, and I need it done quietly. I know how to shut him down quickly and cleanly; I'm sure I can find a suitable knife in the kitchen. He's already unconscious, so he won't feel it even for the moment or two it'll take.

OK, wipe down the scene, get the knife, get gone. I let go of the target and stand up. He doesn't move; he stays slumped in the position I left him. *OK, gotta go.* As I put on my gloves, my hands are shaking. My whole body is shaking. I pull the gloves on and wipe the sweat from my face on the back of one of them. I grab a pillow off the bed and pull the case off. I turn to the window and use the draw string to raise the blinds.

My eyes catch on a shard of glass hanging from the top of the window frame. There's a touch of red on it—blood. I remember the hot line I felt on my head when I crashed through the window and, now that I'm thinking about it, I can still feel it. I take off my right glove, reach up and touch the top rear part of my head gingerly. The hair there is matted and sticky, and my scalp stings when I touch it. And the baseball cap I was wearing is missing. "Shit," I whisper. I look on the floor: no hat. I look at the bed—fortunately no blood there, but no hat either. I turn back to the window, reach for the blood-stained wedge of glass, then remember to put my glove back on. Then I break off the red-tipped triangle and put it in a coat pocket. I unlock and raise the bottom part of the window and poke my head out. The cap is lying on the fire escape close to where it meets the side of the building. I grab it and put it on, gingerly covering the wound on my head. I stick my head out the window again and look down the alley at the street: no one there. I climb out on the fire escape and use the pillow case to wipe down all the supports I might have hung on to with my bared hand before I crashed through the window, then I look around some more. Probably I left hairs inside the apartment somewhere, but what can I do? "Fuck it. Good enough."

Back inside I drop the pillow case. The target is still motionless. I remember he grabbed my hair during our fight, so I check his hands—both hands, both sides of each.   He must have grabbed at a different part of my head from where I'm cut, because there's no blood on his hands.   There are some blonde hairs stuck to his left hand's fingers; I remove a glove, pick them off and pocket them, then put the glove back on.

OK, next go to the kitchen, get what you need.

I leave the bedroom and enter the main living area again. The kid is standing by the door, watching me. "OK, almost done," I say, trying to keep my voice steady.   I think I succeed, but maybe I'm just kidding myself.   "Just another minute and we can go."   In a way, it's good the kid's here— keeps me focused on the steps I have to follow to get done. I look to my left and see the narrow kitchen area, demarcated by yellow walls and tile on the floor instead of carpet. I walk quickly in, scan the counter, then start pulling open drawers. Tableware, random junk, and then cooking utensils in the third drawer. Along with a ladle, spatula, and three wooden spoons, there's a knife. It's a paring knife, the narrow blade three or four inches long. I pick it up, test the point through the cloth of my glove. It's pretty sharp. *OK, let's do this.* I cross back through the living room, holding the knife against the side of my leg where the boy won't see it, and avoiding looking at him, though I feel his eyes following me.

Back in the bedroom, the target is still motionless on the floor in the position I left him. He looks like he could be dead now, but the sense tells me otherwise. "OK, let's do this," I whisper shakily. I step over to the body and kneel down. His hair is trimmed short, making it easier to see where I have to put the blade. I put my left hand on the back of his head and apply some pressure to cant it forward and stretch the back of the neck slightly. I see the slight bulge at the base of the skull, and with my left thumb I find the small bump that marks the end of the skull and the start of the spine. I close my eyes, and want to keep them shut until this is over, but I need to see what I'm doing. It occurs to me he might wake up again if I take too long—that gets my eyes open. I place the tip of the blade against the skin at the top center of his neck, just below where my thumb is resting.

What the hell am I doing? A wave of nausea sweeps over me. I turn my head and fight hard to suppress the vomiting. I scrunch my eyes shut and feel a couple tears squeeze out. *Get a grip, get a grip.* I think of the boy waiting for me, of how skinny and pale and defenseless he looked in his underwear. I remind myself there were four bodies found in the woods, and that I've already probably wrecked this guy's brain. Doing this is the best course of action for everyone.

Except maybe me. *There's no coming back from this.*

I open my eyes again, look at the blade, think of my training, and, in a moment of will, push the blade hard.

There's some resistance—the blade isn't as sharp as it could've been—but it moves steadily in without stopping or deflecting off the top vertebra. A little blood seeps out, but not much. I push knife all the way until the wooden handle comes to rest against his skin, then pull it back out an inch and wiggle and saw the blade, severing the brainstem completely.

I hear a soft exhalation, from him I think. The screaming pain below my heart vanishes.

I don't want to see the blade come out, so I leave it. Letting go of the handle, I press a couple gloved fingertips into the cavity next to his Adam's apple and just below his jaw. There's no pulse of course, but I press deeper to make sure I'm not just missing it. I'm not; he's gone. Really, I only needed the sudden lack of pain behind my old wound to tell me that. I stand, feeling strangely, disturbingly empty inside. I glance around the room, and once more at the wooden handle sticking out the back of his neck. I turn and leave.

Thirty-Eight

Out in the main room, the child is watching me. "OK, let's go," I say quietly, avoiding his eyes and instead looking at the door. My voice isn't shaky anymore, just tired.

"Is he going to be OK?"

The question surprises me into looking down at his face, at the gray eyes gazing up at me. I hesitate a moment, then look back at the locks on the apartment's door. "He's gonna stay here a while, and then the police will come and take care of him." I reach out and twist the lever to open the deadbolt, then reach up and slide back the bolt in the simple barrel lock. I put my hand on the knob, then look at the apartment and mentally retrace my actions one last time. "He was a bad guy, but he's not going to be bad anymore. He's not going to hurt anyone ever again."

"Can I still be friends with him?"

I look back down at the boy and want to shake some sense into him, but he just looks sad, and that makes me feel sad too. "No, he's got to go away now. He wasn't really a good friend. A real friend wouldn't try to take anything from you or use you. Or lie to you.

"All right, let's go," I say. "You have everything you came with?"

He nods and I see he's got his little backpack and his coat on.

I scrub the knob with my gloved hands, in case I touched it when the kid was trying to run out earlier, then turn the knob and open the door a few inches. I look down the stairwell and listen: It's silent. I rotate the button on the knob to lock it, pull the door wide, and step through after the kid, pulling the door shut behind us. We descend the stairs at a normal pace and without speaking. The boy opens the front door and we take the last few steps to the sidewalk. "Take a left," I direct, and the child obeys, heading up the sidewalk toward Stacey with me following behind.

It takes a minute or two to travel the couple blocks, but when we get to Stacey I still hear no sirens.

When I turn the car onto Hamilton, I glance over at the kid. "You OK?"

He nods. "Yeah."

"Little freaked out?"

He says nothing, but when I look at him, he's nodding again.

"Me too," I say. "It's been a pretty weird day. Is anyone at your home now?"

"No, my mom is at work."

I take it that means dad isn't there either, but I don't ask. I brake for a red light, then make eye contact with him. "Listen, don't tell anyone about me, OK?   That's really important. If you can avoid it, don't tell anyone you were here, but if you have to, or feel like you really need to talk to someone about what happened, don't mention me. Say you just ran away and went home, OK?"

"OK."

The light turns green and the late afternoon traffic carries us along.

"So are you like a secret agent or something?"

"What?" I glance over and see him studying my face. *This is so weird.* "Uh, yeah, something like that. I'm a secret. So don't tell anyone you saw me, or anything about me. It'd be really bad for me if you do."

"OK, I won't."

The park appears on the right and I look for the street we walked down an hour or so before. *An hour—seems a lot longer than that. A fuckin' lifetime for—* The image of the knife handle sticking out the back of his neck flashes across my mind. Like a lot of other bad stuff that's happened, this is gonna be with me for a long time.

"Are you a Phillies fan?"

I look quickly at him, then back at the side street coming up and put on the left turn signal. I wonder what the hell he's talking about, and if maybe he's really freaked out and talking crazy now. "What do you mean?" I ask cautiously.

"You know—the Phillies, the baseball team."

I wonder why he would ask that and what its relevance is. Maybe he's trying to make conversation?

"You know, the hat you're wearing?"

"Huh? Oh yeah," I respond, flicking my eyes up at the bill on the baseball cap I chose randomly a couple days ago to obscure my appearance. Except for avoiding the Red Sox, which I know have a red B on their hat and would have been an obvious connection back to my home, I really didn't care what team I chose. The one I bought has a P on it, apparently for Philadelphia. Or Phillies. "Um…I guess…"

"That's cool," he says, settling back into the seat. "I guess I'll be a Phillies fan too."

"OK, that's cool," I say, feeling vaguely complimented but sensing that thanking him isn't appropriate. "So you're gonna have to give me directions from here."

"Oh yeah—keep going. We have to cross that big street with the traffic light, and then take a right at the building that looks like ours—like the one I live in, I mean."

"What's *that* look like?"

"It's red and made outta bricks and kinda square-shaped. And big. Well, pretty big."

The light at Greenwood Avenue is green, so we coast through the intersection and then I see the boxy apartment buildings he was describing. "Take a right here?"

"Yeah."

I turn and he points to the second identical building on the left. The street is wide enough and Stacey's small enough that

I'm able to do a U-turn in a stretch with no parked cars. I stay close to the curb on his side of the street and shift to neutral. I look at the boy with his little backpack in his lap and think as bad as today's experiences were, they'd have been a lot worse if they hadn't happened and this kid were dead now instead of about to go home. He looks back at me, meeting my eyes and looking like he expects me to say something. "So, you're definitely OK, right? Because if you want to talk about anything, we can. Like, if you have any questions…"

"Why did he want to hurt me?"

The question doesn't surprise me. It's the first and only thing I asked the bastard that attacked me when I was a child. "Honestly, I don't know. Maybe he was just messed up. Or maybe someone hurt *him* when he was a kid, and it confused him, made him grow up wrong. I wish it weren't true, but sometimes it happens that way."

"That's sad."

I nod in agreement.

"But he's gonna be all right now, right?"

I look away, out the windshield, check the rearview mirror, see the street's still quiet—no passing cars or pedestrians. "Well, he's not going to hurt anyone else, and he's not going to be confused or unhappy anymore. Maybe that's the best he could do."

The kid sits thinking about that for several seconds. "What are you gonna do now?"

I look at him and smile a little at the thought. "I'm going home, just like you."

Thirty-Nine

I sit with my face in my hands, letting my bladder drain. I finally got to bed—my own bed—early this morning, and had a few hours of sleep, but with my first conscious thought a few minutes ago I was right back to trying to process what happened yesterday. I can't shake the thoroughly creeped out feelings, but I guess that's not surprising. I keep remembering key bits and pieces, especially the part with the knife. The unwanted memories make me feel woozy, and for once I'm glad I have to sit down to pee.

The microwave clock showed the time as a little past ten when I woke up this morning. I suppose I could go into work, but that's not happening today. Tomorrow yes, but today I need to get squared away, do laundry, get my head together. I wince as I remember the gash in my scalp.

I need a shower. I wipe, flush, and step over to the tub. I slide open the translucent plastic door to the tub and turn on the shower to get the hot water up. Then I remember the people at the hospital here in Arlington telling me something about not getting the stitches on the top of my head wet. "Crap." I turn off the shower and go out into the main room. The sheet of instructions from the hospital is on my table. For the first 48 hours I'm supposed to change the wad of gauze a couple times a day and keep the wound dry. I don't own a shower cap, but I get a plastic produce bag leftover from grocery shopping and a big elastic band the mailman left with the mail a while ago.

Back in the bathroom, I tip my head so I can see the dressing. The cut is on the top of my head but pretty far back, so I can only see part of the tape and gauze. Curious, I pull that part off, then remove the rest by feel. Underneath the hair has been buzzed short and the stubble feels soft and fuzzy. The cut is about two or three inches long and feels crusted over but still slightly moist, and the stitches are hard little ridges to my fingertips. It almost doesn't hurt at all unless I press on it, which I do only once.

I put on my makeshift plastic hat and look at my reflection. "Oh yeah, extremely dorky," I mutter before turning away and pulling off my T-shirt and underwear. I turn on the shower again, get in, and make the water as hot as I can stand. I scrub vigorously until my apartment's little water heater can't keep up and the water turns cool, then cold, then icy, breathtaking, and actually slightly painful. I turn the water off and slide open the shower door. The air in the apartment is cool enough that normally I'd want a sweatshirt and jeans, but now it feels warm on my chilled, reddened skin. I grab the towel off the bar on the outside of the shower door and use lots of friction as I get water off me. I guess I'm clean now; I just wish I felt it more.

Maybe it'd be better if I could wash my hair. I pull the field expedient shower hat off and run my fingers through the lank strands, remembering yesterday when the hand grabbed my hair and pulled. I think of Sergeant Pike back at West Point, wielding his electric clippers, giving the guys haircuts before they went off to Ranger School, and how I wished I could cut my hair off too. And why not? Back then I wasn't allowed to get the Rangery "high and tight," or even a crew cut—"airborne" we called it—because either would've been considered, by Army standards, a "bizarre haircut" for a woman, and therefore a violation of grooming standards. But now I'm free to do what I want; hell, I'm practically unemployed. Cutting my hair off—*that* sounds clean. Plus, it'll make it easier for me to change the dressing on my head.

And no one will be able to grab my hair in a fight again.
Yeah, that too.

I put on fresh underwear, a clean, stretchy tank, T-shirt, sweatshirt, jeans, and coat. I think about putting on a stocking cap to cover the wound. *Screw it.* I pull on my Chuck Taylors and I'm about to descend the stairs to my door when I see, sitting on the half wall separating the stairs from the rest of the apartment, the shard of glass responsible for the zipper on my skull. I pause, thinking about what to do, then pocket it.

Really, I should have gotten rid of it earlier this morning, before I went to bed. I started to clean up: I unloaded the Glock and put it and the ammo and other gun stuff in the metal ammo can I bought at a surplus store. But I was falling asleep as I did all that, so I put the can in the crawlspace next to my apartment and went to bed. Now, as I walk down to Spy Pond, the piece of glass is heavy in my mind, if not my coat, and I'm eager to get it away from me. I incinerated the credit card, driver's license, and wallet—cash and all—in a rest area barbecue pit on the way home last night, so this is the last thing tying me to that apartment in Trenton.

Spy Pond is deserted. The benches in the park area are empty, the Little League field nearby is devoid of people. Even the usual geese, ducks, and swans are absent—must be in a different part of the pond for now. The ground is covered with brown, dormant grass and slightly squishy with absorbed water. The pond is smooth and gray under the overcast sky. I step close to where the tiny waves lap the shore and take the glass triangle out of my pocket. Holding it in my gloved hand, I rub both sides of it on my jeans to remove my fingerprints. There's a little dried blood left on it, and it doesn't come off when I rub it against the denim, but I figure that will rinse off in the water. Then I wing it sideways as far out as I can, as if I were trying to skip it. It doesn't skip; instead, it slices the surface and vanishes silently into the pond.

I thought I'd feel better, relieved, with that piece of incriminating evidence gone, but I still feel depressed. I should be psyched, right? I saved the kid, and other, future kids who would have been victims. They'll never even know they were saved, and that's good. I killed, yes: planned to kill, thought it through, and did it. But he was a really bad guy. I remind myself how that little boy looked, all scrawny and pale in his underwear, and about to be abused and murdered by that bastard. And those other kids they found dead in the woods— *He was a really bad guy; it's good he's dead now.*

And I figure I've gotten away with it, as long as I didn't leave any fingerprints behind. *Have to wear better gloves when I do this again—gloves I won't need to take off.*

Maybe that's the problem: that there'll be a next time.

Without wanting to, I think about the feel of the knife as I pushed it into the base of his skull, and of the small exhalation that followed.

I look out across the pond and study the tan and gray tree trunks and bare bushes on the island and the surrounding shores, working to replace the mental image of the collapsed body and wooden knife handle.

Is my life about killing predators now? Is that who I am?

I close my eyes against a wave of nausea. I want to go back to my apartment, lock myself in, and take another shower.

Feeling suddenly uneasy, I open my eyes and look around, but I'm still alone. "Fuck," I whisper.

I look back at the water, then turn and walk up the gentle slope to the turning circle at the end of the road, and keep walking up the street toward Mass Ave, on my way to Walgreens.

About a half hour later and back at my apartment, I unpack some bandana cloths I'll use as kerchiefs to cover the gauze and tape on my head so I don't look too freaky when I go into work tomorrow. I figure the least I can do, after quitting on short notice, is help the architects out until they hire someone new, and then help orient my replacement. Also in the plastic bag is more tape, gauze, and antiseptic ointment, a small mirror I can use with the one on the bathroom wall to see the back of my head, and a new electric hair clipper.

The clipper comes with instructions, but it's pretty obvious how to use it. Unlike Pike's, mine has a built-in rechargeable battery instead of a cord, so I can take it in the tub and close the shower door. This way I won't get cut hair all over the place. The clipper's plastic guide can be adjusted to vary cutting height. I put it on the shortest setting, hesitate a moment, then click it on. It hums and vibrates a little. I press the plastic guide to my forehead and sweep the clipper back through my hair, which immediately starts falling to the floor of the tub.

Forty

Fresh mug of coffee in one hand, Mike lifts the lid on the box of Dunkin' with the other. He scans the selection, and is glad to see there's still one Boston cream donut left. *You're all mine.*

"Hey Mike, Shailene's back," Sam says, walking into the kitchen.

Mike has been wanting to hear those words for over two weeks, but it seems more like two months, so it takes a second for the meaning to fully register with him. "What?" he asks, turning around.

Sam looks him in the eyes as he slides up to the counter. "Shailene—she's back. You can quit doing her job for her."

"Oh—It wasn't like that; I was just helping her out."

"For over two weeks? Whatever, man, she's back." Sam flips open the donut box and takes the Boston cream donut, but Mike barely notices.

He follows Sam out and turns for Shailene's desk, looking for her honey-colored head. Instead, he sees a blue paisley head, but he can tell it's her—something about her posture, maybe the way she holds her shoulders when she stands up. She looks like she's about to go somewhere, so he quickens his pace. "Nice bandana."

She turns and it's like the image of her face clicks into place in his mind, and everything gets a little brighter.

"Hey Mike," she says, but her tone is flat and her face neutral.

"That's it? 'Hey Mike'? I don't even get a smile?"

"I *am* smiling," she deadpans.

"Ha ha, very funny. So welcome back! How are you? What's up with the bandana? New look?"

The little thin-lipped, crooked smile appears, but Mike can tell it's forced. "Yeah, I'm into kerchiefs now."

"Is this something that started in Pennsylvania?"

The smile drops and she looks puzzled for a moment before going back to neutral, or maybe a little grouchy—it's hard to make that distinction with her. "Yeah I guess. Listen, thanks for covering for me—I really appreciate it. I'll come and talk to you later, but I want to talk to Henry first."

"You gonna try to get your job back?" Mike asks, suddenly serious and hopeful.

She shakes her head. "No, nothing like that. More like I want to apologize and ask how I can help out until my replacement gets here. I'll stop by later and get the tapes and talk to you, all right?"

She sounds impatient, so Mike doesn't try to delay her. As she turns, he notices something white through a gap in the back of her kerchief. "Is that a bandage?"

She touches the place on her head as she looks back at him. "Um, yeah. I'll talk to you later, all right?" She turns and heads for the partners' corner of the office, leaving Mike feeling uneasy and wishing he could talk to her now, but instead he just watches the back of her head, though her hand is there now, smoothing down the flap of cloth.

* * *

Mike eats his sandwich at his desk while flipping through an oversize book about the mills of northeastern Massachusetts. The project he's on now is refurbishing a mill complex into a mixed-use facility with retail space on the bottom floor, rentals on the second level, and condos on the top, but the client—the city of Lowell—and the partners here at the firm want to preserve the distinctive, historic aesthetic of the building. So technically he's working through lunch, but Mike doesn't mind because he loves old buildings and the stories they embody. That's why he sought out a job with this firm. For the last few years the architects here have been locally recognized as the "go-to guys" for figuring out how to adapt old industrial buildings for new uses. With the abundance of closed nineteenth-century mills around here, this kind of project has become the firm's bread and butter.

What Mike appreciates most about these buildings is the attention to detail and beauty that is absent from modern industrial architecture. He seriously doubts anyone will ever convert any factory built since 1950 into living space. These days no one cares about aesthetics when constructing manufacturing facilities and warehouses, maybe because they're usually segregated into industrial parks, away from communities. In the old days communities were built around factories so the workers could walk to them. At least, that's one of his theories for why the owners paid extra for arched windows instead of square, and for all the extra brick detailing in the façades. Of course, some of it was practical: the sheer number and size of windows, for example, was dictated by the need for light before there was reliable electric service or effective industrial light fixtures. Nowadays most factories have no windows; they're just big metal and concrete boxes. There's nothing interesting or fun about designing those, and nobody would ever want to live in one.

He closes the book and puts it aside, and zips up the now empty squared-off insulated bag he carries his lunch in. Before rolling his chair back in front of his computer again, he looks down the length of the room and sees Shailene's blue cloth-covered head in front of her monitor. He can't tell what she's working on; maybe she's going through her email backlog. He wishes she would talk with him again. He's felt her pulling away since that weekend they had dinner together, and he doesn't get it. Working out together in the morning seemed to go really well. He smiles at the memory of her concern after she caused him to pass out, and how that had turned into dinner together in the evening, which, as far as he was concerned, was a date. A good date.

So what happened? Something with that trip—she was different that Monday, and she was already leaving on the trip then. Something must've happened between their date on Saturday night and Monday morning, but what? What would make her run off to Pennsylvania? And what was so freakin' secret about it? Even Henry seemed to be in the dark about it when Mike had hinted around at asking him. It's a mystery...the mysterious and alluring Shailene Campbell. He smiles at the thought of her—no makeup or jewelry, dark-colored guy clothing, flat chest, hardly ever smiles: anything but the usual picture of attractive. And yet...

I gotta get her to go out with me again. He figures if he can get her away from the office, just the two of them, she'll open up, tell him what's going on. *Whatever it is, she probably really needs a friend now, and I can be that guy. I am that guy.* But until she lets him in, he needs to play it cool. He knows his tendency is to push too hard, and that'll backfire. She obviously needs some space, needs to do things on her terms for now. *OK, whatever.*

He rolls his chair back to center, hits the shift key to wake up his computer's monitor, and starts working on the south façade again, flipping between the drafting software and the digital images of the existing conditions, noting repairs that'll need to happen, spec'ing the windows and doors. Actually, some of the doors, the originals from 1882 that survived, would be worth restoring rather than replacing. They're in good shape, and add a lot of character to the structure. He lingers on a photo of massive oak double doors with heavy iron hinges. The wood is obviously weathered and in need of treatment, but definitely salvageable. The hinges will need work too, but they're still better than anything he could replace them with.

"Hey Mike."

He looks up suddenly, surprised he couldn't sense her nearness before she spoke. "Hi, how's it going? How's it feel to be back at work?"

She raises her eyebrows and nods. "Really fantastic, actually."

"Yeah, I know you don't want to talk about your trip, but I definitely get the feeling it wasn't a fun time."

She starts to nod and opens her mouth to say something, hesitates, then finishes the single nod and says simply "No, it wasn't. So you want to talk computers now? Is this a good time?"

"Sure! Sure," he says, pushing away from his desk and pivoting to face her. "So let's see..." he tells her about the problems they had with the printer, and how the technician that came in solved them, and about the weird noise one of the servers started making. "Oh yeah, and Emily had a hard time getting her graphics to come out the way they usually do, but I had no idea what to tell her. I don't know if it's her computer, or the printer, *or her*." He smiles and gets the little crooked smile, very briefly in response. "So you should probably talk with her when you get a chance."

"OK. So you might as well give me the backup tapes— did you have any problems?"

"Nope. I mean, I don't think so—I wasn't really sure how to check the jobs."

"I'll take a look," she says, accepting the cartridges. "Thanks again, Mike, for doing all this."

"Hey, no prob—what are friends for? Of course, this friend wouldn't say no to a friendly cup of coffee after work sometime..."

She shifts her eyes away briefly and looks...sort of... is it sad?

What's going on?

He realizes his face's reaction must have been equally obvious, because when she looks back at him she recovers almost immediately and says, "Yes, I—I think that'd be a good, um, that'd be good." She nods and sort of presses her lips together, as if trying to smile.

Shit. Now he doesn't really *want* to go out with her, because obviously it's going to be bad for him. Still, maybe if they can just talk about it—maybe it's some kind of misunderstanding, something he said wrong. Whatever it is, he can't talk about it here in the fishbowl office, with co-workers all around, some just a few yards away. "Um, OK," he says, suddenly tired, unhappy, and just wanting to get it over with. "How 'bout today? After work?"

She frowns a little, then seems to realize she's frowning and consciously moves her face back to neutral and nods. "Sure, after work. Uh, Au Bon Pain again?"

"Sure."

"OK then." She nods again, and he notices she's nodding a lot. "So see you later." She turns abruptly and walks quickly away.

"Shit," he whispers.

Forty-One

*C*rap. I'm staring at my computer screen but not really seeing anything on it because now I'm freaked by the prospect of the heavy talk I agreed to have with Mike after work. I just want to go home—being home still feels like a shiny, dreamy novelty after two weeks of total suck in Trenton. But I owe Mike this at least. *Why did I go out with him in the first place?* Things seemed different then; I know that. Maybe, if it weren't for the sense and the way it reminds me of the Bad, maybe something normal could have happened between us. Hell, if it hadn't been for the Bad, something might've happened with *Derek*, back in high school. I might even be *married* to him by now.

I actually feel my face react to the thought, my eyebrows drawing together, my eyes squinting at the bizarreness of the idea. The last thing—well, maybe not the *last* thing—but I don't want to be close to anyone now, least of all a *guy*. I just want to be left alone; I want to go home, lock the door, and be safe in my room, with no one touching me.

I need time to sort things out. I mean, what I did—when I climbed that fire escape a couple days ago *(only two days?!)*, I knew what I was going up there to do. That makes this time in Trenton the first time I thought about killing before doing it. The other two times—the Bad, and that night in Florida—I was defending myself. There was no time to think; I was fighting for my life. This time, holding the arteries in his neck shut while knowing what it was doing to his brain, and then carefully inserting the knife into the base of his skull, I was aware of my actions and consciously choosing to do each of them. Then the pain under my heart suddenly winked out like a candle being snuffed, and I knew, I *felt* what I'd done, and there was no undoing it.

What does that make me? I shiver involuntarily.

I keep reminding myself what he was, and how long I took to make sure of it. I took risks—*major* risks, including to my life—to be absolutely sure he was what the sense told me he was.

He was killing kids *for fuck's sake. That boy with the gray eyes and freckled nose is alive today because of me.*

So I'm one of the good guys, right? Killing him was the right thing to do, right?

Well, one thing's for sure: he won't rape or kill any more kids. That's good.

What makes something good or bad anyway? Where does an atheist look for her moral touchstone? Well, wait: I've lived a bunch of years as an atheist, but still tried to do things like respect life and be honest. God isn't a prerequisite for a moral code; in fact, maybe it helps *not* to have religion and all the prejudice and superstition that often comes with it.

But I'm not sure I'm an atheist anymore. Back in New Orleans I started questioning that. I'd meant to seriously think it through, but somehow that never happened. If there is a God, does that make a difference to me and what I'm doing? Would that change the moral calculation regarding my new career of finding and killing bad guys? Maybe, but to be honest, even if God exists I'm still stuck in my head, making my own decisions. It's not like God's going to walk up to me and hand me my answers.

But what if the violence is warping me? Can I trust my own judgment?

Well, I guess I have to.

* * *

At some point I glance up from the software manual I'm searching through for answers to Emily's printing problems, and I notice it's about half past five. I look around: most of the architects are gone, and a couple more are walking out. I crane my neck and see Mike's arm, the rest of him being hidden behind the big monitor on his desk. As I'm looking, though, his shoulder shifts, and then one side of his face appears. We make eye contact, and he smiles a little. I find myself smiling back, though I'm not sure why. I put up my index finger in the universal "one minute" gesture, then pivot in my chair and shut down my computer. I stand, take my jacket off the back of my chair and put it on, and stuff my empty lunch bag in one of the pockets. I walk over to Mike.

He watches me coming his way—just watches. It makes me a little uncomfortable; I don't like people looking at me. But it's Mike, and he's smiling slightly, and there's something about his face, especially his eyes, that seems safe. For a second, being with him seems the natural, obvious thing to do.

"Still up for coffee—or in your case, tea?" he asks.

His voice is casual, but suddenly it feels not casual anymore, and the weight of everything else reasserts itself on my shoulders. I nod. "I'd like to talk."

"Oh boy, that sounds like fun," he says sarcastically.

I roll my eyes and am about to respond when we hear the rustling and jingling keys of someone approaching from the other side of the office.

"Looks like you're the last ones—you got keys to lock up?" Kate, the office manager, asks.

"Yeah," Mike and I say in unintentional unison.

Kate smiles, making me feel embarrassed and inexplicably guilty. "You know the alarm code, right?"

I hesitate, but Mike speaks up. "Yeah, I do. Have a good one, Kate."

"Good night," she says, still smiling at us.

"See ya," I say, wanting to move her and her smile along. We watch her walk across the office to the door, then I turn back to Mike.

"Shailene, would you mind if we didn't go out tonight? Like, maybe we can just talk here."

"But I owe you—the least I can do is buy you a cup of joe."

He looks away and down, and smiles, but he looks sad. "I'm not the most perceptive and intuitive guy, but I'd have to be a brick, or maybe a piece of granite façade, to not know this is going to be a heavy and, at least for me, unhappy conversation. If it's all the same to you, I'd rather get it over with and just go home."

I notice I'm clenching my jaw and pressing my lips together, and consciously relax them. "OK," I say quietly, knowing he's right.

"So take off your jacket, pull up a chair, and let's talk. You say you owe me; this is what I want: a few minutes of your undivided attention, just us, talking openly."

"OK," I say, and shrug out of my jacket, which I toss on the desk behind me.

"So what I don't get," Mike starts to say.

"Hold on," I interrupt. I pull the chair around from the desk that's holding my jacket, and sit on it backward so I can rest my arms and head on the back of it. "Now you have my undivided attention."

Mike opens his mouth to say something, but I interrupt him again.

"And before you say anything, I want to apologize for sticking you with my job for the past few weeks, and for being so mysterious about what's going on in my life."

He looks down and opens his mouth again.

"And for being such a cold bitch lately. I'm really sorry about that too."

He looks at me and smiles a little.

"What?" I ask, feeling uncomfortable and wishing he'd stop looking at me.

"Anything else? Or is it my turn now?"

"Go 'head—you go first."

I'm not sure how to interpret the look he gives me, but then he says "Well about that cold bitch thing—what happened?"

"What do you mean?"

"I mean, we seemed to be," he turns an ear toward me and nods his head a little while gesturing as if he wants me to help him with the words. I don't say anything, so finally he continues, "You know, I mean, things seemed to be good between us. I thought we were getting along well—really well. We had coffee, did a little karate training together, you made me lose consciousness, we had dinner—all good stuff, right? At least, it seemed all good to me. And I kinda thought it was mutual."   He looks at me, his eyes wide and questioning.

I don't know why I'm making him spell it out. I know what he's saying, but I guess I don't know how to say it myself. "Yeah, it, uh, it *was* mutual, Mike. I like you— you're a great guy."

"Oh shit, past tense and the 'great guy' speech."

"What? No-no-no, listen: I've, um, I have a hard time with people…guys…with being close to people…especially guy people."

"Now it's the 'it's not you, it's me' speech."

"Well, it *is* me—my problem, I mean."

"All I know is before you decided you had to go on your super-secret trip, things were going well. Suddenly you come in that Monday morning saying you have to leave, you can't tell me, or anyone else apparently, what it's about, and you've been in cold bitch mode—sorry, but you said it—you've been in cold bitch mode ever since. It's like you're somewhere else, even now, sitting here in front of me. So what is it? Tell me honestly: Did I do something wrong or hurt you in some way? Did I do something that made you want nothing more to do with me? What *was* it? Because I'll be honest with you: I, uh…I think you're awesome. I really want to know you better, and not just in the biblical sense, though I'd be—"

"Stop!" I don't intend to say it so loudly, but it comes out as a shout.

Mike freezes, his dark eyes large and round.

"Just," I say quietly, "just—you're embarrassing me." At least, I think that's what I feel. No, it's more complicated than that, but it's a way I don't want to feel.

"I'm sorry," he says. "I was just trying to lighten things up. I didn't mean to sound, I don't know, crude, I guess. I didn't realize you were so sensitive about that stuff. Is that the problem? Did I say something like that before? Because if I did—"

"No. I mean, you didn't say something like that before. But that is the problem." It's not that simple but there's no way I'm going to explain it to him, so I give him a distilled version of the truth so I can be done with this: "I just, Mike, I did get the feeling you wanted to, I don't know—"

"No, I don't want—"

I hold up my hand. "Hold on, let me finish. I did get the feeling you wanted to be, you know, for us to be, uh," *Shit, I don't know how to say this.* "A couple, I mean, like boyfriend-girlfriend, that kind of thing. Even the other, physical, part aside, I'm not ready for that right now. For a while I thought maybe-possibly, but some stuff I'm really confused about has come up, and I need time to sort it out."

"What stuff? Was it something that happened on your trip? What *did* happen?"

The image of that knife handle sticking up flashes through my mind; I shake my head. "Don't even," I say, meaning it. "For the last time, I'm not talking to you or anyone about the trip. But yes, some stuff happened on the trip and now I need to figure it out."

"Well, fine," he says, spreading his arms and opening his hands. "Take all the time you need—I'm in no hurry. Can't we be friends?"

"Friends, yes, but listen, I don't want to think you're waiting for me to be ready for a relationship. I guess this sounds selfish, but I have enough to deal with now without the pressure of you putting your life on hold while you're waiting for me. And to be honest, I really don't see the relationship part changing: I don't want to be anyone's girlfriend, and especially I don't want the physical stuff that goes with a relationship. I don't see that *ever* changing. Do you understand what I'm saying? Yes, I can be friends with you, but only if you understand, believe, and accept that."

He stares at me.

"What?" I ask, feeling irritated.

"Did something bad happen to you?"

That's it, I'm outta here. I stand up. "I've said what I needed to. I'm sorry it has to be this way, but it does." I wheel the chair back to where I got it.

"Shailene, you need to get *help*, not *isolate* yourself." His voice is raised now.

"My past is nobody's business but mine. That's not open for discussion." I put on my jacket.

"Shailene, listen to me!"

"I'm sorry Mike, but this is how it has to be. I'll see you later." I turn to walk away and feel a tug on my sleeve. I jerk my arm away and spin to face him. "Don't touch me! Just don't touch me! You *know* not to touch me!" I'm shouting, and it's like that day in the gym again. Somewhere deep inside a little voice is trying to be heard as it reminds me this is Mike, good guy Mike, not someone bad. "Just—I'm sorry. I just—I gotta go. Bye Mike." I turn and walk fast out the

door. In the corridor I run past the elevator and take the stairs
down to the lobby.

Epilogue

Arlington, Massachusetts
18 May 1997

It's one of those perfect spring days with bright, clear sunshine making the small, light green new leaves on the trees glow and stand out against the deep blue sky. There's also that springtime scent of clean, wet soil, and something else harder to describe, but I think of it as the scent of new life. It'd be quicker to just walk up Mass Ave to the library, but I choose a longer route away from the heavy traffic which travels that road even on Sunday. Instead, I go down to Spy Pond, pausing to watch the geese and ducks browse the grassy bank and float in the shallows. I turn and follow the packed dirt path along the shore, passing by two dog walkers, an elderly couple sitting on a bench, and a father playing catch with his son. In the tree branches above me and the dense thicket of shrubs to my right the song birds call and flap noisily and occasionally dart out in front of me.

All this softens the usual dread I feel when I make my weekly library trip to check for news of serial predators at large. The temptation to blow it off and skip a week is always there, but if I give in to that it'll be easier to skip next week too. The progression from there to sporadic checks to not checking at all is obvious, and my negligence could lead to more victims, like the gray-eyed, freckle-faced boy who would've been killed in Trenton. So I'm going, doing what I need to do, but today I can focus on the beauty and good things around me as I'm walking. I pass by the small playground, and there are kids playing on the swings, slide, monkey bars, and sandbox while their parents watch or, in one case, join in.

The library trips are easier to get motivated for now that checking for new missions isn't the only reason for these visits: I'm also looking for Harold.

When I was a child I thought God's name was Harold. I got that from the prayer: "Our father, who art in heaven, Harold be thy name." But what kind of a father would allow the Bad to happen? What kind of parent would allow his good, loyal children—namely my parents—to be brutally murdered? And as horrible as the Bad was, I know that's not nearly the worst this world has to offer, not in terms of what happened, and certainly not in scale. There's no shortage of victims. That's why I became an atheist: If Harold does exist, he's an abusive parent, and I'd rather be an orphan.

But about a year and a half ago I started thinking about all the patterns and regularity in the world. It's in the new leaves and flowers forming on the trees around me now, and it was evident in the sense that led me to that apartment in Trenton a couple months ago. There's just too much order everywhere in the world to reasonably call it all coincidence and attribute it to random chance. An accidental universe doesn't seem any more plausible than one cared for by a kindly bearded father in the sky.

I've thought about why hunting Harold makes me, a lapsed but still skeptical atheist, feel better. Although I'm coming around to the idea of an ordering force existing in the universe, I know better than to think it's Harold's love that's cheering me up. Whatever God is, it doesn't give a shit about me or my interest in it. I think what I like about my research is the hope I might make some sense out of my situation, that my world might be understandable. Maybe that's overly optimistic, but believing in the possibility makes me feel good. We humans are wired to want to understand. Solving puzzles and getting answers to our questions is deeply satisfying. I guess that's what we're made to do.

There's a non-atheist statement for you.

Well, whether we were made or we just happened, the hunger for answers remains a reality.   More than that, I'm hoping I'll find there's some value to my life, some point to the fear, pain, and bad memories.   One of the books I've checked out lately was written by Viktor Frankl, a psychiatrist who survived the Nazi death camps.   According to him, humans have a fundamental, inescapable need for meaning, and one route to finding that meaning is through suffering. It's positively exciting to think my life and all the bad stuff in it is worthwhile.   Frankl says the need for meaning is proof meaning must exist, but I'm not so sure.   It'd be just like Harold to make us want something fictional and impossible to find.   But I *hope* Dr. Frankl is right; I hope I'm not disappointed.

I follow some tree-lined residential side streets past large, closely-packed nineteenth-century houses and a gothic stone church, out to Pleasant Street.   I cross, and enter the Old Burying Ground.   Here are the remains of many of the town's early citizens, including some men who gave their lives on the opening day of the American Revolution.   The grave markers are all thin, dull slabs of white and gray—no polished marble or elaborate carvings.   It's a peaceful place with enormous old trees that have amazing color in the fall.   No one gets buried here anymore, so the ground remains undisturbed, but the grass is thin because it lives in the shade of the massive trees and their canopy of leaves.   I pass through the gate in the stone wall on the opposite side, and come out in the narrow dead-end roadway that leads to the library's parking lot.

I walk down the street, climb the broad stone steps, and enter the almost cavernous lobby.   Passing by the checkout counter, I go straight through to where the public-use computers are.

Lately I've been getting the bad stuff over with first, using the Harold research as an incentive to get me through the work of checking for trouble.   I sit at an unoccupied carrel and bring up the Altavista search engine. I type in search terms like "homicide," "ongoing," "murder," "string," "investigation," and "serial," then scan the results for hits on news sites like Reuters, CNN, newspapers, and local broadcast affiliates.

Typing the terms and scanning the headlines makes me think of Lambert. More, though, I find myself thinking of the person who killed him: that calculating, almost cold, woman who pushed a paring knife into his brainstem. What kind of person does something like that? Am I that kind of person? I recite all the rational, good reasons for killing the guy, but it doesn't change the feeling that I've been...compromised. I feel different now, in a bad way. It's like I've thrown another shovel load of dirt on the innocence of the fifteen-year-old girl whose parents were murdered eleven and a half years ago.

I notice my eyes are scrunched shut; I open them and resume scanning the screen.

After a few minutes I realize I'm going through the summaries too quickly, simultaneously anxious to find nothing and perhaps, subconsciously, wanting to miss seeing what I'm looking for if it is there. I go back to the start of the list and read more carefully, but still find nothing. There are lots of articles about killings, and some are unsolved and another is a series of murders, but none are both open investigations *and* related strings of homicides. I scroll down further, and my eye snags on the word "Trenton":

Trenton Boy Held on Murder Charges

For the first couple weeks after I got back I found articles about Lambert—his own murder, and speculation about and confirmation of his responsibility for the deaths of the boys whose bodies were found in the woods in south Jersey. This article makes a passing reference to all that, but the incident it reports is a new and unrelated one. A three-year-old boy was found bludgeoned to death in his back yard. The murder weapon, a baseball bat, was found nearby with the victim's blood and an eight-year-old neighbor's fingerprints on it. The short article hints at other evidence, and features statements from a couple neighbors, one who said the suspected eight-year-old boy seemed "sweet and quiet," and another who said he "had a temper on him." It gives the address where the victim was found. I can't recall exactly where I found that boy and the dying cat, but the sick feeling in my stomach is guessing it was in the same neighborhood. My mind flashes on the image of the baseball bat I almost used to euthanize the cat, and on the cat's broken back and leg. "Holy fuck," I whisper, my tongue sticking and clicking in my suddenly dry mouth.

I wonder if they had a problem with cats going missing there for a while before this.

I wish that voice would shut the fuck up. How the hell could I execute a kid?

Could the woman pushing the blade in that apartment in Trenton do it?

I close my eyes and lean back, the palms of my hands sliding across the stubbly hair on my head. I feel dizzy, like I'm on a carnival ride but I can't make it stop so I can get off.

What about Harold? If this world *is* created—what the fuck kind of God makes a world where children beat other children to death?

What is this world making *me*?

About The Author

Like Shailene, Max Salt is a graduate of the U.S. Military Academy and a former helicopter pilot. He now lives in Rhode Island in a re-purposed Grange hall on an acre of land he is working to transform into a tiny nature preserve. This is his second novel about Shailene. You can learn more at www.maxsalt.com.

www.ingramcontent.com/pod-product-compliance
Lightning Source LLC
Chambersburg PA
CBHW020611260626
47157CB00003B/958